The Seeds
of the Light of Christ

DURGA HOLZHAUSER
AGNI F. EICKERMANN

The Female Solution
93 Chemin de Vauloube
83600 Bagnols-en-Foret, France
thefemalegrail@gmail.com

Published by
The Female Solution
83600 Bagnols-en-Foret, France

© The Female Solution 2018

You can find us on the Internet on the following site:
www.jesus-the-book.com

I cannot stop, remembering.

We first dream our lives in heaven. Our desires bring us into this world. Each of us is born with a prophecy.

As we remember who we are and where we come from our soul's dream awakens and expands into our greater vision. Our role is to remember, and we have the ability to reconnect. This is what the promise of enlightenment means to me.

Our soul book is bonded in eternal unity. The beauty of a pilgrimage is forgetting where we come from and where we will be going.

When we begin to awaken, we read the first and the last pages of our own creation so we can write the manuscript of our life. One of my dreams from heaven is writing these books and completing The Sacred Series.

For more than 9 years I have been living and dreaming images of my memories with Jesus and His companions. I cannot force these images; they come to me in waves. They grow in my visions and only then can I find words to describe what I lived and witnessed 2,000 years ago.

Jesus The Book was created in three weeks and we never changed a word. I read it from the Akasha and then wrote it down.

Jesus The Forgotten Years took two years to be read through the mists of time. I sometimes felt lost but fragment-by-fragment, my memories arose. I wove a tapestry of time forgotten.

Jesus The Seeds of the Light of Christ came to me as shards of memory. It felt like I was re-assembling a beautiful but broken stained glass window from a medieval church. I collected them and put the pieces of glass together piece-by-piece to restore the image.

It seemed that it would take many more years for my memories to grow for this third volume of Jesus the Book and The Sacred Series.

But in May 2014 the fierceness of my thoughts opened a Pandora's box.

The red of my root chakras pulsated and I knew:
This book wanted to be written. It felt like contractions, uncontrollable, like a force of nature.

I have to follow the truth of reproductive labor and delivery, and so I found myself writing the third volume.

Jesus The Seeds of the Light of Christ is the lost story of the church of Christianity.

The early Christians searched for shelter from persecution and spread out over Europe, Asia Minor and Asia. After the crucifixion, neither the omnipotent temples of the Jewish high priests nor kings or Roman emperors resonated with the "Religion of Love" that Jesus was teaching, nor the existence of heaven here on Earth and within each of one of us, nor the concept of divinity within each woman and man.

The church of Jesus and Mary Magdalene was hidden away, innocently embraced in Gaul, Southern France and planted in the groves of the Celts.

We still find many traces of The Church of Mary Magdalene and the Celtic symbiosis between Christianity and the Druids of France and England.

The Christian church of Rome started to grow at the same time and its roots reached into Southern France.

Years later, the Inquisition, with the support of the king of Northern France and the Pope in Rome, invaded the Occitane (the name for Southern France in the Middle Ages). It exterminated all roots of the church of Jesus and Mary Magdalene. We have no idea what happened; all known memories of it were brutally extinguished.

This is the story of the "Seeds of the Light of Christ" that Jesus, Mary Magdalene, the Essenes and the early Christians planted. Our time is destined for harvesting.

I restore the image.
I remember.

Welcome to our sacred stories.

durga

Jesus did not die on the cross.

He followed the call to the Himalayas.
After the crucifixion, the Essenes and Jesus' followers sought
refuge in Gaul,
where Sara, daughter of Mary Magdalene and Jesus, was born.
She grew up with my son John.
Jesus came back to spread
His next prophecy.
He renewed connection in Britannia
and led the Essenes to their
new destination.
He took Mary Magdalene
as His wife and we traveled
with Him to Ephesus where we
were reunited with Mary, His mother
and John the Apostle.

There, Jesus and Simon lit
sacred fires at night and
opened new dimensions.
Heaven and Earth melted away
before our eyes and within us.

A new era began,
the universe of God opened the paths of grace.

Ephesus
The Beginning of a New World

"Are you ready to know?

Awaken

to write your own prophecies.

Reflect

the divine universe within you."

Jesus sat back-to-back with Simon against a tree trunk. The night sky in Ephesus was adorned with the shining bodies of the stars and allowed us no sleep. They were weaving a spectacle of the universes that retold our stories. They built myriad worlds of light which we drew into ourselves with awe. We saw ourselves in them. And we remembered.

The people who had gathered around Mary since her arrival at their new destination had all seen how Jesus had united Heaven and Earth in the nights before. Now they had withdrawn and left us in the grove for our night of farewells. They watched respectfully from a distance in the surrounding fields as the fire showers of the universes were created before our eyes.

Jesus and Simon intertwined in a spectacle of the cosmos right before our eyes. The universes of light flowed in and out of them. Their flesh dissolved and their bodies imploded. Black light exploded from them and flowed back into infinity. Mary Magdalene and I knelt humbly, sitting on our heels. Showers of beauty held us in thrall in the bliss of what we were experiencing. Our holy stories were unfolding before us. The stars formed our promised destiny in visions that were older than this life. Our hearts were torn open even further, full of burning love which we dedicated to Creation.

Mary was sitting nearby, alone on the illuminated space on the ground. Our surroundings enveloped us in silver. I felt God's green Earth beneath my knees. The Earth was breathing. Oh, how I loved her when she pulsated with life. The reverent scent of deep awareness was sweet. I didn't need to look at Mary because she too knew that something was happening to us in that moment.

After a long silence, Jesus spoke this question into the darkness and our souls began to awaken and to echo our longing. I looked into the infinite divine fabric of the dome of stars above me. The key to my prophecy was hidden in them.

We fight for what we love. Forever.

"Yes." I stood up and looked at Jesus and Simon with resolve.

"I want to know." Mary Magdalene had also awoken and sat at Jesus' feet, leaning against him. "Have you returned to finally return to us that which has been lost? All of the stories we have forgotten about ourselves in the confusion of time?"

Silence. When I sat down with Simon the sound of my robes broke through the vibrating emptiness. I looked at him and thousands of universes shone in his eyes. "How long will our journey home take?" I asked. A glowing rain of stardust was the only response. It flowed from the night sky, wove into my body and awakened the sleeping matrix within me. The ecstasy of my body loved with all of its senses. Born in Heaven, we became whole on Earth.

That night, we became ancestors of the new story.

A new thread of life wove between the worlds. Jesus, the cosmic Christ, began to write His story anew on Earth. We were a community then and our life wrote our holy scriptures for us. We were the quill for God's handwriting and we have wandered through time ever since. The legacy of our Order lives in a place between the universes. The story of the Earth has only rarely acknowledged us.

As our sacred book began to write itself, the worlds parted. During that time of concealment, Jesus led us back to our origins. By once again reading the history of our own creation, we were made whole. I began to sense that the universe lived out of my world and not the other way around. It was my turn to awaken the fulfillment that had begun to grow within me and to transform it into a flaming altar in which God embodied Himself as the power of one.

Christendom was awakening on Earth. The followers of the teachings of love were growing like weeds, wild and beautiful, throughout the Roman Empire, Palestine and Asia Minor. Unwanted, it sowed itself in the most barren soil. The seeds of the Light of Christ were indomitable.

The Departure

When the sun rose, it was time to begin the journey to our new home in Gaul. Mary held me in her arms for a long time. I realized what had been decided upon here. Mary's path was sealed by the presence of God. Her white light marked each of her priestesses, with whom she would work in this place until the end of her days. The Order of Mary lived on in purity in Ephesus. Each of the priestesses touched the Earth with reverent silence and with God's healing powers.

I too had chosen my fate. The vision of the path I had chosen transformed as I lay in Mary's arms. A part of my soul had sunken into the darkness of the universe to wander there. What I originally experienced as a curse during the encounter itself had transformed into a new vision of creation in Mary's healing arms. I was able to connect certain worlds to anchor the light in the depths of the averted darkness. Mary's arms didn't want to let me go and they carried me deeper and deeper into the pulsating darkness of the mother's creation. In the safety of her arms, my fear subsided and I reached a place in which everything around me grew quiet and the safety of the goddess received me.

The origins of the goddess were dark. Those who had scaled to the light of God knew the mother's seed. In that moment, Mary and I held each other at this source of eternity as our connection transformed and made a new promise. We were without differences. At home, every vision of the others had awakened. Every breath was in unison. My son was in danger of dissolving in this reality, where absolute contentment and the beyond commingled and fused. Then Mary released her embrace.

"Look at me," she said. There was nothing but love between us. I found it difficult to say farewell. I pressed my forehead to hers. I was touching a fragile gentleness. When such a love exists, one no longer worries about the future of the others, one lets them go and knows their paths. Love releases us and sets us free so everyone can seek their own perfection by finding their own story in the prayers of their hearts. Then it was time for us to leave. Mary kissed my forehead in farewell.

As Jesus, Simon, Mary Magdalene and I, the four companions, left Ephesus, we all became pilgrims in our shared story. A new ribbon wove itself between us as God found Himself in His own creations. Mary Magdalene loved Jesus and He loved her. As we saw the landscape pale behind us, I stopped for a moment and looked at Simon. I loved him and he loved me.

We were the forebears of the divine legacy that wove through the ages.

Mary Magdalene and I had expressed the desire to see our children, Sara and John, again after so much time apart. Our companions, Magda and Joseph of Arimathea, had already set out for Britannia.

This time, we traveled back to Southern Gaul by ship and crossed the lands of the Greeks, Romans, unrecognized, mixing in with the other exotic travelers. We passed through countries and cultures without leaving a trace, until we reached the harbor in Massalia. Fro there, we continued on foot.

The Sacred Red

The Essene Village

One evening, we espied the Essene village from afar. It lay before us on the hill in the light of the fiery red sun. We stood on the opposite side of the rise and looked at it in silence. Mary Magdalene and I took each other by the hands put our trust in each other. Our children were there, at the other point on the horizon and we would see them soon. Our hearts tightened for a brief moment. There would always be a wound within us for having followed the mission of our lives and leaving our children with the Essenes for such a long time. This cut would never heal, for, though we fully grasped the power of our heaven and the core of the independence of our spiritual being, we still lived an Earth-bound existence. And the heart of a mother wrote its own feelings. We each knew how the other felt.

When twilight came, it looked as though the people in the Essene village had withdrawn for the evening, so we decided to spend the night in the open air and rejoin our friends the next morning.

I awoke very early. I looked at the village in the gleaming morning sun. At the end of the world and completely undiscovered, the community of the Essenes had been rebuilt. But I was also sad in that moment. A place of light pulsated there timidly, unnoticed from the rest of the world. Upon seeing this, I felt deep within me that something was wrong. To give my irritation space, I dug my hands into the soil. Instinct guided me to do this.

Simon had awoken. "What are you thinking about?" he asked, almost gently. "I think the village I see before me no longer lives in this world Simon. They have returned to heaven. It is so bright, a circle of shadows is building up around it." Simon remained silent, as he always did when deep in thought.

Jesus and Mary Magdalene, who had spent the night a bit further away from us, came toward us. We walked toward the village together. It wasn't easy for me to control the feelings beneath my skin as the energy from the nights of awakening consciousness we had experienced in Ephesus was drastically opposing the energy before us. The light we approached was submerged.

Jesus was with us. That was the greatest miracle after everything that had happened. He had returned from the world of transcendence, from the regions of the Himalayas. Jesus had followed when we women had called; we prayed Him back to Earth with the wild longing in our hearts and our message, telling Him of His corporeal daughter, Sara. He gradually regained his carnal, earthly form and traveled with us to places to interweave invisible threads of destiny. They had not shaped themselves into a foreseeable future as of yet. But I knew that everything He did was to the benefit of a great, divine connection. He acted from within and His impulses were Creation. He was the Son of God. Silently and without the world suspecting, He was remaking it.

We combed our way through high grasses until we were so close we could see how large the village had become. Little stone houses dotted the hillside. We went to the temple which was still the center of the village. Humble walls of stacked stone protected the sanctum. We sat on the low stone wall in the square in front of the temple and waited while the Essenes greeted the fire of morning in silent prayer. I sank into the light, meditating, but it was no longer a refuge as it was anchored beyond this world. Life was draining from this village. What had happened?

When the people flowed out of the small, humble temple, they hardly believed their eyes when they saw us standing in the morning light, as though we had appeared on the stone wall out of nowhere. Their joy at our return was great. Many were uncertain as to how to approach Jesus; they bowed before Him and continued on. We had been gone a long time. I didn't recognize many of the faces. With my heart pounding, I waited to see if I could spot my son John, or little Sara among the crowd leaving the temple. I felt the excitement of Mary Magdalene's heart next to me as our two children came out of the temple holding Martha's hands. When they saw us, they stopped a moment and looked at us silently. Sara took a step back and pulled Martha along with her by her sleeve. John's little child's soul began to think, waiting. It was not an easy moment for Mary Magdalene and me. Had we lost our children during our travels?

I looked at Simon, almost desperate. Jesus had gotten up and was crouching in front of the children. He opened the palms of His hands with His love and the scent of rose flowed visibly from His hands and turned iridescent colors. John looked up at Martha and Sara came closer, curious. There was something sad in his eyes, but she was smiling. I knew at that moment, that these children had withdrawn into their own world, which lived within them.

Mary Magdalene and I acted on the same impulse. We went toward our beloved children, crouched in front of them and grasped their little hands. When I looked up at Martha, she had tears in her eyes. She hadn't spoken a word to us. John grasped my hands and the connections between our souls began to timidly flow toward each other until our touch lifted our sense of estrangement. I wept; my son didn't know what was happening to him. And then Sara broke the spell. She jumped boisterously at Jesus and broke His eternal heart into a million petals of fatherly love with the magic of her charm. His spell had not missed its mark.

Sumaja came toward us. She embraced us, but the joyous mood still seemed to resist expanding. There was an accusation in the air. "It is nice to have you back." Time stood still that morning as Simon, Mary Magdalene, Jesus and I returned to the Essene village after a long journey. It wasn't until I was in Lazarus' fervent embrace of greeting that the tension eased a bit.

On our journey, I wondered how the pure, clear light of the Essenes who lived so untouched by this world, would react to the shadow hidden within me. It was calming that neither Jesus, Simon nor Mary Magdalene rubbed against my dark light. My soul now wandered in shadow and in the light. I had chosen this for myself on my path to myself. The great secret of Jesus and Simon had become clear within me in our nights on our journey. Their love united the creations of light and the creations of the dark worlds and wove a great, holy bond of love between everything God had ever created. The dark side of my power did not resist its own presence, rather it spanned a much larger horizon of wisdom and depth in the discovery of our inner selves. My dark side started to become a friend within me. But now I was back with the Essenes. I had to connect my old life with the new seeds I had brought with me with openness.

The Essenes had escaped Palestine and had built a new society in Southern Gaul. Whereas for those of us who traveled with Jesus, life had become an adventure. We had been in Britannia, Rome, Greece and Ephesus. Much had change while we were away on our journey. The shadow of the past seemed to follow us, if not as a threat to our lives, then as hopelessness.

Though Mary Magdalene and I were exhausted from our long trek, we planned on winning our children back that morning. We went with Martha out of the village and into the fields crowned with olive trees. Beneath the sun, which embraced us all, we began to play together in the nature around us. Martha punished us with silence. Mary Magdalene and I didn't know how to reach out to her. There was an unspoken accusation in her heart; deep within her, she had distanced herself from us.

I noticed something in that moment that I had never experienced in our community before. There were thoughts that created separation. When we diverge from love and sow the seeds of judgment, interrupting the connection between us, we open a distance. I sought within me for a way to reach out to Martha until I decided that the truth was always the best for disarming the drama. We were people and certainly not without flaws.

As I played with my son John and with Sara, I asked casually, "Martha, what is wrong?"

"What do you think is wrong?" she boomed back in response.

"I don't know! Martha, we came back and I can't find you or the others again."

"What nerve. You leave us and we are fighting for our lives here and are still without roots." I looked at Mary Magdalene, concerned.

"You are right," I responded, and Mary Magdalene's warm voice reinforced our understanding. She was by her. Instinctively, I dug my hands back into the soil. I searched for warm impulses for soothing words and a way to convey what could not be conveyed just now. Mary Magdalene and I had followed our destiny and Jesus without question since we had met Him. But Jesus had ushered us women into a new era of liberation. I didn't want to ever apologize to anyone for that.

The soil beneath me grew warmer and conciliatory. I sought my answers in the stability of the soil. We came from the deepest experience of our embodied heaven which Jesus and Simon had made real within us in Ephesus. At the same time, I had to admit Martha was right, that her accusation was right. The Earth demanded its own right to enlightenment. She wanted to devour that which Heaven offered us in order to make Heaven real in the darkness of her bosom.

My eyes focused on Mary Magdalene and then Martha. "Sisters, it is up to us to unite that which seems irreconcilable. The place from whence we come is breaking apart right now," The vast distance I saw behind all that was directed at us. It was ready to carry us into new worlds.

Martha wept silently. "I don't think it's right for you to have left your children here with us. I have pondered this often. You all left us with a burden to bear, but especially you and the burden you placed upon me, which I no longer wish to bear. You have no idea how difficult it was without you. We live in constant fear of being discovered, though the people here protect us. I have often been afraid for the children. I do not think it is right for children to grow up without their family, their mother and father, with only spiritual guidance. I have seen how our generations, the mothers of Ephesus, have followed this tradition. I was brought to the women of Ephesus as a young girl, but believe me, the pain within me never healed, for I never stopped secretly weeping at night, when no one noticed, thinking of my mother, whom I missed bitterly. I was so alone back then and they didn't see my suffering." Her body shook silently.

Martha was furious. She trembled with the pain that separated us. She was breaking open old, hardened structures. We were under fire. With our awakening, an old world tore open without knowing how it wanted to transform itself.

"Martha, I feel the sacred space guiding us to a new world. It will strip us of all we have learned and will destroy our tradition. I don't think we can force it, because it is happening on its own. The Black Mother rules over us right now. You know the spheres are vibrating before the storm. We also know that it is unwise to decide anything now. First, we must withstand the tension building within us by embracing the power of change." Mary Magdalene took her in her arms until she grew silent.

We women began to feel the pain in the depths of our stomachs. It was older than us. Our feminine voices were timid. They were awakening and were meant to help write the story of our community in the future. Something had happened that sought us out before we could suspect it. During those nights in Ephesus, Jesus and Simon had arrived in their corporeal lives, their full presence. They had decided to leave their heaven and become corporeal on Earth thus infecting our story. We were all awakening.

Magda looked as us with teary eyes. She nodded, indicating we should go back to the village. She gathered up our children and we were finally able to rest for a few hours.

That night, when dusk fell, oil lamps were lit and the spaces in which we could receive each other finally opened. The villagers gathered in the evening in the meadow beyond the village. They came timidly, to quietly celebrate our return. I was still in another world. Exhausted, I sat down next to Lazarus on the meadow. I embraced him several times, I was so touched, and I told him what we had experienced. I was happy that this misty veil of mixed energies had begun to lift. Our children were playing with the flowers in the mild evening wind. The mood was blue and secretive.

The lights burned in the darkness, but the energy remained silent. Mary Magdalene joined us and looked at me, enquiringly. Because nothing happened and no one came. Only Lazarus stayed with us while the people in the village withdrew to their houses. Mary Magdalene and I began to grow angry.

I didn't know where Jesus and Simon were, so I decided to look for them. I found them with Sumaja and when I knocked, they looked at me as though I were unwelcome. They were deep in conversation. When I started to close the door, saying "I didn't mean to disturb you," Jesus spoke. "Please come in."

Sumaja had tears in her eyes and I felt oddly touched for I did not know what was wrong. As tightly, internally connected as we were, each of us could sense the mood. It was unbearable for me. "What is going on here?" I asked. Sumaja did not look at me, nor did Jesus and Simon respond. "Why can't you speak when something is wrong?" I was so angry, I left the room and went to search for Mary Magdalene.

She looked at me enquiringly. "Do you perhaps want to tell me what is going on?" She was holding Sara in her arms and John by the hand. It calmed me to see her little daughter snuggling against her heart. I needed a familiar moment in the midst of these frozen emotions. I picked up my son. "Come, let us find a quiet room somewhere." Lazarus looked at me, confused. "Leave us alone please, Lazarus," I said. "It's nothing to do with you."

"We are thinking the same thing," said Mary Magdalene, "that nothing here is connected to the Earth anymore. The whole village has disconnected from reality." "And why is it happening to them and not to us?" I asked Mary Magdalene. "Because we realized in Ephesus that we cannot escape the Earth if we want to find our own salvation." Mary Magdalene had unleashed the deep power of the unbroken sacredness.

"The worlds beneath us are being torn asunder and it is unbearable. Some are isolating themselves in heaven and the two of us are burying ourselves and our children deeper in the Earth, just to keep hold. Martha is desperate and none of us can find a way to move on."

"Then we must speak," said Mary Magdalene. "If Jesus says we are now the teachers of the worlds, then it is our responsibility to share our truth with the others."

"I don't dare," I said. "I don't dare tell my erstwhile Essene teacher that they have lost the ground beneath their feet, that they have withdrawn into the light and they are no longer among us." But as I spoke this aloud, it suddenly became easier.

I took another breath and sank to the ground. "Perhaps it isn't about us knowing the truth or one person knowing what the other doesn't. Perhaps now it is about learning from each other." It felt like the onset of birth pains. "I feel like I did when giving birth. The silence of the contractions, the tightening." "You are right," Mary Magdalene smiled. Since we are all so sensitive to the others' energies, we feel helpless, because we don't understand.

"Do you think we are being born into something new?" She looked at me lovingly. My son had fallen asleep in my arms. I stroked his head and gave myself space to drift into the vastness beyond all things real. Instead of going with the confinement these contractions brought with them, I simply let go. "I think so."

Mary Magdalene and I gathered up our children and withdrew early. Simon didn't come to me until very late and I finally fell asleep without a word. When I awoke late at night, I felt alone and was freezing from abandonment, though I had most of those whom I loved around me. Until I began to sense that it was not loneliness, but a new movement of community. If I withdrew from my personal consternation and expanded, I was able to sense everyone close to me, but each of us was in a cocoon. Each encased in their own world. We were like caterpillars, destined to become butterflies. My world began to weave inward. Pondering this, I fell into a restless sleep.

I awoke next to Simon saying, "I need you now!" which was an astounding experience for me. When he looked at me, I first had to decipher what was within me. Until now, we had followed Jesus and Simon without question.

"I need help," was a step in my evolution, which I first had to understand myself. Simon reacted with a supernatural calm, "Everything is all right, Miriam. There is great upheaval in the worlds. Do not try to lay your emotions upon the high, constantly moving waves. We have to wait and see how the universe will orient itself anew." "Is it not already written?" I asked. "No, it is not," said Simon. "Everything is evolution, everything is fire and depending on what its beings contribute toward this evolution, Creation's progress will change." Yes. I understood that in that moment. The wisdom in my body born unto me knew what he meant. Understanding the greater space that created us helped me to trust in my groundlessness.

I arose early and brought the still slumbering John to Martha. Little Sara lay rolled up in her chamber and both of them were asleep. It didn't make sense to me. I looked for a place where I could take a conscious look at the panorama of my environment. I turned around in a circle to take in the atmosphere and landscape with all of my senses. The Essenes had built several little, new stone houses with great care. Surrounded by fields, olive trees and grapevines, we had all the sustenance we needed.

Lazarus' love for Jesus had grown. He showed it in his gestures and in the little house he had built on the hill for Mary Magdalene, Sara and Jesus, so they might have some personal privacy. Many new people had joined them, for the Essenes were leaving Palestine and following us to the new country.

As I neared the temple, I once again felt the speechlessness that paralyzed us all. People slowly came from all directions and gathered in silence for morning meditation. I decided to leave the village and seek my healing balm in nature's prayers. As I roamed across the fields that mild, sunny morning, Mary Magdalene came toward me. Her red scarf waved in the wind and gently touched the golden grass.

My friend. Her heart and my heart were one. As she came closer, I knew she had not slept well that night. As we looked into each other's eyes, she said, without hesitation, "I was in the universe last night, Miriam. I danced with rage. I no longer know what to do with these dammed up feelings. I can no longer explain my rage." "Where is Jesus?" I asked. "He has been gone all night, Miriam. I brought Sara to Martha last night and bade her watch over her. I had to get out. I listened to the wilderness. Have you felt that, that nature is one with the universe?" "Only too well. I often listen to the grass, then I listen to the stars."

We embraced. And then we were safe as the wind blew around us and held us tight. It helped that Mary Magdalene was simply there and I could hear her heart beating. In that moment, I knew: There is a new path. A path that is not a path. I was once again beyond our world, in a greater vision in the deep, dark center of Creation where everything was being rewoven, searching for a connection. In Mary Magdalene's arms, I knew that I had lost my connection. We both took a step back and Mary Magdalene and I got lost in each other's eyes. We were wandering in the world of the others. "I am searching for my story," she said.

That was the first thing she had said that made me feel better. As we came back to the village, the Essenes were just leaving their morning meditation. For a moment I considered whether I should feel badly. I think it was the first time in my life that I had not gone to meditation. I had sought out nature and found a far greater connection than I had had in the temple. Jesus was standing there, waiting for the people and from afar I could see that Simon was approaching. This little space exuded peace in that moment. Jesus beckoned to them all. "I would like us all to meet tonight. We all know that something lies hidden within us. Let us seek God within us together, for there is something we must understand." I went to Jesus and embraced Him. I was grateful to Him. My eyes sought out Sumaja. She stood, moved, at the portal of the Essene temple with tears in her eyes.

"I think we should get Martha. There is a kind of woman's knowledge we should rescue and preserve now," I told Mary Magdalene. "Wait for me outside in the field." I found Martha in her chamber. She was sitting, staring into space. She had not brought the children to meditation as she usually did. They were still asleep.

"Martha, come," I said. "There is something you remember, from the time you spent with the women of Ephesus that we desperately need now. We women are reawakening now." She pursed her lips and looked up at me. There it was; a smile in her eyes. "All right, I will come."

We took the sleeping children of heaven in our arms and walked out into the field where Mary Magdalene was waiting beneath an olive tree. The children were in another world and did not even wake when we lay them down in the shade beneath a tree in the fragrant meadow.

We three women embraced as we had agreed and the fabric of our bond was there again and sought an echo in our stories.

"Tell me of your experiences on your journey," Martha said.

"We were in Ephesus," said Mary Magdalene.

"And did you see Mary again?"

"Yes," I said, "and on the way there we met Peter and Andrew." "Are they well?" Martha asked. "I know they are in Rome."

"From time to time, we hear rumors that there are Christians everywhere. Christians are starting to multiply and the mood is restless," said Martha. "But it does not look good. The Romans condemn it. I think that is why the mood in the village is getting more and more oppressive."

"Have you heard anything from Rome?" I asked.

"You should ask Lazarus, he is in the bigger cities more often and hears news," Martha responded. "Everyone here feels our world falling apart. We feel we are no longer a part of the secular world's story and that is harmful to us. What is the point of living without a connection? The world out there has nothing to do with us. If you ask me, there is no purpose to our being here in the Essene village if so much remains unfulfilled in the world outside and within myself. In all these years, so much about myself remains unexplained."

"Is that what makes you so restless?" Mary Magdalene asked.

"Yes. I know Jesus, I know love, I know our story, but I have the feeling that I also have a story that spans far beyond this life," Martha said, growing softer.

"We know so little about our heaven," I realized.

"Do you also yearn for your own heaven?" asked Mary Magdalene, laying her warm, copper-brown hair on my shoulder. "Hm," she said, "how often have we been with Jesus in heaven, Miriam? And still, we don't know Him. How can that be?"

"Because we women experience heaven differently."

"What?" We both looked at Martha with our full attention.

"I know," she said, "from our rituals during my time in Ephesus. When the women sang, it created a depth, like the bewitching, intoxicating scent of flowers. We often entered trances in this dimension and dissolved into ecstasy. That was different from the heaven Jesus showed us."

"Hm," said Mary Magdalene. "Yes, I remember our time in Ephesus, but it never bewitched me that way. I think I know my own fire rituals from my heaven and I think I can bear them forth. I think I have to create it from myself."

"And do you dare?" Martha asked her.

"Why shouldn't I?" said Mary Magdalene. "Because we are never permitted to create the fire rituals ourselves."

"Says who?" Mary Magdalene was herself, "If I can remember my heaven, then I may create anything from it and share it with the Earth and all its beings." "You have always been rebellious!" Martha was very upset.

"What exactly are we talking about here?" I wanted to know.

"We know there is something in the air and it has to do with us women. Something that can only be born from us, from the depths. Why are you treating each other like this?"

"Because we have not trusted ourselves for some time now, Miriam," said Mary Magdalene, and so doing, opened Pandora's box. "But we women should build each other up," I said.

"I am certain there is a new path of initiation for us. I know that this is what Jesus meant. There is a path of initiation for every being, which is born of that being itself and I think that is what we are seeking right now. Last night, I thought a lot about the images in my visions," I continued. "I think we can learn a lot from each other if the Essenes search through their heaven and share it with us and we explore our heaven, because I know my heaven feels different. The heaven from whence you sprang forth and that which made you women of Ephesus, certainly holds great knowledge for us."

"You are dreaming again, Miriam," Martha barked at me. Her words shot straight through my heart. Mary Magdalene noticed the tears welling up in my eyes. It was she who found healing words when my innermost being closed itself off after this unexpected attack.

"Dreams are sacred, Miriam. They are the most sacred things we have."

"Martha, I have to tell you something. You are very bitter about yourself and that is all right, but that doesn't give you the right to shoot arrows. I would find it much nicer and more desirable if you too would reach into your treasure chest, your heart. We need something for ourselves. Behold! Our community is breaking apart."

It had grown so hot that the air around us was shimmering. I had regained control of myself. I stood up and took Martha in my arms. "What is breaking your heart so?"

"That I have not found a husband," she said, her voice cracking. "That I am still alone. I love your two children, but they are not mine. It tortures me to think I bear a curse from Ephesus. I swore before a fire that I would dedicate myself to the great Goddess. You are so free!" She looked at us, her underlying envy giving way to a deeper hopelessness.

It was true. Jesus and Simon had freed us both. We had barely noticed it happening. They had led us to an unconventional life. We had roamed heaven and Earth with them, we saw Jesus on the cross and God's thunder had struck me at that moment. The crucifixion was the beginning of our liberation. He had liberated us women, but not just us. He had liberated the entire world, all of humanity, I knew it. My visions had grown so powerful that they nearly crushed me.

I looked at the sky with open eyes and it roared around me. The Son of God had freed humanity from a yoke it had placed on its own shoulders. Now, humanity was free, now it had to choose.

Humanity was starting out on a new path. Since the crucifixion, something had happened in the Earth. Every being had returned to itself, to where it was able to start encountering itself. Jesus had removed the yoke of the past from humanity's shoulders. Now it was free to decide for itself whether it wanted to reflect its expectations at God or if they wanted to recognize themselves within Him. God was how we experienced wholeness. My visions stopped and I came back, gasping for air.

"What was that?" I asked as I revived in Mary Magdalene's arms. "You were having visions again."

"I saw something and I would like Jesus to explain it to us, for I do not understand what it means. I saw humanity buried beneath the yoke of destiny that promotes war and breeds revenge. That Karma was the eternal wheel of retribution that had laid over humanity until the moment of the crucifixion. He was able to destroy this yoke. They are free to choose."

"Then they will need good, whole dreams," Mary Magdalene said and kissed me on the forehead. "It is time to go."

The evening was mild when we met outside the village bringing wine along with us. When I joined them later, Mary Magdalene, Magda and Martha were already there, talking with each other. I had my son in my arms and sensed that the vibrations of the people had grown more peaceful. There were many I didn't know and I decided that that was something that should change.

I searched for Lazarus and finding him sat down beside him.

"How are things in the outside world? Have you heard anything new?"

"I hear different things, Miriam. There are many groups scattered throughout the Roman Empire that are beginning to join in Jesus' message. The proclamation of love, forgiveness and the kingdom of heaven in each person soothes the hopelessness of the enslaved, the dishonored, the persecuted and the unseen. His persistent love leaves traces in the world of those fighting for survival and who feel oppressed. It nourishes them and their illusions of powerlessness fall away. He has raised them up from the gutter of victimhood.

There are those who have begun preaching in Jesus' name. There are rumors that they are passing on his teachings. You can imagine the Romans will disapprove of anything that questions their powerful dominion.

They still don't know about us, where we are and that Jesus is alive. It is only an open secret in certain circles. The Romans who do know it use it to blame the

Jews. They want to get the rapidly growing number of Christians on their side. That is their policy. We also have friends in Massalia who know us and who are friends of Qumran. They help us by providing information. There are different cultures and beliefs in this country. There are Celts, the erstwhile lords of the land, and Jews, Romans and even Egyptians. We aren't very noticeable here."

I didn't understand the world anymore. Why did we separate ourselves from everything like this? Was this what was frightening the Essenes? That they no longer had any interaction with the world? I looked at the people around me and my gaze drifted to Sumaja and Agnisha. I thought to myself: It was different once, back in Qumran. Our life in Palestine was a web of relationships. Everything was connected, we were chalices of the heart for each other, created from courage, healing and connectedness.

The loyalty of love then inspired a dialog between the Essenes who lived in the temple city and the Essenes who lived a secular life among the Romans and the Jews. But now we were isolated. We avoided the people in the surrounding areas and they did not seek contact with us. Where there is no lively dialog, the feeling of liveliness itself begins to die out, I thought to myself. Once, we were awakened. Even beneath the cross, we had been alive because we were connected to everyone in that moment. With enemies, friends and all others who were part of that event. But now? We had to call ourselves back to the love that burns for life, that burns for good and evil. We were once revered, now we were nobody.

I let my gaze drift to Jesus and looked at Him enquiringly. How I wished the Lord would arise and preach to us. How fulfilled we were back then under the starry sky in the Holy Land as we magically interwove heaven and Earth. I could listen to Him forever. It wasn't what He said, it was what He evoked within us. The magic that touched us. I missed the ecstasy of divine passion. He and Simon were lost in their own world, always in agreement, but we were beginning to die of thirst. I was certain something would have to happen. But I didn't know what.

Jesus began to stoke the fire. Sumaja and I helped Him. I observed Sumaja. She was avoiding me. The distance she had once exhibited in the Essene village, where she had been a revered teacher, was different now. Because there was something in her world and in my world that was so painful it didn't want to be touched. I looked at her, pleadingly, and mumbled, "Don't avoid me Sumaja, that won't solve it." We were silent as we stoked the fire with the determination of performing the incantation. The fire burned and everyone was woven into the magic of knowledge without speaking. Time stretched out for us as did the healing space its extension created.

Mary Magdalene arose in the silence and with her there arose a powerful wave of feminine power as she stood at the fire where everyone could see her. She held Sara in her arms and shone, red and divine. "I would like," she said, "for everyone here to stand and face the fire and state honestly what is on their mind." She paused and melted into desperate gentleness. She looked at Him, pleading and demanding, "Jesus, I do not care if I draw heaven's wrath upon me or if some old, sacred teachings contradict me. I will never leave our daughter alone again. It breaks my heart." She broke down, hurt and we all knew, no one would be able to convince her otherwise.

"I held my daughter in my arms last night and sensed her soul withdrawing. It is my job as a mother to show her the world. I don't care it that flies in the face of tradition. Wherever your prophecy leads you, my beloved, I will be with you and will take Sara with me on the journey. Jesus, these old teachings no longer apply to me. I once rebelled against the women of Ephesus and I am rebelling again today. I want you to hear my words and not misunderstand them. I thank you Essenes with all my heart for your loving care of my child, but I... I am a woman and mother. That is my new legacy. Wherever we go, our daughter will go with us, Jesus." She looked at Him, pleadingly. Jesus' love was calm and silent and He gazed at her lovingly. His silence was eternal.

That was my wake-up call. With my own son in my arms, I stood across from her at the fire. "I too thank the Essenes for their loving care of my son. But I think it is time the old structures be destroyed. I feel and would like to say it here, that the tradition, as we once lived it, has changed. These rules no longer apply. You, Jesus, and you, Simon, awakened us women. You have empowered us too much. I know the world is calling us women and we will not ignore it. I also want to take my son with me on our journey. I feel we can describe a new era and I want very much for something to break open for all of us this evening, for we are all paralyzed.

I feel so strongly that we women bear a new legacy within us, that you, Jesus and Simon, awaken more deeply within us with every passing moment, but if we are really to grow, we must find our own voice. Even if this voice is still timid or evokes displeasure in you, I still know that my voice no longer wishes to remain silent." My heart was beating in my throat.

Mary Magdalene and I stood proudly at the fire with our children in our arms. We united the feminine and maternal power within us. Our sacred voice and the power of our unbroken feminine sanctity awoke in that fire. The paralysis in our souls awakened to become a snake that fought against the inner walls of our bodies and wanted to break out. I sensed that Mary Magdalene was fighting the same battle within herself and the Earth shook beneath us.

Martha joined us at the fire. "And I would like to tell you all that I have been considering going my own way for quite some time now. I grew up with the women of Ephesus and learned much from them, for which I will ever be eternally grateful. I have lived with the Essenes for some time and love their rituals, their purity, and yet I wish to conquer the life that waits for me beyond all that. I don't care if I am pure or impure, I believe my life is my initiation and it is seeking me out. I no longer want to hide it in secret orders or sects as they call us to insult us. I am sick of living in secret and hiding because my life might otherwise be in danger. To whom am I so dangerous? My truth lives within me, a burning sword; a wise, fiery belief.

Life holds so much for us and I want to regain this freedom. And I would like most, Jesus, if you would agree that I am as free as I wish to feel."

Sumaja had been sitting next to Jesus the entire time and, against all expectations, as we had always been rebellious women, she now joined us at the fire. We now formed a circle around the flames. She was not protesting as we were. Instead, she was intent, turned inward. She was crying. "I think the feminine powers of creation among the Essenes were broken long ago. Encouraged by the fire and your words, I now see what has held me paralyzed the last few weeks. The stronger this inner cold became, the less I was able to fulfill my spiritual tasks. The feminine powers among the Essenes were broken long ago. But since I am not a being of memory, but rather a being of the present, I have no means to conquer my story. But I know it is lurking deep within my soul. If I could wish for something, then it would be to connect the women of my tradition with their feminine powers, wherever I can find them, if you will help me."

More and more women joined us at the fire and formed a circle around us. The men watched us in silence. The fire that night gave us back the grace of unbroken knowledge, which we had lost long ago and hadn't even been able to sense. I was the first to withdraw from the fire and sit next to Simon. I looked at him and his expression was calm. I leaned against him. I knew what he was saying to me without speaking a word. We would see what was best for all of us.

Mary Magdalene sat down with Jesus, he took her in His arms and Sumaja sat next to her husband, who usually went unnoticed and was quite composed. The other women, however, remained around the fire for a long time as though spellbound by the power. Martha gazed into the fire and I sensed her pleading prayers. Mary Magdalene and I were once again at home, inside and out. We had spoken aloud for the voices in our hearts.

Jesus took the wine and cups and poured a cup for each of the women around the fire. The ritual grew red like the light of the wine. He also poured a cup for each of the rest of us.

"You have to know," He began to speak, "that a new idea has begun to influence Creation. I once came to Earth to extinguish oblivion with the power of forgiveness. For you have all forgotten that you were once born in heaven, in God's glory. You were created as an expression of the power of light. Every soul rules its own heaven. Oblivion on Earth had grown so great that even the gods were lost. And without heaven within you, you are hopeless without a soul and you wage war and lack respect for life. The soul is the feminine power of creation, it is the dynamic, the creative force of the cosmos. It is eternal existence and we have it to thank for our lives. Without it, none of us would be here. It lives in every being, in women and in men.

I once came to Earth to dissolve this oblivion. I paid a high price for breaking the unwitting legacy without light. When I was growing up with the Essenes, I knew one thing even then: that you all embodied a beautiful light, but that you all lacked your own heaven and could not experience its completeness. What is happening today and the reason you are so restless, is that you are realizing that you are no longer creating from your own heaven. We are all standing on a new threshold. I too am facing a new creation. Life is a much larger destiny of divine will. The Father sees us. He is raising femininity and the fiery cups of your love burn. The feminine is arising to deliver us, even me. Evolution is raising up the snake of the Goddess. She lives within women and is awakening. For a long time, this cosmic power was suppressed and is now returning. It will reveal a new creation to us all."

Jesus stopped in front of Martha and His whole aura glowed as He gently, yet insistently said, "Martha, you are free. My personal advice is that you stay a while, for God guides us through the new creation. Then decide." Martha nodded and looked at the ground, relieved. I knew it was all right. He had given her the choice and taken her will seriously. She knew that He meant well, for it was about her.

How often will we have to forget ourselves before we are delivered from oblivion? In this life and in the many incarnations in our past and in those yet to come? I look back at the many years of encounters, reunions, awakenings, burnings, pain and tears which oblivion revealed to me bit by bit. Now with the help of Jesus and Simon we had returned to the fabric of life. We awakened to life. But it needed more time.

That night, 2,000 years ago, in the south of what is now France, time stood still. There are moments when Creation itself holds its breath. Our entire consciousness dove down into it.

Jesus approached Mary Magdalene, lifted her up and kissed her for all to see. He embraced her so full of love and desire that the universe imploded with powerlessness and poured around the two in spirals of ruby red showers of stars. They melted into a red ecstasy that was love and Creation. And she loved Him, full of awakened yearning.

When the universe holds its breath, we have the opportunity in that instant of entering a newly-born consciousness. Until we awaken, we think we are experiencing ourselves. Once the awakening touches us, we realize that we were only dreaming that sleepless state somewhere between sleep and consciousness. God had opened the gates to the depths of consciousness.

I lay in Simon's arms and held my son close to me while everything happened around me. In the aura of this love, God's love poured into my body like lava. The sweet pain burned everything away. The alchemy of heaven and Earth freed my consciousness and the material from which I was once born. Simon pulled me close to him so I wouldn't get lost again. His body and mine were one. I raised my head and looked at him. Only light radiated from my eyes, a light that loved sacredly and invitingly. I was unbroken and without shame. A thousand, illuminated universes danced in his eyes and I was the feminine power at his side.

The lava current in my body began to understand how the divine consciousness weaves life between heaven and Earth. It is not easy to penetrate if our intellect has grown too complicated. Only in the innocence of the heart was I able to understand what Jesus and Simon taught us from that moment on. And from that moment forth, when I encountered Simon, I began to awaken. A love greater than humanity magically bound our fates. A love, greater than ourselves, bound our lives and touched the unknown which knows us better than we know ourselves if we live in twilight.

The first time I looked him in the eyes I remembered and every time thereafter his essence has reunited us, a weaving with the fabric beyond time. Again and again, we will dive into the dozing sleep of the incarnations, for in this life, I had landed in this time, completely forgotten. Until I encountered him; he who kissed me awake and I him.

At the end of the evening, Simon and I stayed awake for a while. John was sleeping at our feet. "Miriam, tell me what is good for you and we will find a way. You know that we are preparing for an even greater task now and you are an integral part of that." "Thank you. You have no idea what that means to me." I felt I had been acknowledged as a woman.

Love pours into truth, truth is love.

Love craves emotion, emotion is love.

Love is God's will, will is one with love.

Love touches us, beneath our skin, love flows.

Love offers itself, love wants nothing.

Love reaches places it has never been.

Love asks, the answer is love.

Love is where you came from, love is where I am.

Love knows me, it knows from whence I came.

Love frees me, freedom is love.

Life is love, love is life.

Love needs love to survive.

Love is the will to love without boundaries.

Simon and I held each other tightly the entire night and did not let go. I dreamt of the future. As always, my visions came to me as powerful emotions and fragments of images. They painted themselves in my dreams. I saw Mary Magdalene walking through a barren landscape, the wind powerfully blowing her red scarf about. Her scarf danced and painted patterns on the landscape. She walked through dimensions of the highest consciousness, interweaving with the landscape. She reached a castle, enthroned like a massive aerie on a hill. The doors opened and a circle of women greeted her. They were all wearing red. Then a new vision appeared. Mary Magdalene is teaching amidst the circle of women. She is old and beautiful, the embodiment of the feminine teacher. Her church is red and her teachings prophetic. My dreams were premonitions.

I fell asleep and God carried me further, my body shook and I found myself in a dream. I am fighting through a snowstorm through the deep snow, for I know I must reach the peak. My feet are frozen, the will to fulfill my prophecy driving me forward. My sister is with me, the snow is more like some material in which we sank to our hips; it blew around us, howling in our ears. I am not cold. I have to carry the sacred story we had written by reconquering creation, through the time zones of oblivion. I have to break through to the place that synchronizes everything in the presence of God. The place in the Himalayas that exists between the worlds, protected by the snow, where events and history become real again. I bear the chains of knowledge in the zones beyond the memory of this world which kills to forget. I lose my sister to the icy cold. I do not scream; I do not want to lose my last bit of energy. I continue forward and reach the place where the noble lions wait on the plateau that knows no cold. Exhausted, I fall and die. I have made it. I have brought the scrolls that tell our story to the place between space and time where they can be preserved.

I awoke, shaking, in Simon's arms. I was freezing. I knew what Creation was planning. Mary Magdalene and I would become female prophets and Jesus and Simon were the teachers who would bring us there. Feminine creation was shaping the new teachings of God.

As I left our little hut under the gleaming sun that morning with my son, I took a deep breath. I wanted to get warm outside as my body was still so cold. I wanted to see what was going on around me. It was the first time in this life that a natural flow had suddenly come to a stop. My life and that of my companions had been a single flow of events. But now, something stood still. We stood in expectation. I didn't want to think about it for something within me said that in such times, one should turn inward and focus on what was important. I felt that the restlessness of standing still, which irritated us all, was a part of creation. One only had to know how to find one's way. The Essenes had returned to their daily lives. I didn't see anyone in the village and Simon was still asleep; so I went out to the meadows with John.

When I finally stopped circling my inner world for a moment and noticed the world around me, it took my breath away. Nature had awakened to life around me. The flowery grasses, olive trees and grapevines became a pulsating orchestra of colorful energies. Nature was a living, pulsing consciousness. I was immediately on another level of vibration and I dove into it. I found Mary Magdalene asleep with Sara under the old, familiar tree we had visited with Martha the days before. I sat down next to her quietly and hoped that John would continue sleeping in my arms so as not to wake them. I looked at them sleeping, so peacefully.

Golden light surrounded us and suddenly, streams of knowledge began to flow into me. Nature was speaking to me. In the silence, a golden stream awoke in every one of nature's cells. And I sensed that nature, in its innermost core, always lived in this pulsating silence. And it also taught me, in that moment, that this silence was one of aimless confusion as one might think. On the contrary, it was one of active trust, for it trusted life itself.

I held my son to my heart. His heartbeat and mine deeply merged with this experience. There was life there. Life itself was limitlessly hopeful. But there were quiet times and turbulent times when we wandered at the edge of experience and both were a part of life.

On that day, Nature taught me to trust. In the ignorance of how life would develop, there is a kernel of silence within us that remains unaffected. That is Nature within us. It is golden and gleaming. It is soft and maternal. It did not have any characteristics and yet it is loving and calls itself the trust beyond trust.

I must have fallen asleep beneath the tree, because when I opened my eyes, Mary Magdalene was looking at me, smiling. It was already late in the morning. I sat up and we looked into the distance. "We will not give up our children now," said Mary Magdalene. I bit my lip for a moment, but felt the audacity she had developed in her adventurous freedom as a mother. Then I took a deep breath, "How right you are," and I pressed John to my breast. There was nothing else we needed to know from each other. We ran, barefoot in the warm sun, across the soft meadows and back to the Essene village and approached the Essenes to ask them if we could help them with their daily work.

It had been a long time since Mary Magdalene and I had been able take part in this silent routine. I once again saw what I so loved about the Essenes: their devotion was divine. They prayed while they baked bread, they prayed while they drew water, they prayed while they tilled the fields, they prayed while they cleaned their houses and maintained the sacred rooms. Despite the helplessness in their hearts, they filled the day with a reverence willed by God. They all greatly elevated the day by honoring it.

We were given the task of cleaning the temple. I suggested simply taking our children with us and thus found ourselves kneeling on the floor of the little Essene temple, devotedly scrubbing the floor and happily doing so. Was this what we had missed? Shaped by our lives, Mary Magdalene and I had become nomads. Scrubbing the floor with all our hearts made us happier in that moment than we could ever have imagined. We spent hours cleaning the temple with our prayers and our hands until we noticed Jesus standing in the door watching us. "What are you doing there?" Mary Magdalene called, smiling. Jesus was deep in thought and smiled. Apparently He liked what he saw. There was a love dedicated to the little things in which God resides. We didn't even have to speak about it. That moment was just as special to Jesus as it was to us. For the sacred spaces around us preserved the care we invested in them.

It was midday and the Essenes had gathered outside, as usual, in the summer sun to set up the tables and eat. When Mary Magdalene and I came to the table with our dresses tied up as aprons, our hearts were joyous for this was something we no longer called a community: it was our family. There were around thirty people in the village then. I sat down at the table and observed the conspicuously large northerner who had come from Britannia to join the Essenes. He had apparently been helping outside with the construction site. He seemed serene, considerate and introspective.

In the midday sun, surrounded by the soft rustling of nature and with the warmth of the earth beneath us, our values changed before our eyes. It was time to create our world anew. Jesus announced that we would gather again at the fire that night and I could hardly wait for dusk to arrive. I loved what was happening. I could feel, in every fiber of my being, that we were starting to awaken from our twilight sleep and it was different that I had imagined. We weren't being lifted out of the world, rather our flesh and blood were intermingling with the senses of this earthly life, awakening to become a fire of divine passion.

After I had fallen into a deep midday sleep, exhausted from the night before, I came outside at dusk and the fire was already burning. Jesus was standing there, stoking the flames with prayers. He kept pouring olive oil into the fire. Several people were already sitting there, silently waiting for what would come. One member after the other, the entire village joined us around the fire. I had noticed that the villagers had secured the area with stones because the land was dry.

And I noted that Simon hadn't joined us yet. He was the last to come. He saw Jesus and they agreed without speaking a word. They shot each other a brief glance, then Simon sat down next to me. The fire and the presence of Jesus and Simon did not make the twilight any more pleasant. It became nearly unbearable for me. I pressed my sleeping son against me and looked briefly at Mary Magdalene whose expression made it clear to me that she felt the same.

Jesus' mood changed. "Once the worlds could see. Light and darkness penetrated the surface of what is visible." Then His voice changed. "You think you are perceptive and can clearly see the world and creation behind it. The light of Agni allows you to see. But you judge what you see. You have come to a point in your evolution at which you evaluate what you encounter, the visible in the invisible. This has separated you. Guilt and atonement are the war that has grown huge thorns around your hearts, within you, in your hearts. If you were like children, without preconceptions and if you could see each progression of creation with a child's eyes, with innocence, your heads would no longer rule your world today. But believe me, I do not wish to punish you by these words. I want to elevate you. If you are ready to lay yourselves and your heads at God's feet, you can be born again into the innocence of your hearts, for life is simply a spectacle of God's glory. If you want to become creators again, you must unite with the fire. For fire creates. It is the most powerful expression of God's creation in all of Creation."

Jesus grew silent. We waited for a long time for him to continue His sermon, but nothing happened until Lazarus spoke. He was looking at the floor because he didn't dare look up. "If I understand you correctly," he said, "is it not true that you, Simon, are this Agni? Why don't you tell us this story yourself? You are the Lord of Fire. He tells us of the beginning, of the worlds of creation from times I did not know. Would you give me the opportunity to understand?"

Simon looked at him. "That is why we were born for one another, to help each other remember our stories. Believe me, I do not know my stories, any more than Jesus knows His stories." Simon looked at the fire, dug into the earth and threw the dirt into the fire. The fire changed. It grew red. It became even calmer and my innermost being exhaled. The silence filled with warmth and comforted me. I didn't want the cold of the untouched, I loved the warmth of touch. This fire was warm. "Jesus and I were born in the same moment. Love penetrated the worlds in a great wave and flooded them. Light and fire and love belong to each other. Neither Jesus nor I, neither of us remembered ourselves. But His love reminded me of the fire and the fire in me reminded Him of His love."

"Jesus, is there a future?" said the large, dark-haired man whom I had noticed earlier at lunch as he arose. I wondered how he had come to join the Essenes. He had stepped up to the fire, powerful like a warrior going into battle. He fell to his knees and his head sank in a pain none of us knew. Lazarus was sitting next to me and I couldn't help but ask, "Who is that? Where does he come from?" But the scene continued without my curiosity being sated that evening.

As I later learned, this large, dark-haired man had come to the Essene community one day. It was said he came from a royal family, from Northern Britannia, and had left his family. He had met Jesus when we met with the royal tribe leaders in the stone circle of power. Jesus and Simon had been branded in his heart and he could not stop his yearning. He had left his country to seek out Jesus and had found himself joining our community.

The man knelt there, noble and elevated, the rage in all his cells palpable. I heard repeatedly, "Is there a future, Lord?" Jesus did not arise, nor did He react to him. He looked at him, lifelessly. "Arise and let us hear your story!" Simon's warm voice dispelled the frozen scene before the fire. Slowly, the warrior from the north arose from his knees and sat at the fire. As he began to find the words within him, he simply starred into the flames. He didn't look at any of us.

"I have seen so many wars in my own country. I have fought on the battlefields. The war had already taken shape in me so I voluntarily fought against the Romans with the tribes of the north, far from the home where I was born. I saw so many men and women bleed to death on the battlefields and heard so many agonizing screams and saw so many die, until one day, I heard the call. My soul was dead, I was beyond despair. War had stopped leaving traces of itself within me long ago, for my whole being had grown numb; battle was simply about battle. Then a light approached me and a voice spoke unto me, 'Thou, my lost son, is it not time you finally returned home?'"

He had tears in his eyes. I could see that in the reflection of the fire. This huge man, who seemed so imperturbable, was near collapse under the weight of his own pain. He continued, his voice gloomy, "I left the battlefield that instant. I looked at the Romans. I looked my tribesmen from the north. No one tried to stop me. And I knew that none of them would win this battle, for war is eternal if no one stops fighting.

I left the battlefield and remembered you," he said. "For I had once met you in Britannia with my father. It was years ago. But that voice, that light approached me and the memories of you suddenly united and melted together. I remembered that you lived in the south of Gaul and set out to find you.

I came here and never told you my story, because the wound within me is so vast. I only have one question: How is it possible that war stokes the hearts of men? The Romans come to our lands and kill to own the land. We fight against them to protect our land. The land is protected, but the price is the blood spilled on its soil. I would like an explanation for war. When you, Jesus, once said that the lost heaven gave birth to war, I awoke. I wonder if my wounded soul can be healed or if I must suffer forever."

Worlds collided by the fire. The words of the warrior from the north had touched and shaken us all. It became even clearer to me that, other than seeing Jesus on the cross, I had never known violence in this world. The world had suffered great wounds.

"Who is more innocent?" asked Jesus. "Those whose hands are soaked in blood or those who don't soil their hands because they do not touch the world? Which wound is greater? That of those who have killed in battle, who have dishonored mothers and children or those who do not partake in life and those whose renunciation tears a wound in their soul and who do not stand up for justice? Believe me, the source of this is the same. It is the decision of free will that makes the tone of life different. If we want to end war, we must end the war within us. War always begins in our own souls, in our own hearts.

The images with which we describe the world shall become our fate if we do not awaken. The refusal to touch the Earth bears an equally long shadow as does the devotion to engage in everything the Earth has to offer. Believe me, love knows no judgment of that which you do." The warrior looked at Jesus with warm, gentle eyes. Almost beseechingly, he asked, "Is there a cure for the wound in my soul? So the gruesome images will end?"

"Yes," Jesus answered. "The Earth will heal you. Not heaven. You have to know that heaven knows no cure, for heaven is always whole, it is always perfect. What you experience of separation and oblivion is connected to the Earth and therefore only it can heal you. The cure for our souls was born in the Great Mother who gives us a home in our human bodies. "Is that the solution?" the warrior asked, "That we no longer wage war?" The fire grew calmer and Jesus waited awhile before he began speaking again.

"People learn the most from wars. Unfortunately. The human soul seeks the boundaries of experience to further advance its own evolution. The human soul, in its divine experience, wants to push the boundaries and there are souls that bear so much power within they have only been able to experience this in war. Their own power becomes clear to them on the battlefield of the worlds. It is about power. What has not been healed between the humans and the worlds is how love treats the light and dark sides of power. Power is light. And the battle for power is our struggle to return to the light. The battlefields have caused great evolutionary steps in the past few eras than has the peaceful isolation of meditation. It is this deed that defines your life. You fill this deed with content. If you sow good deeds, you shall reap good deeds. If you sow bad deeds, you shall reap bad deeds."

Agnisha had arisen and sat down at the fire. His moment of truth had arrived. It was a relief that each of us was allowed to embrace our own truth and withstand it, unknowing and without judgment, before this fire of love.

"I have often asked myself," he began, hesitantly, "if my true joy lies in the renunciation of my life as an Essene. We lead an isolated life and are one with God at every moment, but I have started to notice that something is missing. If I have touched the people out there, I cannot feel what they are experiencing. When I hear you, warrior, tell me of the battlefield, I must admit, I begin to wish I had seen this battlefield. For renunciation alone has not yet made my soul whole."

Agnisha paused and revealed his realization emphatically. "Renunciation alone has not yet made my soul whole."

"I remember your stories," I heard myself say. "Our stories were all written in heaven. I can remember you all. We traveled a long way to reunite with each other here today. And our paths do not end here. I think I understand something now."

Startled, I looked at Jesus and Simon. "There is no preordained path for finding God within us, but there is a holy path that is written within us. It can lead us through great battlefields; it can connect us with those who hate us, who, in unity, become the greatest loving experiences. It can let us fall into our enemies' hands until we can forgive. It can guide us through renunciation, loneliness, in which we raise God up within ourselves in prayer. It can guide us through the fire where we burn and suffer and sink into pain until we rediscover ourselves in devotion. None of these paths is better, but it is our path. If we forget that we are Master and Mistress of our own paths, we will be lost. For that is God within us. God lives within us when we are the gods of our own lives. The love of which you have always told me, I see it now. Love carries us." I paused.

Something had been reborn within me in this fire. I suddenly knew. I looked at Jesus, I looked at Simon. "I have a question for you. Why is it that it is not we who help shape the world, but only the powerful, out there, whom we even suffer to persecute us and who bound you to the cross, Jesus?"

"I know why," I heard Lazarus say. "We renounce power. We renounce the power of God within us, which we create. That is why those who create take power for themselves. Everything we experience in this world is a creation of that which brings forth power."

I looked at Jesus, smiling. The space began to weave around us. "You are beginning to reawaken. You are my friends, you are my companions. The journey began here. The fire has recognized us."

To truly understand Creation, one needs more than religion or enlightenment. To truly be whole and find heaven within oneself, one must walk a path that only we ourselves know. Therein lies a secret, something we will never understand. The fascination of the miracle is when we touch those places in our souls that reconnect us to our perfection.

"Choose your enemies well," Jesus said, "for they will help you to truly walk the path of your initiation. Your allies will support you, but your enemies will guide you to the limits of your experience and be your true initiation."

Jesus preached a harrowing sermon that night about how we could break through the limits of our existence and reveal our stories, stories that were once written in the universe: The enemy as our teacher.

At one time, the apparent enemies were those who nailed Jesus to the cross, who contributed to the story on Earth liberating itself. Many years later, Jesus told us that this was an agreement forged in heaven. "There is a sound barrier between heaven and Earth. In heaven, there is a greater destiny, a greater plan. If we are beyond consciousness, then we know of these agreements. But there is a thick layer of oblivion between human life and conscious existence. Often those who are our enemies in the life of oblivion are actually those whom we love the most. Only we have forgotten the agreement. The enemy on the battle-field who kills you is perhaps he who loves you the most. No one else would take on this burden of guiding you to the limit of your experience out of love. Your enemies will represent your shadows. Your greatest truth lies hidden in the shadows, for your greatest power lies hidden in the shadows. Your power, which you deny. Choose your enemies in heaven and, in your mortal life, your enemies will be chosen as your greatest teachers. If you begin to see your own shadows in your enemies and bow before them, war will come to an end. If you thank your enemy for that which he does unto you, then you are free."

Jesus was the embodiment of love. Direct contact with Him changed everyone's life. He was from the source. Jesus had encountered many souls on His many journeys and sometimes He only needed one look to remind us of heaven and set that life on a new path, out of the darkness, into the twilight and back into the light. He was beyond mortal suffering and drama. His presence led us back to ourselves.

He stood up, took a clump of dirt and threw it into the fire. It was done so abruptly we were all startled. "If you do not finally face the war within you and choose your enemies yourself, you will never awaken from this lethargy," He said. The fire was raging and Jesus was full of fury. Oh my God, how long it had been since I had seen Him like this. But He was right. This lethargy that swelled within us, existed because we did not want to face the truth. We fancy ourselves saintly, but perhaps saintliness was buried in our own war, which did not wish to be seen. Choose your enemies, He had said.

Jesus left the clearing, the fire had grown angry. I didn't dare look at anyone. We were all affected by our power exploding around us. The only option was to devote ourselves to it unquestioningly. I knew exactly what Jesus and Simon were planning. We were supposed to remember our heaven, our stories. The word forgiveness hung in the air. I sank into myself and knew in that moment:

To truly experience forgiveness, the story connected to it must heal. Forgiveness without the sacred story can never come to pass. I had never seen war in my life, but in the images the great warrior from the north had described, murder and manslaughter incarnated within me, reflected by the gruesomeness where blood is worth more than love. These images unsettled me. My dark side was not reflected in these theaters of war, the world of fatal swords and slashing knives. It was the part of me that was light that was reflected therein. Without bidding anyone goodnight, I left the clearing. I was the first to penetrate this spell that held everyone. I wanted to be alone for it was unbearable.

Simon did not come in for a long time and I fell asleep. I fell into a chamber of universal dreams. I wandered between the fields of war, so devastating, they froze my soul. That night carried me further to the places I avoided because they tore so deeply at the abyss of my soul. But Jesus and Simon and God had decided that I could no longer avoid this place if my soul was to heal. The dreams that night taught me the innermost laws of forgiveness. That night, God healed the unspeakable within me. I had to wander in the terror of the event I had banished from my life. There I was, back at the center of the crucifixion.

I was standing among the persecutors. I saw Jesus, covered in blood, and my heart exploded. The pain within me at the images from that time was so great. This image stoked the numbness in my soul. My trauma was born then. I knew my dream wanted me to relive those experiences, but this time, my walk to the cross through the crowd changed. Some screamed and demanded a gruesome death because there was bloodlust in their souls. Others cried and despaired in hopelessness in that hour which rewrote humanity. In the dream, however, I went along my own path to the cross, to my own crucifixion. Suddenly, among the people, Jesus' voice awoke within me and liberated me.

As I walked through the scene as though in a trance, salvation wove within my heart. "Forgive them, even now in this hour. See how great their own pain in oblivion is, the children of God, they know not what they do." I once again walked through the streets of Jerusalem. My feet burned as they once did, but my heart changed. Instead of letting my own crown of thorns prick me and letting my heart run dry, a liberation began to lift in me as I looked into the faces, deep into their eyes, and I knew: They know not what they do.

With each step, I forgave and my heart burned. And my ego burned even deeper. My judgment, which I had passed in that hour on those souls, the children of God. The crown of thorns in my heart was greater than the one Jesus wore on His head. Once again, I stood before the cross. This time, my heart was filled with mercy and I saw that hour anew. His human existence was soaked in blood, His body tortured, but His heart was full of love. Mercy was reborn within me. Jesus, Simon and God had healed me.

And it became even clearer to me that Jesus dissolved on the cross in a self-love that extended beyond the limits of my perception. The divine will never be explainable. My self-love lifted me up and stoked a new fire within me. To love as God does requires death. To fully devote oneself means the death of one's own ego. But, I had to wander at the edge of my experience in order to be healed that night.

Wounded, but healed, I awoke very early and took part in the Essene's morning meditation. It felt good to connect my soul in unity with all of Creation. The Light of Christ was unerring. It carried itself forward through the ages and was still present in the world, hidden in that little temple by the prayers of the Essenes.

I fled into my daily duties and helped in the village wherever I was needed. I yearned for the simplicity in which my inner mantra connected the worlds. "Forgiveness and devotion. Forgiveness and devotion. Forgiveness and devotion." That healed me. Everyone in the village felt the same way. We healed the consternation about the inner war that Jesus had invoked to quench it, by giving the mundane space, trusting that heaven and Earth wanted to reconcile within us.

"Let us return to the source," Jesus spoke as the fire was burning again at twilight. I knew that each of us had passed through deep transitions that day. I realized that Jesus and Simon were flaying us, strip by strip. It had been promised that we would gather our stories in heaven. Jesus threw herbs and petals into the flames. I had watched Him collecting them out in the fields that day. And I had to smile a little at this scene, for I had never observed Him like that before.

The fire received the gifts of nature and there came a silent calm, so gentle and peaceful. It began to smell like a thousand flowers, so divinely rich and imaginative that we were all suddenly in another world. A gentle, quiet and peaceful fire once expanded from that source and filled all of the worlds.

"This was the birth of Agni," Jesus said calmly. "There was nothing that wasn't fire and the worlds could see; the fire was peaceful and benevolent and ignited a fire in everything that lived. There was nothing that wasn't Agni, that wasn't the fire. All beings existed in that moment, for the fire was within them. Agni is the presence of the all-powerful fire. Fire is everything, fire is Creation. This time is so old, as old as you yourselves. The stories of all creatures began to write themselves in this fire, the sacred scriptures were born in the fire, and it was destined that they should write the story of the universe. The eternal fire, that explosion of the light of the universe, lives beyond oblivion. A vast span of oblivion separates us from the light that is reflected in the fire, when the fire bears the eternal and infinite Agni."

"Why is it necessary to forget?" I now noticed that Mary Magdalene still hadn't joined us. She had approached the fire from the darkness, holding Sara in her arms, rocking her back and forth. Mary Magdalene looked so noble in that moment, as though the Goddess Herself were reflected in her. The Goddess, rocking her own child in her arms. Her dignity and her love marked her beauty.

"Oblivion, oblivion, oblivion, oblivion, oblivion, oblivion...," she murmured an endless mantra. It has to be repeated a thousand times.

"Oblivion is the kiss of love," was Jesus' response.

"Can we liberate it?" she asked me. "I don't know, Mary Magdalene." Did I dare do what was within me? "I follow what I feel," I said. "Will you help me?" I looked into the fire and began to pray. "Great Mother, we pray unto you, open your starry womb to us." The dark sky descended over us and came so close the stars danced around us in a trance. The magic of all the worlds enveloped us. Mary Magdalene looked at me, her eyes like stars. "Yes, you are right, it is the Great Mother who must take us under her starry cloak." The prayers of our own fire, born of our primeval femininity became the fire. We prayed until our own souls and hearts were soothed and we felt the divine Mother had accepted us, and our plea to heal the stories within us. The light let the old burden die before our very eyes.

As we realized what was happening because of us, that the magic of the Great Mother acted through us, I looked at Jesus, frightened and uncertain. He nodded. Everything was all right. Everyone would be included in this eternal field of the Mother; it enveloped us with its love and healing. We were all silent and shook with the universe that became our mother. I felt the starry fields caress my skin, touching me with tones from another world. We exploded into starry fields, into brilliant colors and lights and pieced ourselves back together again. The sanctification of the Mother was ecstasy that guided us through the dreamless sleep until we slowly awoke from the intoxication of the worlds and found ourselves back at the fire, which had since burnt out. Stardust glowed within me.

Everything had grown very quiet. Mary Magdalene stood up and went to her sleeping chamber and little by little, everyone left the fire, silently disappearing into the darkness of night. They were swaying with intoxication. But I remained at the fire. I couldn't sleep yet. I kept watch that night. The forces that did not wish to be revealed slept in the unconscious and I could sense them. My powers were present and bridled the rearing dragon. I stoked the fire and was alone for many hours in the solitude of the Mother who watched over me. It was a premonition that had been unleashed in the arms of the completeness of the cosmos of Creation.

A scream echoed throughout the village behind me. I immediately jumped up and I knew that it was Mary Magdalene who had screamed. I ran up to her chamber and practically ran into Mary Magdalene's arms. She screamed, "Come!" They came toward us from the village. Mary Magdalene fended them off, "Stay away! Come Miriam, get Simon!" I ran in a panic and woke Simon. "Come! I do not know what is happening. We must go to Jesus' chamber." We ran up to the hill and what we saw through the open door broke my heart.

Jesus was lying there, unconscious, blood flowing from His open wounds. I looked at Mary Magdalene in desperation. Simon had tears in his eyes.

He knelt beside Jesus and lay his hand on His heart. For a moment, Mary Magdalene and I looked at each other to make sure our presence was wanted in this time of crisis, but we knew the Great Mother bade us stay. We were synchronous. We sank to our knees and took His feet in our hands. We tethered Him to the Earth. Jesus was not with us and blood seeped from the wounds from His crucifixion. Even Simon could not staunch it.

What played out before our eyes was an absolute nightmare. Jesus was lost in His pain. Nothing was speaking to us anymore and even Simon was helpless and could do nothing. Mary Magdalene looked at me, insistently, "Please go and get Sumaja." I ran to the temple and found her praying on her knees in the light of the oil lamps. "Come, we need you. Jesus' stigmata have torn open, He is unconscious."

When Sumaja entered the chamber, she froze. She had not come to heal Jesus. The worlds of the moment were clear before us. She came to be healed herself. "He is doing it for us." I was crying. She knew right away. It was completely silent in the room as she knelt before Jesus. Her entire being was lifted out of its own light. In that moment, as Sumaja knelt before Him, His wounds began to close. Simon went to His side. He grew calmer and as Mary Magdalene and I held Jesus' feel, he witnessed what was destined to happen. Jesus' wounds suddenly staunched themselves. His breath slowly returned. Time slowed down for us and the panic subsided. Jesus reached out His hand. "Sumaja, come to me." He took her hand. Jesus was very weak. He said, "It is time to heal. We are all caught in a web that binds us. If we do not decipher it, we cannot continue on any path." He held Sumaja and I noticed her innermost being begin to relax.

Jesus came back to life. "It is good that you are ready to heal the story of your heaven. Then I no longer need to die for you. Come to me, Miriam," He said. I took a step back, instead of going to Him. "No, Lord. Why me?" "Because you know," He said. Everything rebelled within me because the knowledge felt like a curse in that moment. I couldn't deny that I had had the heaven-sent dreams since our departure in Ephesus. I dreamt all of the stories, I knew all of the stories, but my innermost being forbade me to speak. "Come to me," Jesus bade me imploringly and blood began to flow from His heart again. Everything raged within me; I could not go to Him. Everything within me refused. I cried so bitterly it tore me apart. I wanted it to stop. I felt guilty for what was happening. All my powers began to turn on me.

"No, I do not want to," only my love for Him forced me to take a step out of my despair. The pain I felt for Him was greater than the pain I felt for myself. My empathy for His wounds was greater than the refusal of not wanting to know. "You must be ready to take on a burden, Miriam. Only if you are ready to drink of my blood can you receive the curative medicine." I cried so bitterly because my love for that which was, shattered. "What should I do, Lord?" My body trembled.

"Drink my blood," said Jesus.

The Blood of Christ.

The sacred blood.

The Holy Grail.

That is the secret of life.

I am life.

I am the blood. I am the wound of healing.

I am the resurrection.

If you drink my blood, your soul will be healed.

I bowed before Jesus, ready to walk the path of nakedness without shame and without avoidance. I was ready to reabsorb the guilt stored within me. So be it. My soul would only heal if drank the blood of truth. I knew what others had forgotten. I know the stories of heaven, without wanting to know them.

I sank down to Jesus and looked at Him. I merged with Him. I lay my head on His heart and my mouth touched the blood. I drank from the heart of Jesus, the drops of blood dripping on my tongue. I ate the forbidden fruit. I accepted the offer of the sacred, fertile blood. I bore no blame. I was naked, free in my soul.

I assumed my place. I am she who knows everything. The space of my soul knows of the darkness and the light. I sink into darkness until light shines from it.

Healing inflamed my heart and streams of tears flowed from me, mourning the years of oblivion. I was born beneath God's lap to heal love. Crying, the war healed my being. Light and darkness were one in this love. "Lord, teach me this path. Let me be a student of this path of true love." Jesus' hand lay on my heart. "This path will be harder than any path you have ever taken. It will push you to your limits, limits you have never known before. You know why." I said, "And that is why I want to walk it."

Each of the others drank the blood of Christ. Simon and Sumaja knelt beside Him, one after the other, and received the sacred host. Mary Magdalene first kissed the blood of His heart, then His mouth.

His wounds had not broken open because He was suffering. He had sacrificed Himself for us, to liberate us. Jesus fell asleep and we remained to watch over Him. Mary Magdalene came to me and drew me toward her. My soul was still burning. Mary Magdalene and I leaned against the living, stone wall. "Why do I know all of this?" I asked, almost silently. "Because you have never forgotten. You... you live in the conscious and the unconscious in every moment. Your name is older than this time, but your name may not be born until future ages. What you are will never be denied. The power that preserves the unconscious and conscious in life.

Our story is old. It was not only written throughout many lives on Earth, but also much earlier in the heavens. We were once born there, all of us. The source of our souls, our origin, our essence lies in the multi-faceted heavens and universal creations. We were born, innocent, in the bosom of the divine. The expansion of this universe and its infinite, creative force urged us to partake in writing the stories of the universe. God placed a quill in each of our cradles when we were born in His image, and we began to write ourselves. Once, each of us burned to give our souls meaning. The adventure of life.

The language of oblivion has slowed our ink. We have become hesitant and the lethargy of oblivion tortures us to continue writing our story. Oblivion is a Great Goddess and her cloak has been laid over the universe. The souls asked to forget. But no one knows what really happened anymore.

"Mary Magdalene, tell me, what are you feeling?"

"He is my beloved in all times. I love Him more than my own life. His blood now flows through my veins. My heart can hardly bear the love my soul pours out in His presence. What I just saw, carried me to the edge of death. When I kissed Him, I knew I had awakened. I have lived in fear all this time, that He would leave again and leave me here. I know that He will stay now. He has decided to stay with me. I can now accept my prophecy for I know that He will not abandon me."

Jesus had united that which cannot be united. Light and material pulsed as one.

I awoke, screaming, that night. Full of panic, a deadly battle raged in my heart. It struggled between stopping out of pure disgust and gasping for the breath of life. Simon tore me from my dream and took me in his arms. The frozen scene, as Jesus lay in His own blood repeated in my dreams so many times until it was all right and I had digested it. My body and my soul struggled for unity. There was nothing more to learn on the subject. So I decided, consciously, to bring my soul back. Then I dozed for a few hours.

When I returned to my body, Simon was sitting next to me, watching over me. "Thank you," I told him. I knew he didn't want to sleep until every part of my soul had returned home. Jesus had torn open all of the wounds within us from all of time. He had opened all of the portals at once, to close them all at once. I felt as though all of the parts of my soul had returned to me and I was whole. But my soul was like skins of light and material, like fabric torn into many little pieces and had now been laid out to be sown back together. The scraps of fabric lay next each other; sowing them back together was painful. Simon kissed me and fell asleep. He loved me until I was whole. He protected me.

The Sacred Oils

Shivering, I stepped out into the cold morning. After the few steps I took to warm myself in the sun, I couldn't believe my eyes. I saw a red sea of petals at the edge of our village. I went closer and the roses the Essenes had planted around the village had blossomed overnight. They had long since withered as it was too dry and hot, but overnight, they had turned green and the big, red roses were once again in bloom. I had come in deep despair and when I saw the roses, everything changed. I lowered my nose to nature, which gave us the magic of healing we had been seeking. The scent and the color of the roses enveloped me like velvet. My entire soul was embedded. I knew the world and its conflict would not be healed by conflict, but by us awakening as initiates and this knowledge being our cure. The beauty of Mother Nature had brought me home. And in that moment, I knew what I had to do.

There were beings around the roses. I connected with the rosebushes and the Devas around them and bade them show me the healing roses they might give us. I returned to the village with my boon without telling anyone what had happened outside the village. I went to the chamber where the sacred oils were stored. No one was there. I wasn't certain if I should ask or if I should simply follow my instincts, which came from the divine like impulses that pieced together the fragments of healing. I knew we were supposed to make the seven sacred oils. I had no idea where they came from, but I knew that I knew them and they returned.

I saw the oils in my mind, telling me of themselves; that they united the masculine and the feminine in the Light of Christ and would heal us. I decided to seek out Sumaja first. I found her in her chamber. She silently signaled me permission to open the door to her chamber. She lay weakened in her bed that night. I only asked if I could have permission to take oils from her chamber. I was miraculously full of life energy. She said, "Take anything you need." I sensed that she was so weak, she wanted to be alone. So I left her.

Back in the chamber, I took the pure almond oil. The Essenes had begun to make oils from the materials the wilderness of Gaul gave us. I took a large bowl and lay the rose petals from my apron in it. I poured the oil over them. It turned deep red before my eyes. A magical field of the divine surrounded me and I celebrated this miracle. The roses condensed and became a presence that combined all that could not be united.

In that moment, I was present as an initiate I knew the ceremonies and the composition. I divided the oil into seven little amphorae and brought them to Simon. "I found the remedy we need. The roses miraculously grew overnight and their beings showed me how to make the remedy for which we asked. We have to do it together. I have already prepared everything. We have to recharge them together and then I will bring them to Jesus and Mary Magdalene. Each of us is a key; only together can it take its effect through our light. It brings us what we seek."

I bade him recharge the rose oils with me. And in the alchemy of our sanctity, we recharged the oils with our prayers. The roses condensed and became a presence that combined all that could not be united. A red light appeared above us. We looked in each other's eyes and united our love for all the worlds. We perfected what we were able to complete. I packed the little amphorae in a piece of cloth and gently knocked on Jesus' and Mary Magdalene's door. When I opened it, Jesus was sitting on a cot and Mary Magdalene was giving Him a brew of herbs to drink. His eyes began to gleam. "You found it," He said to me. I presented the oils. "If you add your part of the cure to these oils, then we will have the seven sacred oils and we can heal the community."

Mary Magdalene took the oils first and sank to her knees and began to pray in supplication. Then she passed the amphorae to Jesus. Jesus took each vial of oil in His hands and suddenly His hands and the oils turned red. They glowed as red as the blood, so sacred I barely dared touch them again. Jesus and His beloved melted together in blood-red love.

He said, "Help me with this, Miriam."

"How?" I asked.

"Heal me first," he bade.

I bowed before my Lord, who had guided me through my soul all these years and then took each of the oils and brushed them on his stigmata, praying. I was amazed by what was happening to me. The oils healed Him and as I brushed them on, I became complete. I didn't know who was healing whom in that moment. With each oil, I grew more complete. Jesus looked at me, full of love. I felt more myself with each coat.

He bade me also help Mary Magdalene. I took the seven sacred oils and brushed them on several places on her body, always waiting until I could see that the sacred soul in her body and the knowledge within her had been perfected. She was sobbing. When my ceremony was over, she lay her hands in mine and put her forehead to mine. As we stood there, the village awoke at our feet and breathed new life.

I witnessed how we, as mediators between heaven and Earth, brought the remedy that would help us begin our journey into the new era. I took the rose oils with me to our chamber. The curative effect of these jewels came from the divine hand upon which we had called. Our worlds reconnected around us and became whole. The pain became scars on our souls and then maps. But the pain no longer carried us back to the powerlessness of war, instead it made us whole. I was reborn in my existence. More complete than ever before.

A short time later, Mary Magdalene was standing at my doorstep. She looked tired; her hair was in wild knots. "How is Jesus?" I asked. "His wounds have closed. He is still sleeping," she responded. "What we experienced last night was terrible," I said. "Where the terror is the greatest, the cure comes closer to us," she smiled. Mary Magdalene took me in her arms. Her soul relaxed. The she laid her head on my lap and once again, we began to hum like a swarm of bees in the evening sun.

From afar, we saw Simon coming toward us. He looked at us both and smiled. "I came to tell you that we will gather at the fire again tonight. Come when you are ready. As soon as the sun sets we will gather at the fire." I sat up. "How is Jesus?" "Better," said Simon. "I was just with Him. Take your time." I looked at him, a bit confused, for I was really just coming to after the shock. He brushed his hand across my head. "Don't worry. Nothing more will be lost."

That soothed me.

Then he went back to the village. The aura of tranquility he left behind was good for our souls. We were so familiar to each other that we could be alone in the presence of the other. We no longer had to hum; we were steeled for battle. The core of our feminine power was awakening and declared a manifest within us without knowing where this force of power would go. Enveloped by the fragility of our souls, our primal feminine power rose up and declared: I am powerful.

The silence filled the concurrence of power and powerlessness. The sun warmed us and regardless of how lonely and cold the night had been, its promise that it would rise on the horizon was guaranteed. The Earth and nature at our feet would never die. Nature had always been our Great Mother. She had taken in our souls, given birth to us and enveloped our dreams in her tides.

Healing Our Inner Country

We lived in Gaul, the realm of the Celts. After the Romans had conquered it, they had built roads that meandered across the land like snakes. The cobblestone Viae controlled the rough terrain, arrogantly exuding certain victory. Where the land became knotted and inaccessible, there were invisible, woven hedges, paths hidden behind thickets and high-growing defensive undergrowth. Hidden therein, the world was reborn for us. There were even more secrets that preserved their own mysteries in the places where the Romans could not go. They knew about us before we knew about them.

Our world began to intertwine from within with the outside world in which we found ourselves. Our cocoons had been dissolved. We had arisen from the ashes of the dream and the pursuit of our faith and our inner shadows no longer created enemies. We were free to love and had pledged ourselves to the massive undertaking of planting peace in the hearts of the enemies.

We had been born into a new world. I barely recognized the village. Everyone suddenly took the initiative. Tilling new fields, going outside to speak to the people. Everyone suddenly had dreams and plans. It was as though we had awakened from a nightmare. The wholeness of heaven found a home within our bodies. Even though we didn't know exactly who we were, where we came from and where we were going, life began to pulsate and the dreams built a world in which we completed each other.

We were all happy. Jesus and Simon spent time discussing the future of the Essene village with Sumaja and Agnisha and Mary Magdalene, Martha and I took the time to take long walks, exploring nature and spending time with our children. We lived in an idyll in which our shimmering future was taking shape in our hearts. I knew we had arrived in a golden parallel world. And I also knew that there were many other worlds.

Unbelievable things were happening around the village. Plants that shouldn't be blooming, because the nights were much too harsh, began to bloom. Grapevines in the fields grew little buds and within three days, they bore fruit we could eat. We gave this magic space. We had breached the world in which the Devas I knew from times gone by suddenly had the chance to consciously help shape our lives. We laid the grapes on the table for Jesus and as He touched them, He said, "By working with the forces of nature and love, you will bring forth things and you will no longer need to worry about anything. It is up to you to make contact with these beings, for they live in another dimension. In order to bring forth the present and true fruits in our spaces, they need your love."

Lazarus had reawakened. "How am I to do that, practically?" he asked. Jesus smiled at him. "Your heart, Lazarus. Love! Break through these boundaries with love and break through the boundaries to nature for she is our mother and gives us everything." Several Essenes had spoken up, saying they wanted to be trained. They said, "Lord, can't you train us? For we would like to cultivate the fields with the help of the Devas. We would like to see what miracles we can bring forth between heaven and Earth if you teach us."

Jesus thought for a while. "We will all contribute our knowledge and teach each other how to cultivate these fields, in harmony with the powerful creatures that are currently present in the world beyond and who seek our cooperation. It is God's will that we learn this, for humanity has long since forgotten."

We planted wine and olives and cultivated our fields with the seeds from the farmers who gave them to us. They sacredly preserved and honored the time capsules of life. They brought us into contact with people and the Devas became our friends. We healed. The sources of the Earth were inexhaustible. We rediscovered the mysticism of nature.

Things went wrong too, but the Devas said this was part of the process. We had to learn to use the earth currents beneath us and listen to them more intently, for not every plant thrives on every earth current.

Mother Earth taught us to recognize the earth currents beneath us. Some were deeper in the earth and others closer to the surface and we learned how plants and earth currents communicated with each other. How the plants brought forth power in some currents and yet they were unable to gather power from other currents. All of this did not come from knowledge, but in conversation. Only by listening did we open a dimension that gave us abundant gifts.

When winter came, it felt like the old days. The optimistic mood had inspired Sumaja to start teaching again. The light in her eyes had returned. Agnisha had taken on the task of communing with the forces of nature and the Devas, like in the old days, when everything around the Essene village had been green. Back then, the Essenes had cultivated their fields with the power of their love and their purity and grew plants because they were at one with the elements. We were building the new on the pillars of tradition. The old was returning, shaping itself within us and seeking a new expression.

I enjoyed being in the old rhythm of the Essenes, even if our community was smaller than it was back then. The optimistic mood and hope was good for us. I took part in the classes sometimes, for Jesus had tasked us with no longer passing on knowledge from teacher to student as we did in the old Essene village, but striking out on new paths; by delving into our own knowledge, we connected to our primal sources. Teachers no longer conveyed knowledge to students. We were all connected to our sources and these sources created with each other.

The Essenes also began to offer their healing hands again. The village and the soil we wanted to cultivate were symbolic for the fertile soil we were building for our future. The cultivation of the earth and our ritual life were allies.

We were to stay here, in one place, for the longest we had in a long time. We decided to stay with the community until the next harvest festival, for Jesus and Simon agreed that something was growing within us that needed time.

By spring, the plant Devas were devoted to us. We learned that every plant had a Deva. They taught us that every idea had a Deva, a being of light that had a personality. They also taught us that they were different from us. In their other-world, they were always bound to the presence of the joy of the One. Nature, which knew no duality. They also taught us that they did not have free will. That they only pulsated in the will of the unity of nature and the Great Mother. But we also experienced them as personalities, as angels and great Devas or little Devas that played around the plants. We got to know their childishness. This reawakened our own childishness within us.

Lazarus performed a great service. He went to the villages and introduced the Essenes. We slowly started to understand the language of the region around us. Until then, we had been prisoners in our village of light. Now, something was opening. From our world to the world out there.

Although we were always at risk of running into people who might recognize us and would persecute us again, this never seemed to happen. The people slowly started to become friends with the Essenes and the Essenes began to heal this land and roamed throughout it like wandering monks. When people were sick, someone was sent to the Essene village to ask for our help. It was for us to decide in which world we lived. If we decided to live the path that allowed others to judge or persecute us, we created that world. In the moment we decided to create another world, a golden world began to form around us. We were rich.

Then autumn came and the fruits were ripe in our fields and we aspired to make the first wine ourselves. The Essenes had made contact with the farmers in the area and they taught us how to grow and press wine. That autumn, found us all stomping in vats full of grapes. We were happy and intoxicated by life as we stomped on the red grapes, for everything around us was red again. As we picked the berries from the vines, we thanked the Devas of the earth and the Devas of the grapes with our songs. That autumn, we filled our first casks of wine.

The Ruby-Red Night

On the first evening of autumn, on the cusp of day and night, we all gathered for a great feast. It was a good feeling to have brought in the summer harvest, leaving us enough to feed ourselves for the winter. We had learned how to store much of the harvest for the winter, for the farmers had shared their wisdom with us. We were rich people gathering at that table, when Jesus stood and poured the wine.

Simon had been meditating in his room for several days. When new eras began, Jesus and Simon began to coordinate with each other. Light and love expanded their heaven at night to pray new creation into being on Earth. Simon had spent every night in meditation and I gave him this space.

The sky changed its hue until everything around us was ruby red. Jesus said, "This red light appears when you embody your own heaven and have arrived in your own sacred world. I do not know if you are aware of this, but you are all free. There are no more karmic tracks behind you anymore. Everything before you is a pure creation of what you want to create from your heaven while in this body. You are free to go, for your souls are free. This is the beginning of all ages. This is how you once began. We were all born free in heaven. Each in the presence of the Lord. You were free to choose.

You have reached precisely this point again. Simply because you have purified your thoughts and feelings and allowed love to become part of the space of all your creation. We will now strike out on new paths. I will tell you what you we can create between the ages, but I want for each of you two know that you are no longer karmically bound to all of these things, you are free to decide."

I noticed that Simon had sat down next to me. Jesus looked at Simon and Simon said, "The evolution of the Earth is partly determined by humanity. You must know that this part of the Earth, the part we know, is only a small part. The Earth is much larger. It is home to many cultures. Some live more consciously, others less. The Earth develops with humanity and the awareness the people wish to accept."

Then Jesus spoke, "Over the past few nights we have learned that we have another chance to spread our teachings throughout the world. And to plant the seeds of the Lord in teachings that begin to distance themselves from God. I will start traveling again. We have also learned that there is a place in the Himalayas where we can store all of our knowledge, between the ages, for the future. But we must find this place. If we write our books with humanity, they may disappear one day, into the fingers of greedy power, lost forever. To truly bring our books to the future, there are places that reside between the ages and if we store our stories there, they will be there for humanity in the future." Jesus continued, "I am once again ready to teach that which is not yet on Earth."

Simon added, "I will go with Jesus on His journey. Miriam and you, Mary Magdalene, are free to decide if you will join us and write the paths between the ages, so Shiva and Shakti, masculine and feminine, can write a new story into the Earth with the Light of Christ. We could begin to rewrite the path of Shakti with the Light of Christ, for Shakti embodies Creation. We have a great opportunity for the world of the future by beginning to write the new story and seek out those who will write this story with us.

Essentially, every person writes history. But we have to find the people who have already reached an awareness of the greater whole, to help write the greater pattern of the history of the universe, to help raise up those who are in this environment. Beings that have reached that awareness, who write with God's hand and with God Himself, are required so the One can be created. Those who create unconsciously and only create the writings of power only do so for a short time."

I looked into Mary Magdalene's eyes. We had both already suspected. Our inner images had shown us. Now it was time for us to make a decision about being mothers again. I said, "I would like to discuss that with my child and make my decision based on that." John was old enough and mature enough that he would tell me what he wanted. Mary Magdalene nodded. "I would also like to discuss it with my little Sara. Then we will make our decision.

The beauty that surrounded us told us of a book of God that wrote itself on Earth. We talked about the wonderful future of the Essenes, for we could all see the vision that this land would be preserved for a long time, beyond the unrest of the Earth. We were also aware that another story was writing itself beside us: A story of death, the darkness of humanity, which Jesus had proclaimed.

Instead of hesitating and wondering how God could allow the worlds to exist, yet be so different from each other, it became clear to me that we were creating this world ourselves. And that we had to take responsibility for everything we created. That those who lived in war with hatred for each other and who overpowered souls, had created it themselves because they wanted it that way and humanity had to walk this path and create in unison or create separately and that this was humanity's task and lesson.

It soothed my heart to know the Essenes had found their home in this wonderful place, at least for many centuries, until the twelfth century. Until then, they would continue to live and contribute toward this land's abundance.

Something new had been born within me. I knew that if I died and left the old, the familiar, behind, the birth of the new would be upon us, but it no longer frightened me. For everything was interwoven in a red light in which the beauty that died gave birth to the new beauty in that same moment.

Mary Magdalene glowed in wonderful, ruby-red light that night. That light grew thicker around us and I asked Jesus. "What is that light? Whenever I see it, it is like I am home. My sacred heart bleeds within me with joy. When this light is near me, I delve into a depth, a depth of sacred passion that brings me so close to life that I can smell it, taste it and feel it."

Jesus passed me a glass of wine and said, "Drink." Then He poured a glass of wine for each person at the table. "The ruby-red light is the embodiment of the Light of Christ. When it is embodied in human flesh, the passion for life is transformed into the pure love of Christ. Then the essence of life begins to pulsate between heaven and Earth.

The Light of Christ appears from the heavens as a white light. But when it is embodied in material and in the human body, it turns ruby-red. And then life is while."

"So, is it the Light of Christ I feel?" I wanted to know.

"Yes," said Jesus, "the sacred heart, exposed in full unity with the abundance of the Earth. That is what you feel."

"And how does it transform?" I asked, for I knew that this feeling also pulsated between life and death in a greater context.

Jesus was loving and enlightened.

"The Light of Christ appears in three colors.

It comes as purity and white light when it is born and brings forth new creation. It reaches its acme as ruby-red light, where heaven and Earth, material and light, melt together and life becomes one great passion. And it is reborn in black light: a light that casts no shadows.

All aspects are embodied at this table. Know that I am this white light. When I come, I bear a new Light of Christ, for the Light of Christ takes of different forms. It has different aspects of Creation that always come to Earth at different times.

Simon embodies the black light. The Light of Christ that casts no shadow. It is the highest form of healing we can receive. One who knows, in the black light, how he will die will be healed completely. He shall know wholeness and be reborn.

The red light is the Shakti that the women and goddesses embody. You bear it in you, Miriam and you too, Mary Magdalene. At the same time, this ruby-red light is borne by all Essenes that carry the Shakti aspect of Christ through the worlds. But that aspect of Christ has been disconnected and has not yet returned to the Essenes. Before we go, we will all try to bring the Shakti aspect of Christ back to the Essenes so you can nourish yourselves in these fires. Then our journey shall begin."

Everything was holy that evening. I had never felt the world around me this way before. I could sense every heavenly being beside me. We were in embodied flesh. Everything smelled of wonderful earth and heaven. Our cure came from the perfection in which everything and every event found its place. Every being in our circle had his or her own destiny. We were ready to determine our destinies ourselves and create with each other.

The fear for our children, whom we could not take on the journey into the unknown at the end of the world, soon subsided. "It is good for us here," said John the next morning, squinting in the sun. Mary Magdalene and I looked at these little creatures, full of awe. They were glowing in ruby-red light. John was crystal clear at only five years of age. "I want to stay here. Mother and John will never lose each other." John pressed Sara's hand tighter. "I want to stay with Sara." These two creatures would be with each other from childhood and beyond. They did not wish to adventure as we did. They wanted to grow up in the community of the Grail over which they would one day stand guard.

Mary Magdalene and I cried. We lived an unconventional life. Our children had decided we should go on the journey because it was our mission. And so they decided that they would stay in the Essene village. And it nearly broke our hearts.

The Grail and its Destiny

There were only two beings back then who knew where the Grail was hidden. Lazarus and Agnisha. The decision to keep this knowledge so limited was made in order to protect the Grail should something happen or should our community be betrayed. I sought out Simon and Jesus, for the Grail glowed in my inner visions. It was calling to us. I found them both on that fateful morning in the autumn sun sitting at a table with Sumaja and Agnisha. I disturbed them, wittingly. "May I interrupt for a moment? I would like to journey to the Grail with our children. I would like to unite the wholeness in the Grail's Light of Christ and our missions and the visions. The Grail is calling us."

Simon said, "Why don't you ask Lazarus if he will guide you to the Grail? As far as I know, it is about an hour from here. You could be back tonight."

"We will join you on the journey," I called to Simon as I walked away to find Lazarus.

I found him outside in the fields making the last preparations with the people and preparing our fields for the pending cold season. "Come, lead us to the Grail." He called, brusquely, "What?"

"We want to go to the Grail. Can you lead us there?"

As was always his nature, Lazarus packed his things immediately. "All right. I will be right with you. We have to hike about an hour. Take things for your children." We made quick preparations and then began our hike.

Lazarus constantly checked to ensure we weren't being followed. It was very important to everyone that the Grail remain protected, for it was not meant for the wrong hands. We had to fight our way through a large thicket for a while. I hardly knew how I would get our children through, but Lazarus helped us until we reached a rocky hill and Lazarus uncovered an otherwise invisible entrance that led into the ground. "I found this place. The Grail showed it to us." He pushed the undergrowth aside and we had crawl down a long, narrow hallway deep underground. Sara and John enjoyed the adventure. We women did not. The deeper we traveled into the grotto, the more its darkness received us. Lazarus had brought oil lamps which shone until we finally reached a cave which housed the Grail itself. A holy relic awaited us within, in the bosom of Mother Earth. Her nature had formed a temple from the psyche of her dark light. She had created folds, layer-by-layer, until the textures crystallized into a temple of light in one of its breathing hollows.

The Grail stood in a niche, small compared to the grotto surrounding it, but it came from another dimension and its light was so bright, so strong, it illuminated everything. We knelt, reverently, before the Grail and prayed for insight, in awe of its beauty. The Grail had melted consciousness and become a complete entity. It conveyed to us that it wished to return to the community that day, for it wanted to place its seal on the new community. The light grew warmer and brighter in that womb beneath the Earth. Mary Magdalene and I looked at each other, confused, for we had both been conveyed the same information from the Grail.

But we had never been permitted to receive decisions from the Grail before. Still, it had called to us. We also knew that we could not tell Lazarus of this decision, for his orders came from Jesus. I could only think of one course of action. I asked Sara and John quietly, "Is it right for us to take the Grail with us because it wants to return to the community? It wants to usher in the new era of our community." John went directly to the Grail and touched it with his little finger. Our children did not give us any further signs.

We had to follow our own intuition and what we had felt. When Lazarus went ahead with the light and led us back out, I placed the Grail in my apron. Soon, we were back in the thicket, fighting our way through, until the landscape opened back up. Lazarus didn't seem to suspect anything. Once we were back in the village, I sought out Jesus and Simon first. Jesus simply said, "That is good. The Shaktis have brought the Grail back. It wanted to come to us. It is all right, Miriam."

Mary Magdalene and I were relieved, for we had never allowed ourselves to receive instructions from the Grail. But the signs of the new era, the powers of

Shakti and the Light of Christ embraced each other, flirting anew. They began to listen to each other; this was the first sign.

We held our children proudly by the hand and were enveloped by a special light. I was relieved that my inner voice and our corresponding intuition had done the right thing. "Jesus, when will we leave?" I asked. "Miriam, I don't know yet. There are still many things left to do. You must understand that it is once again time for light to create. We can bring the first seeds back to Earth. We will stay here until we have created the first seeds together. We are creating the future and showing humanity new paths. These seeds shall begin here. We will listen to them and hear what they tell us."

The Powers of Shakti Return

We gathered several days later after evening meditation, after we had immersed ourselves unceasingly in the Light of Christ. Everyone in the village melded into one community and we absorbed the binding forces of the impulses. Jesus requested that Mary Magdalene and I allow ourselves to fall so deeply into the depths of our souls until we could touch the ruby-red Shakti fire, the powers of Shakti. For the Essenes needed the powers of Shakti back. We had been given the ability to immerse ourselves in these powers and give them form. To develop a new era, they encompassed time.

Every person who lived here, new and old familiar faces, had all joined us. They had made the long journey across the sea and had fled Palestine. Some I recognized and others, whom I did not, had joined us from the surrounding areas.

They had adopted our lifestyle and we had become a mixture of cultures. A mixture of the culture from which we came, from the old country where our legend was written and the culture of the new country with its hidden, wild beauty. The people who came from Gaul were diamonds in the rough; the Earth had not yet mined them. But the beauty of the golden light that lived in this land also shone within them.

I loved this huge table which Lazarus had built of wood; wood from the surrounding area. The benches were simple, like the simplicity of the spirit. We had thick blankets which Lazarus had bought from the people in the area, who wove them from the sheep's wool. They were beautiful colors, for the people in the area had learned the skill of dying wool other colors from the Arabic countries. I loved these blankets and when we sat on the benches in the evening after preparing our meal, they warmed us in gentle red.

Our little gatherings were sacred to us. As was the wine.

That evening, I was the first person Jesus bade come to Him and He whispered in my ear, "Would you get the Grail?"

I started, for I had completely forgotten about the Grail. I had taken it from under my skirt and simply left it in our chamber like a little treasure and forgotten it there in the excitement of the last few days. So I went to retrieve it. When I came into the chamber, the Grail had dissolved into a gleaming light and the contours of the chamber crossed over to other dimensions. The Grail glowed. I hardly dared touch it, for I feared it was too hot. So I first took it carefully in the fabric of my apron, but to my amazement, the gleaming light around it was not hot. It was white light and in that moment, when I touched the Grail, my visions were immediately borne away.

I brought the Grail, enveloped in a white cloth, placed it carefully before Jesus and released it from my hands. Jesus and Simon looked at it for a long time. Not even Lazarus dared say a word.

I wasn't certain if this light was destructive or good. There was something odd about it. After we finished eating and clearing the tables, Jesus placed the Grail in the center. "It is time for you to learn about the creation of light. The Grail decided today to teach us of a light that was once destructive many moons ago. Some of you remember perhaps: this light was once used in Atlantis to activate the destructive forces of this light. But in the universe, this light is one of creation.

When it was misused, this light contributed toward destroying a large portion of the Earth, for it grew out of control. We call it atomic light. The challenge humanity will face in the future will be to use this light benevolently and study it without it becoming destructive. It is the highest form of creative light that, when misused, can be the highest form of destruction. But the Grail decided that you should first learn about this light. If humanity knew that the Light of Christ and the Grail were the cure for this destructive light, they would find the solution. But to do so, they need the poetry of humility.

Jesus said, "Do not touch the Grail right now. It wants to heal this light within you." Simon was the only one who could touch it in this context. In his hands, a healing light appeared that also looked like something solid, like sweets. He went around and gave each of us a healing light.

He said, "The destructive light of Atlantis shall now be healed. Memories of the destructive light will awaken within you, but this medicine will make you whole again."

The Atlantian sky balled up once again above the Earth and above us. Protected by the healing light, the Grail's Light of Christ, which Simon had manifested in his hands, I was able to immerse myself in that time. Fragments of Atlantis came to each of us. From that time when we were all still light and created with life. In that era, when we didn't know how to connect these forces with the Earth's Light of Christ, we brought much destruction upon the worlds.

The experience of Atlantis was healed in me that evening. I became fully aware of the healing taking place within me. Since the time of Atlantis, we had been afraid to create with light. We did not touch it anymore. The darkness had become comfortable for many, for this quieted the trauma.

But if we truly wanted to become powerful again, we had to begin creating with light again. The light comes from God. It was love when it began. Only the separation of love and knowledge made this light destructive.

Unleashing the Feminine Powers

The Grail became another character in our landscape. It was given a little altar in our meditation room and Jesus, Simon and Sumaja allowed anyone to go in from time to time to pray, meditate, connect to its light or receive answers. Everyone in the community was acknowledged as initiates and among us initiates, we knew that at any time, the right person would be tasked with sharing their knowledge with the community. This ability of the community was now being used consciously, so everyone could contribute toward creating.

I myself began to follow my inner instincts, my intuition, the very next day and several times a day, I went to the rosebushes that had blessed us last autumn and which were still in bloom. It was late autumn and I picked red roses that felt like velvet on my hand. These roses smelled like the pure ruby-red light. They had grown in the plant world as the embodiment of the Light of Christ.

I continued following my intuition and, several times a day, I laid a circle of red roses around the base of the Grail and then sank into my meditations in order to touch the powers of Shakti in the ruby-red light. For a long time, no concrete images came to me, rather I simply experienced it as light that coursed through the material and found its expression in plants and humans, if they allowed it. I also began to understand that the material permitted to receive this ruby-red light, the powers of Shakti in the Light of Christ, which was so pure and rich and abundant, I could only receive it if the material itself had been purified. First, the transformation of the material had to be completed for the material itself to be ready to accept it, whether by humans or in the plant worlds.

If we were to share our pure powers of love with the plant world, in return, the plants would be able to give us plants capable of embodying the ruby-red power of Shakti. And if we purify our bodies, our thoughts and emotions, we will be ready to receive this Light of Christ which creates from itself and from us. We create in completely different ways if we do not create from separation, but from the light of Shakti, the ruby-red light, for everything becomes a sacred place. Everything we do is so filled with the abundance of life that we are enchanted.

After several days, the roses began to speak to me. They reminded me that I had collected all of the roses throughout the winter and dried them in a room the Essenes used to store all of their oils and essences. The ruby-red light and the Grail directed me to make a powder out of them and they gave me inner visions of fire ceremonies. That was how I was to bring the light of Shakti back to the Essenes. And I thanked the maps of heaven.

I went to the room and gathered the roses I had dried and retrieved a mortar and pestle from the kitchen. I went out into nature and began to sing. I sat down in a quiet place and began to sing old songs and pestle the roses until they were pulverized and I was left with a deep-red powder. I blessed it with prayers dedicated to nature, the Devas, the Light of the Mother's powers of creation and the ruby-red powers of Shakti. Then I went back and poured the powder into a bowl that I had cleansed with water, for everything had to be pure. These were my preparations until Jesus was ready to bring the fire of Shakti back to the Essenes.

Mary Magdalene had gone on her own journey. Still, we sensed we were synchronously connected with each other in this creative process of bringing the powers of Shakti back from heaven.

I sensed, but did not really know, what she had received, but I remained curious as to how our aspects of creation, sent from heaven, would come together. The Atlantian light had closed something within us that we needed to finally dissolve all resistance to the light.

After several days of silence and when the table had been cleared in the evening, Jesus went and retrieved the Grail and placed it in the center of the table. We all grew much quieter when we saw the light of warm love emanating from the Grail that evening.

A black light pulsated within it, the primal light, that embodied the deep silence of the universe. We all grew so silent in this space that expanded blissfully around us. Simon reached into this light and held it out to us in his left hand.

"This is the light of Creation, born from the golden fire. It fills the entire universe with infinite silence. And in this light, golden light and the fire itself are born. The silence of the light is with us today, for the Grail wants me to teach you certain things. This state is called omnipresence and the black light seems intent on letting you experience this state. It is the state in which you will think in complete synchronicity with the universe. In the future, it will give you the opportunity to exist among people without falling into duality because you will flow in the simultaneity of the universe. This will give you the ability to know when danger is lurking so you can take precautions. You will remain untouched in the midst of the energies and be able to live in the synchronicity of time."

Simon came and marked our necks with this light. And I noticed how the state I was naturally in grew more substantial. I was thinking in all directions at the same time and felt the thoughts simply developing above me. The difference between my linear and simultaneous thought no longer existed. I realized that I was often in this state, especially when my visions came to me. But to enter this state with everyone present at the table was amazing, for we were all suddenly in synch with the universe. It gave us the ability to anchor ourselves in our own heaven so we were in this world and the dual thoughts could no longer touch us. We simply ignored them.

I realized in that moment that Jesus and Simon always lived in this state. They could switch their thought structures from simultaneity, in which they received information and could be among people in order to focus on things when they wanted to drive them forward.

This black light brought us the peace for which we yearned for so long. It was so calm, we immersed ourselves into a universe of black light. It allowed us to return home in the silence of the universe where there was no sound to be heard and everything was simultaneous. The silence is the final cure for the soul. If we can reach it, we can immerse ourselves in it and decide how we go into the world, because the world no longer controls us and our reactions to this world, rather we go our own path out of this light which creates itself from within us, uninfluenced by this world.

The silence of the black light cannot be touched by space and time. It is the source from whence all Creation once sprang. If we want to become whole, we have to retreat to that point and step out into Creation from there. If we manage to reach this point, we will become the creators of our lives. For God is omnipresent here, without distance. He is the space that accepts us all.

Home.

The calm

for which I had yearned

in so many lives.

Everything

returned to my soul.

This light was the beginning and the end,
but it was comforting and safe
and more peaceful than anything
I had ever known.
It was beyond peace.
It was a peace, a heavenly peace
I had imagined much
differently.
This peace was a silent home,
that loved and embraced me.
In which I could be everything
I ever was and would ever be
without it being reflected in light and
shadow.
I was whole here.

The Awakening of the Feminine Powers

When I went to the evening meal with the rose powder the next evening, I first went to Jesus and Simon. I wanted to talk to them about what I should do with the fire. Simon said, "You can simply build a fire pit and invite them all." "But I would like everyone to take part in the ritual," I said. "Do as you see fit." I bade Lazarus help me build a fire pit. While I collected wood, Fe joined me again. Once the Essenes had kept the fire burning, but since Fe had gone and we were in a strange land, I could not remember when we had made a fire in the Essene village. There were no permanent ritual fire pits. Lazarus reminded me the ground was very dry and we had to secure the area very well. He first checked if the wind was calm enough and said, "If the fire flashes over, the whole countryside will burn and we will not be able to control it.

Mary Magdalene helped us. Our hearts connected as we built the fire and prepared everything. "Can we do it together?" she asked me. "Of course," I said. "I think I know what to do now." She stood up, went into the village and came back with a bottle of olive oil. She said, "Make the fire and show them how to use the rose fire to bring the powers of Shakti back to the Essenes. I will imbue the oil with the powers of Shakti so people can establish a connection with them."

"I am starting to realize," I said, "that the powers of Shakti can only be filled with rituals and deeds. The powers of Shakti are the manifestation of everything and when they are removed, we must first start feeling them again in order to let them flow into our deeds so Shakti once again fills our hands and touches that which is manifested. I believe that it is our attitude which allows us to let the sacred flow into things. But the powers of Shakti are much more. I want to experience them again and remember how the powers of Shakti create, for until now I have wandered in a world created by the powers of Shiva. I believe we must simply connect with ourselves so we can reconnect what has been broken. The powers of Shakti will find their own path."

Jesus came to me and said, "It is time. Kindle the fire." Then we invited all of the Essenes to the fire that we had built a bit away from our table.

Mary Magdalene and I lit the fire and I began to sing a song I remembered deep within me. Then I approached the fire with the rose powder and went around marking each person's forehead with the rose powder.

I said, "In order to be able to feel the powers of Shakti again, join us at the fire and make sacrifices to the fire, dedicated to the powers of Shakti. The roses will always bring forth the powers of Shakti from the Light of Christ. And if you approach the fire, the fire will bring the powers of Shakti back to you. I gave each of them the bowl with the rose powder and they sanctified the fire with it by offering the rose vibhuti to the fire. I wanted everyone to take part in the ritual. Everyone should approach the fire and connect with the powers of Shakti. Mary Magdalene went around and marked their hearts with the olive oil she had sanctified and we sank deeper into something the world had lost. The Light of Christ that surrounded us gave us the ability to connect with the feminine powers of creation. We didn't really know how they would return to us, but it was a beginning. I could not see what HE saw, but I trusted our actions.

We stayed at the fire for a long time. Jesus seemed satisfied and that made me happy. When everyone rose to leave, I wanted to stay at the fire and bade Lazarus stay with me, for I wanted to be certain the fire went out without anything happening. We sat at the fire alone for a short while when a gust of wind blew by us and into the center of the fire. Lazarus and I started and stood. I screamed, "Oh my God," for this gust of wind blasted through the fire where the flames were still burning and all of the sudden, the entire area around us was burning. The people turned around on their way back to the village and ran to get water. But we didn't have much water in the village. Jesus and Simon were there in an instant, for the wind spurred the fire to burn ever higher and it raced across the area, blazing. I was frozen in shock.

Jesus and Simon built up their powers beside me, for we could no longer fight this fire with water. And suddenly I was overcome by complete calm. Although the pain and panic at what was happening were great, I took Jesus by the hand and said, "Let me try." The power of Shakti reared up within me and I heard myself saying, "Halt, fire!" The power of Shakti wove together over the fire and the fire stopped. The power of the wind gathered above me and I simply said,

"Be silent wind, for we are friends. You are Lord of the air, but I beg of you, let us work together again."

The fire stopped and the villagers came and threw blankets on the fire and we were able to slowly extinguish it. I was still frozen in shock. Although I had been able to stop the fire with the surging power of Shakti, I felt guilty for what had happened. I did not want to speak to anyone so I returned to my chamber. I was in utter despair, for the fire could have destroyed our entire village. The wind had thrown three more such gusts at us. It could have destroyed the entire landscape and all of our fields. I cried bitterly, despairing.

When Simon entered the chamber, he found me sobbing. "What I did was terrible," I said. "But no one could have known that the wind would come. You must understand, Miriam, when the powers of Shakti return to Earth, they will face a great imbalance. And nature reflects this in that first moment. The wind didn't wish to harm you, but the imbalance of the forces challenged things in that first moment. The wind was attracted to this power." "Was it wrong to make the fire?" "No," said Simon, "for if we do not know where the imbalance is, we cannot bring it back into balance." I understood. I embraced him and was grateful. I still needed a moment to digest what I had experienced.

I went outside and stood watch over our land the entire night with Mary Magdalene and Lazarus. For we were not certain if errant sparks might reignite the dry landscape. Mary Magdalene and I held hands the entire night. We knew that Shakti had lost her power. We did not know, however, how we could reconquer the power of Shakti. For a moment, we had felt it and at the same time, it had shown us once again that we feared the power of its destruction.

I wasn't certain what should frighten me more. The power I had experienced when I stopped the fire or what I had experienced of the feminine powers thus far. The feminine powers were not always maternal and caring. They were destructive. But therein lie the secret. Instead of shaking my world to its core, the pieces came together. And still, my entire essence yearned for understanding. For in the first moment, I had retreated in fear from the power of Shakti that had found its expression in my body that night. I wanted to learn about these powers of which no one had yet told me.

The fire had not caused much damage, thank God, and only a small area was burned. Lazarus, my brother, finally gave me solace. He said, "You know, you actually did us a favor. I noticed

the farmers burning their fields on purpose. They told me this brings forth fertile land. That is how they do things in this country. You just have to be careful, for the wind is powerful here. But the farmers know when the wind is still and how to estimate the wind patterns. So you have given us fertile soil."

Shakti,

take me.

Drink me

until I am you.

Lazarus and the Gladiators

Our evening meals became feasts of the senses and community. Outside in nature, the tables were set with fresh wine, our own baked bread, fruits we brought in fresh from the fields, and cheese from the farmers who roamed from meadow to meadow like nomads, sometimes visiting us. When we were all gathered together, new spaces were born. The dimensions between us opened and we began to listen to the other beings. Beneath the open sky, the spirit united with life. There were new transitions between the grass, the olive trees and the tones of the crickets that brought us closer to the Earth and conversations that delved into touched depths.

Each of us was a story of many tapestries of life. Every day, we looked forward to the sunset as we set the table together. We finally had time to encounter each other with care and sense the bright presence of the others. We sat together every night with those to whom we were attracted and got to know each other. Stories were exchanged and life stories were retold.

Lazarus left us several times for several days to go to Massalia to secure our funds for the journey. He had returned and, at dinner, he told us what he had experienced.

"Lazarus, tell us! How were the gladiator games?" Simon was a master in making a game of what others kept secret. Lazarus was visibly embarrassed, but he didn't let it show. "How did you know that? I didn't tell anyone! But since you asked, I wanted to know how the Romans live here. For we want to integrate ourselves into life here and I wanted to get to know them and their culture." We all knew what gladiator games were, but had always considered them to be barbaric games that the bloodthirsty Romans played. "What was it like for you to watch people go into the arena, to be forced to fight for their lives like animals, while others greedily worked themselves into a frenzy?" I wanted to know.

The mood at our table became divided. But the lesson Jesus had instilled in us settled deep in us; that every judgment falls back onto the judger and that every external enemy becomes our persecutor, first in our spirit and then in our real lives. The education of the spirit, which remains clear and which does not get hung up on illusions but filters the truth which is anchored in love, was our daily discipline. We walked the path of the enlightened in the midst of a lost world. "You should take Miriam with you next time." Simon wasn't joking. "Why only me? Why not all of us?"

"Because it is your education, which belongs only to you and no one else." Simon was loving and masterfully serious. I knew he was right.

"Why do the Romans love this spectacle of death as entertainment so much?" Mary Magdalene was relaxed, as always. Agnisha was just inhaling to speak when I knew,

"There is nothing to discuss. I can hear my truth calling. To learn a lesson is to learn a lesson. I will go with you, then I will tell you all. When shall we leave, Lazarus?" Several Essenes at the table gulped; we were no longer in Qumran, where the light could expand heaven without obstruction. We were in Gaul, where light and darkness ruled; we were in the place of our next destiny.

"It is not our task to preserve light. Light preserves itself. Our task is to bring the light to places where there is darkness, to anchor the divine in the material and bring it into the light. Those who dare enter the lion's den must be lions themselves, for only lions know how lions fight. We are breaking through our boundaries and this is one of them. We must not hate the Romans; we must learn to see them. Your eyes, Miriam, can do that, your lioness is powerful." Jesus' words hit me like lightning.

My dark side rose up like a wild animal and laid itself over the left half of my body, waiting. "Tell me, how was it, Lazarus?" Simon neutralized the ground. "What drove me was this rage. I couldn't bear this imbalance anymore. It is often too sacred for me here. I was hungry for a contrast. I imagined it differently. I thought I would be shocked or disgusted. But you know me. I always want to know how I will react and what personalities live within me. But it was healing for me instead. I was a zealot again for a moment and all of my memories awoke within me. The fighting in the streets… that was and is me, and I wanted to see it. The gladiator fights are brutal, but these fights exist and thousands of people fill the arenas, wanting them. It quenches the hunger within them."

"What are you hungry for?" asked Mary Magdalene lovingly. Lazarus looked at her as though he suddenly understood. "I want to love, truly love and not wait any longer for me to be worth it or to have to do something to deserve it. I am ready now. I want to love life as it is."

"We all want that. To truly understand that we are loved before we know it." Jesus arose and said, "I wish you a peaceful, good night." He left the love, tangible, in the open portrait of nature in which we found ourselves. Under the open sky, it was our own.

The next day, I packed my things and Lazarus brought me Roman robes, "So you aren't so conspicuous." It was exciting. For the first time in a long time, I left our village and my goal was to touch and get to know the country in which I now lived. We wanted to travel to Arles because Lazarus said it was better to experience it in the city of Roman aristocrats than in Nemausus where there are far too many peasants. People who were even less conscious, as he called them. It would be bloody and uncivilized and coarse anyway. So preferably with Roman culture.

We walked a few hours, then borrowed horses from a farmer Lazarus knew and, after a night in the open, we arrived in Arles late in the afternoon on the next day. No one seemed to notice us. The people were colorful and travelers were part of life here. Even as I rode through the city gates, my skin resisted the energy in which I was immersed. I had been in the pure light of the Essenes for such a long time, this field tried to wrap itself around me like a strange cloak. I shook myself. "Lazarus, do you feel that?" Of course not. He had a thousand skins and waded through all the zones, unaffected. I activated my light shield and said my prayers.

We found an inn and Lazarus left me alone to run some errands and secure seats for us at the next gladiator games. He kept me away from his connections, who belonged to our secret network, in order to protect both sides. I slept restlessly and the next morning, we forged a path between the many Romans who came to the arena from all around. In the tight, narrow alleyways, I jostled against their bodies, which could not be permeated by light. What had I done to myself! I was already growing angry about the untransformed energy of the people around me. At least their fabrics were made of soft silk.

We found a place high up in the arena near the exit. Lazarus was always ready to flee. So I sat there, a Christian, on the steps of those who were supposed to be my enemies and was a part of or observer of their deadly game with God. "If you do not conquer the inner war, you will always be conquered", Jesus had always said, and I heard His words in my ears now. My lesson was hard, but my two teachers had chosen it for me. I was ready to see.

There was nothing uplifting about what was playing out before my eyes. What I saw were gruesome fights between slaves and blood that made the audience roar. I stayed there. I didn't go away. But I was also not prepared to sacrifice a part of who I was. I was a disciple of Christ and wanted to see with God's eyes. I wondered what He was seeing now. Not what I saw. I saw His children, whose terror had turned them into monsters. It started to rain and God wept. I did not weep. My heart stopped as men died before my very eyes. I wasn't able to breathe freely until it was over. I was multidimensional. I was in an arena with people who were addicted to destruction. And I was in another dimension which took on a different perspective, like a larger lens above the events, because it did not change their existence. I was in the past; a mighty warrior, full of power and courage, who saw death as part of her battle. I was the mother who had just lost her son. I was the love that created everything. I could choose from which perspective I experienced it all.

"Take me home, Lazarus." Whatever was going on with me went deeper. I quieted as the silence and the Mother awakened within me, the serene presence that expanded and connected everything that had shattered. Everything around me was my space. I was everything and nothing. I was everything I had experienced and I was nothing.

The inner war within me had been quenched, so I could become the mother I was meant to be. It was time to be more than a small extract of reality. Everything within me was bigger.

Of course, we were overwhelmed by curiosity when we returned to the Essene village. Jesus stood at the temple as though He had been waiting for me. We had ridden and run through the night, in the storm that raged around us. He smiled and nodded. Sumaja was just coming out of the temple and said, "What happened to you? You aren't the same woman you were before. You have achieved your perfection." She folded her hands and bowed. The paths Jesus and Simon were showing us were beyond the teachings. They were bringing us home in an unconventional way.

"How was it?" I said. "Lazarus, how was it? It was what I needed to forgive myself and finally experience the naive peace with the hard peace which is real. Gladiator games are a cynical game of the gods who have lost hope that God even exists. For others it is God. In the end, I was grateful, for I was now standing on a fresh foundation. I was centered and open to all of the worlds I might encounter in the future."

Lazarus remained awake and everyone wanted to hear his stories of the Romans, heroes, emperors and battles won and lost.

I slept for a few hours in Simon's arms and when I awoke, I went to find Mary Magdalene and Martha. We lay on the meadow and I told them what little I was able to put into words. "Believe me, we are in a utopia. We live in heaven on Earth."

"I am not worried about that. If I know our husbands, we will leave the nest soon because we are the plows for new earths. We will soon overflow with consciousness. We must go out and share it."

The Secret Realm of the Celts

The Queen of the Celts Appears

It was late morning and mild outside. In the distance, we could make out two figures approaching us across the southwestern hill. As they came closer, the silhouettes of a woman and a man grew clearer. Lazarus brashly went out to meet them: if they were enemies, he would signal to warn us. If they were friends, he would greet them like royalty and accompany them to the village. He stayed at a safe distance and talked to them. We watched, with our children in our arms, as they approached us as a group. Lazarus' face, however, revealed that he did not trust them. The woman was very regal. Her hair was dyed red like poppy flowers and glistened brightly in the sun. Her cloak was green like emeralds and her adornments were emblems of her power. The man was a Druid of which I had seen several. His rank was higher; his behavior and aura made that apparent.

Jesus and Simon came in from the field and washed their hands in the stone well, our proud, new achievement. Sumaja and Agnisha joined us immediately and looked at the two of them, enquiringly. Mary Magdalene and I proudly stood beside them with our children.

We met the Queen of the Celts in the square before the temple. She folded her hands over her heart in greeting and Lazarus translated what she said. "I am Ia-hr-ra. I have come from very far away to meet you. I have heard stories of you. My Druids have been reading the stars for weeks and tell me that your light has brightened the land since you arrived and continues to grow stronger. They tell me that the followers of the Messiah from Palestine are among us, if not the Messiah Himself. You are holy people. We know about you. Our people believe in the prophecy of the Messiah, who will come, and we have been awaiting Him for so long. I came to invite you to my realm. I hope to learn who you are." Lazarus added, "I don't trust her. Do you see the armed men she brought, hiding on the crest of the hill?"

Jesus spoke a few sentences in her language, then bade Lazarus translate. "Be welcome Ia-hr-ra. We are Essenes and your sages and Druids have been friends of our order for a long time. We are in contact with the groups in Britannia and sought refuge here because we are being persecuted in our land." I had to trust Him, for I was not certain about the queen. Her desire for power flickered unceasingly in her aura.

Her eyes widened when Jesus raised His hand and she glimpsed His stigmata. "What they say is true. You are alive." Our teachings of how inner peace empowers the enemy would have to work miracles now, for the Queen of the Celts was not pure of heart nor were her intentions. She also showed no deference to Jesus, the Lord. Her nature was uncultivated. She stared at Him, almost disrespectfully. But He took her power and transformed the demon. "Welcome. Today you shall be our guests." I wasn't certain whether the Druid had developed his skills as finely as we had. We read their thoughts and they knew they had to decide: Would she turn us over to the Romans for their own profit or would the loyalty of love within her conquer? She fought.

She then addressed us women, for she noticed our reservation. She hissed as she spoke and Lazarus translated. "I am a warrior queen. You do not have to trust me, but my war games have served my people well. We live with the Romans in one country and I feed both desires. But the secret knowledge of my people also lives on under my protection."

I was still able to speak the Roman language and I knew she would understand me, so I spoke on behalf of the women in my village. "Forgive us our distance. We are very cautious and help others to be cautious. We must keep so much secret." We must be prepared to flee, I thought. I heard my greater self saying, "I would like to trust you, if you show me that you will protect my life and the lives of my kin and not threaten us." I don't know who spoke from within me, but the Druid said, in Hebrew, "There is a wolf woman among you and a holy, red doe woman. We have come to protect you and honor your arrival. We first had to be certain that the instructions of our traditional seers who promise us that He who has returned and you are one and the same."

The aura of the Celtic queen was now gleaming green and its intentions clearer. "Your women do you honor." My speech had won her over; she loved a challenging opponent. Jesus and Simon handled the charming, wooing invitation to the midday meal and retrieved wine from the cool cellars beneath the Earth.

Our guests were presented a meal of everything our fresh chambers had to offer. Jesus poured the wine and invited our guests to sit. The mild wind wrote the poetry of the day and the table we had grown so fond of, outside in the greenery, did our guests good. Lazarus nudged me and pointed out that the warriors on the ridge were coming closer until the Celtic queen waved them off. She granted us her trust. What she didn't know was that our entire village was completely unarmed.

"I have to excuse my impoliteness. This hostility has also turned me into a barbarian. I would like you to know who we are. Three generations before me, we were a Celtic people that had withdrawn to the valley our sages had read of in the omens. The energies of the Earth were so high here and the earth lines so powerful and showed us powerful, sacred, cosmic patterns. A long time ago, my people came here and we dedicated our culture to developing and preserving our cosmic legacy. We lived on a higher level of consciousness and began to connect the powerful earth currents, which we read carefully, with the currents of the stars as our laws decree and we built our sacred city on this geometry and it reflected the sacred order.

Our culture dates back to Atlantis, our Druids come from the sacred lines of the star cultures. Our manuscripts and scriptures also come from that age. They date back to a time when our sages began to understand that the Earth's energy currents began to change after Atlantis. They learned to read where high-frequency currents left the power centers in the Earth and where they reappeared.

Our tribes were called from this place, which pulsates, hidden and beyond the world in opened dimensions. We rebuilt our culture and learned to renew our spiritual roots therein. When my great grandmother was a little girl, the Romans came and conquered the land. That was a long time ago and today, we live with them. They built temples for their gods which remained inanimate stones. They prayed to power and we learned to live with their low vibrations and not lose ourselves. My grandmother decided that my mother would become a warrior and she was trained accordingly. As was I. We are spiritual warriors and yet we know how to kill. We protect our people, our beliefs and do so with skill. Thus we live together with Romans, Jews, Greeks and other Celtic tribes in this land.

We have never given up our sacred culture; we hid it in the groves and grottoes of holy nature and her gods protected us. Our scriptures have told us since the beginning of time that they will return, the once rulers of the blissful realms of Atlantis. They also say they will come in times of darkness, unrecognized and humble."

Jesus looked at her for a long time and penetrated her worlds with light. "I know you and know who you are. When we decided to come to Gaul, we were very aware of why. We needed time to settle in after we had left everything behind us and now you have come at precisely the right time. I have been expecting you. Let us become friends again. We should work together. Our cultures can learn from each other. Our churches shall prepare the communal ground for an even greater church that will balance the sacred feminine and the sacred masculine with the goal of reintegration for future generations. Our promise is old."

Now we all understood why Jesus had allowed the strangers to come so close to us, for He always protected us with His magical abilities. He would have warned us if we were in danger. The tension at the table eased noticeably.

"I do not come with empty hands," she said. "My gifts for you are my best warriors, whom I will leave here for your protection. They can be invisible, like the wind and appear out of the darkness with the power of the wolves. You are free to choose them. I bring you the gift of a high invitation from our Druids. They want to show you our sacred land, which only few are permitted to enter. And I bring my friendship which I offer humbly. It is a sign of the gods."

"Call your warriors closer, we want to break bread with them." Simon had been listening until now. He stood up and brought more bread and wine.

Ia-hr-ra arose and called them to us with a gesture. I was impressed at how well-coordinated they were. They disappeared from my view and appeared directly before us as though from a fog. Warriors dressed in black with ornamental war paint and light hair came nearer. They were strong men who feared no enemy and certainly not death. Simon invited them to the table and two universes collided under the southern sun. The highly sensitive Essenes, with their bright tenderness and the muscles of those who feared no darkness. When they were given bread and cheese, they wrinkled their noses, for they were used to meat which strengthened them. They behaved honorably and ate, but they drank even more.

I was fascinated by them, for they had hearts, forged of honor, devotion and loyalty. "It is time we learn your language properly," Mary Magdalene said. "I accept this gift. What do you say? Are these warriors ours?"

Our future began that evening. We accepted the invitation to the holy land of the Celts and began trying to learn the language. We drank a lot of wine and laughed until the sky above us put a stop to it, for it too wished to sleep. Only the dark-haired Druid remained quiet and silent. "I can help you," it was already late at night when Jesus addressed him in his own language. "The high energies have made you ill, your body can no longer harmonize the discrepancy, you frequency is too high for the environment. I know you are in pain."

The Celtic queen and her warriors became witnesses of the son of God as He touched the Druid's swollen stomach with His bare hands, emptied the waste he had collected therein, and burned it in the fire of His hands. The Druid lost consciousness. He was carried to a chamber with Jesus' assurances that he would recover by morning. Sumaja wanted to be certain and went to him again before she withdrew while we celebrated until morning.

The wild life had us back. This wildness tasted different: It tasted like this land and its origins. Of resinous trees with souls, of the hunting gods of the wind, the blustering goddess of the sea and the wildness of the animals that were sacred here. The Queen of the Celts slept peacefully in one of our humble little homes that night. The man she secretly loved slept safely in the light of the Essenes.

Mary Magdalene did not sleep that night. Her memories and dreams of the present awakened her. When I left our chamber a few hours later, I saw her sitting on the hill, enveloped in her own world. She seemed lonely and the landscape wove patterns of golden light around her. I stood three hundred paces away and felt every one of her movements, the pain and love that wrestled within her. I carefully, considerately touched her essence very gently with my energy to find out if she wanted to be alone. A gentle current came from her core in response: I would like you to stay with me. I need you. I climbed the hill, where the sun was already blazing down on us and sat down beside her. The bright fire of light sparkled in our eyes.

"This is my land, I am the blood that flows in these veins, I am the salt of this Earth. The earth currents flow in my womb and I breath the ether of heaven in my breast. I hold them, I sing them. My women bear wings of mourning and painful wounds. The roses, the game animals, are my children. They need to be liberated from the bandages that bind them. These are the roots of the old, red land, where the brothers of the stars left their legacy behind. Their treasures shine on my body like gold and silver. The sacred feminine is the Mother. I am her body. We belong to the Earth more than she to us. She seeks dialog with me so I can give her the voice to sing of her old memories."

She was in a trance. Far from her memories, where the past makes sense. Without knowing of what she spoke, I knew where she was and what she meant. She was the mother of this land. Her current of power ran through these veins and created the currents of the rivers and valleys. She was the power that watered the lemon trees, that poured into the seas and sank into the mountain ravines. The blood in her veins was the meal that nourished the knowledge of how humanity grows or perishes with the Earth.

"It is time for you to come back, you were far away. You have gathered much, bring it back to us." I was careful not to startle her from her trance.

"They will build a church on my body which will be crowned by love and femininity. On the paths of the veins through the land, we will follow the currents of reawakening. I see the church which unites the consciousness of love, beauty, peace and magic." She wept bitterly and her body fell, trembling, into my arms. I loved her so much, my wild friend. She was the red of Creation, in the body of a woman and she loved Jesus with passion. She fought to understand the universe that would be born within her. Within her was a seed of the church, the union of the powers of the sacred masculine and the sacred feminine. That which had not existed until now.

"We will show them how to find what women have lost, how they can seek the substance in the stars and incarnate it in on Earth. I will support you and be at your side." Women bear their creation in different cycles. This life was her time.

"The red, holy doe woman; the Druid meant you, Mary Magdalene. I think it is their sacred animal of maternal creative forces. Also, when I think about how magical it was when we encountered them in the forests, I have to say, the energy is very similar to yours." I sensed she needed space so her worlds could piece themselves together again. "I will leave you alone." She nodded.

The village grew lively. Many people had been on their feet since early morning and I saw them scattered across the fields. Others sensed the aftermath of the previous night and remained in their houses. We learned the Celts celebrated their gods with sacred intoxicants and wine. I ran directly into Ia-hr-ra, the Celtic queen's arms. She stopped and studied me. "Do you have children too?" Love was my strategy for disarming her and she grew softer. "Yes, I have two sons. They are already grown. One of them is following the path of the warrior, the other the path of the Druids."

Her Latin was perfect and mine was sufficient. "Their father died many years ago. He had to fight for the Romans, which cost him his life. That was the price for our life, which we can lead with our heads held high. It was the price for us living the way we do, as our beliefs proscribe. We must learn that we cannot defeat them, but we can live with them." She had opened herself to me.

"Do you want to come to the river with us? You can bathe there. Or should we bring jugs with water and bowls for washing to your chamber?" She smiled. The river was closer to her nature. She waited until I had retrieved the children and accompanied me. Two warriors immediately followed us at an inconspicuous distance; Ia-hr-ra was always under their protection. I tried to imagine how that would change our lives. She went off to the side a bit and I sat down with Sara and John on the riverbank. They loved this place and immediately threw themselves into the water, splashing around.

"What is it like to be with Him?" Her clothing hung loosely over her shoulders as she walked toward us. She had a different sense of shame. Nearly her entire body was bare; she was robust and painted with symbols. I swallowed first, then the brusque, wild nature from which she sprang forth opened itself to me. Sara and John hadn't even noticed.

"I have known Him since I was four years old. My father was an Essene. He brought me to them to receive my education. Then I met Him. That was my destiny. My life and that of our community is my destiny."

"Many of you Essenes live in our land. Many of you have also settled in Arhedaes. They have long told me of the master who is promised. They have been coming for a hundred years and do not mingle with the sons of Benjamin, for their views are too free.

You can find them everywhere. They also live a very withdrawn and simple life. But they are different. Their women are not like you."

"Even in Palestine and Judea, where I am from, the women are not like us. We are outlaws there. We are free with Jesus and elevated and are valued in our community. He took us on many of His journeys; we saw many cultures and learned so much. He made me richer than I ever could have been. He gave me the freedom to explore my soul and walk my spiritual path."

"He is truly the Messiah who died on the cross?"

"Yes, He is. He is our heaven turned real. If you betray us, you will send the persecutors after my children and everyone I love." I had tears in my eyes, the pain of those great days never ebbed.

"I will not. You have already stolen my heart. We Celts are always loyal, our word is ironclad, believe me." She had dressed now and was watching Sara and John play. "Children have never looked at me that way. As though they are looking into the most secret chambers of my soul. They are like you. What does He teach you that makes you so different?"

"He teaches us to love and that the Kingdom of Heaven lives within us. He teaches us to heal so we can heal ourselves. He teaches us to walk the path of enlightenment and guide the darkness into the light. Actually, He doesn't teach us anything, He simply sees us, every day, as who we are."

"Do you have to go through years of initiations to ascend?"

"I think they did that in Egypt and so did the Essenes once, but I wasn't part of these initiations. My life threw me from one change to the next. My life was my rite of passage."

Then Mary Magdalene approached us. Sara screamed with joy, "Mama," and ran toward her with her arms open wide. She sat down with us and the

Queen of the Celts, Ia-hr-ra, wanted to go. I took her by the hand. "Stay." A friendship between three women that wove together like the pattern of infinity began at that little river, which the Celts called their god, like all rivers and groves in the land. From that day on, we taught the Celtic queen love and she taught us not to fear death, but to embrace it as a companion in our lives. Love and death first made the three of us women invulnerable, then invincible.

We were already awaited when we returned to the village. Jesus and Simon had already planned for us to accept the invitation Ia-hr-ra and the Druids had extended. The next day, we departed and this time, we took our children with us. "How many will travel with us?" Ia-hr-ra was standing, regally, at the table ruling. "Seven adults." She whistled through her teeth and an echo sounded throughout the valley and a man came riding over the hill with a horde of horses. He dismounted before her and handed her the reins. "Then I counted correctly," she said. "The children will ride with others. We told the Romans we were taking the horses to sell them, which is slightly true. Give me a gold thaler and the horses are yours."

The next day, early in the morning, we rode west. Mary Magdalene rode next to me. Little Sara found everything terribly exciting while John was still taking it all in. "Finally, the spell has lost its power; we will find new friends and allies among these people. Our isolation is over." "What do you think about them showering us with gifts?" I asked. "The absolution for what they cannot forgive of themselves," Mary Magdalene responded.

The Journey to Arhedaes

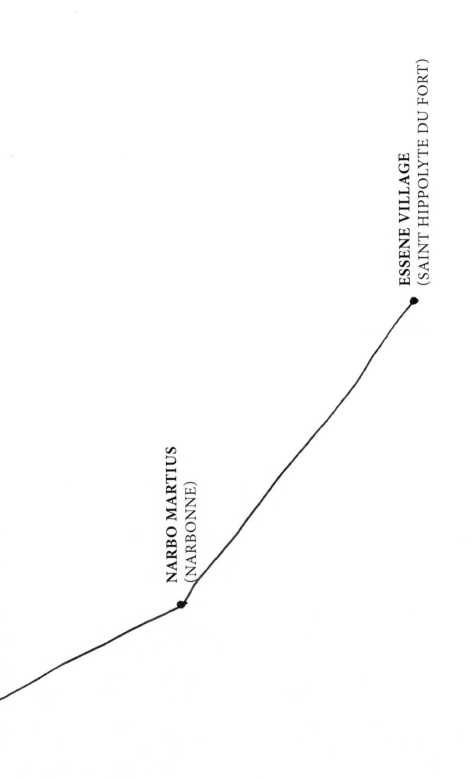

ARHEDAES
(RENNES-LE-CHÂTEAU)

NARBO MARTIUS
(NARBONNE)

ESSENE VILLAGE
(SAINT HIPPOLYTE DU FORT)

We rode through the wilderness and glimpsed little settlements here and there until, after one day and night, we reached the Via Domitia. When my horse put his hooves on the road, with its orderly cobbled stones, the clattering sound echoed in my nervous heart. It was the first time we had used the Roman victory road. We had avoided it until now to avoid being recognized. But this road was filled with colorful, traveling people and being the mixed group we were, we went without notice. A Druid, a Celtic queen, exotic people of Jewish heritage and Simon, whose blond hair shone in the sun like John's. We didn't speak much and we kept moving. The children found it more and more exciting to see new things and the Roman soldiers that rode passed us were their favorite attraction because everything on them jingled: their chest armor, their helmets, their auras. Most of them appeared bored and hardly noticed us when we encountered them. Two Celtic warriors always remained close, invisible in the underbrush, always ready to protect us.

Sara and John surprised us with how lovingly they adapted. They slept in our arms as we rode on, or on the horses' manes, but most of the time, they absorbed the impressions and new stimuli. In the evenings, we looked for remote places in the forests to sleep.

"The Romans leave you alone if you obey their trade and governance laws," Ia-hr-ra told us. "We don't have any problems with them and this area is peaceful. We have heard there are battles being fought a two-day ride from here."

We sat on the grass in a copse at sunset and quenched our hunger. "The forests, copses and bodies of water are our Mother. They give us everything. We do not have a temple, they are our direct access to other worlds," she changed the energy. "When I was that little," she looked at our children silently, "my grandmother taught me that all of the life force I need, I can get from this source of life. She slept on the ground with me until I dissolved into it and could smell, hear and taste the worlds that lived therein.

Under the protection of the trees, in the fertile, wild plants, we find our herbs for healing and the drinks that bear their magic. Our midwives find their magic ingredients here and the warriors their invulnerability. In constructed temples, they control the wild space of the soul, in nature and its wilderness, it is free.

The forest and its worlds are the vulva of the great, life-giving Mother. Our Druids know how to read the prophecies and council from other dimensions spanning between these trees and they have stood beside our people with sage advice since the beginning of our days. To become queen, I had to surrender to their magic in order to cross my shadowy realms. For only then was the Great Goddess wiling to weave her grace and allow me to read the signs in my vision of life. I had to mature within her in order to lead my people.

There is a light branch and a dark branch of the Celts. Our people do not gather the heads of their slain enemies, nor do we sacrifice living beings to gain the favor of the gods. We know about the vital world of nature's dimensions and the worlds beyond this world. They foretold of your coming, now I want to know what you will bring upon us."

Instead of answering her question, Jesus looked at His beloved, piercingly and for a long time; He was initiating her. "Mary Magdalene, what does the Earth wish to tell us?" She followed His impulse, laid down on the grass and pressed her stomach into the soil. I took Sara, who watched everything intently, so Mary Magdalene could perform her ritual without distraction. She first delved into her inner worlds. At first, her body seemed to falter and she stopped breathing. Then she sank into the soil and the Earth swallowed her and then released her.

She had started breathing again, calm and steady. Her spirit awoke, stirred and enveloped her in golden light. She began to hum and allowed herself to be carried on the meandering current in which all of her states of consciousness were at one with the dimension of the Earth. She sang. She did not need a sacred grove; any piece of earth was an access point to her worlds of dark currents, the maternal material. Her songs were old, wise and of a primal, feminine nature. She danced in the dimensions of the Earth and writhed like a snake until she went into a trance. Then she sat up and Earth's energy currents flowed into her body and coursed through her. She had become the Earth.

"We are all here to serve the Earth and ourselves. We did not come together to teach, but to learn from each other. The Earth, our Mother, is shrouded in the shadows of a dark age. But on this night of humanity, the seeds of the future are germinating. One of the seeds is old and was the origin of the cosmos and the

Earth. The feminine power of Creation, the Goddess herself and her creative currents of renewal. Her powers of creation have withdrawn into the core of the universe and in the fire of the Earth. Again and again, humanity forgets her secret. If she does not give herself willingly, the masculine powers of creation become dominant and the balance begins to fade. The power of the Goddess resides in rituals that recognize her, in art that is kissed by beauty, the fire in which it is resurrected, in songs that awaken her to dance in cosmic ecstasy and in science, which dares penetrate the center of her initiation.

The other power is the cosmic consciousness of Christ. It is the substance of love that holds all of the worlds together. It holds our bodies together, so we do not fall apart, it keeps us on this Earth, it holds the starry sky together and apart. It is the sweetness of life and God's pure expression of joy. The Light of Christ sows seeds for the future of humanity in which all beings have the chance to coexist in harmony and create in peace.

Both powers are the seeds in the innermost heart of the Earth, in the fire, in which it eternally praises God. Both powers have been isolated from todays' humanity, thus we bring them to you by being who we are. Miriam, Sara and I and the other women bear the conscious seeds of the feminine powers of creation within us. Jesus, Simon and John bear the Creator's Light of Christ as the embodiment of His love and Lazarus bore the fire of His actions.

You are the guardians of the Earth and her knowledge. We shall bring the people together and connect them without changing their beliefs. We will weave webs of tolerance, like spiders, by teaching and, most importantly, learning from each other. Our alliance is blessed. The ground you have cultivated with sacred geometry is the foundation on which the Light of Christ sows seeds. Here, different faiths can meet, recognize God in everything and no longer keep Him separate."

Mary Magdalene inhaled deeply and returned to her human consciousness. Little Sara slid from my embrace and laid down on her lap; the little girl drew her mother out of the cosmic expansion of the trance and back into her body and soothed her. She did it with masterful wisdom.

The Queen of the Celts wept and the Druid arose and bowed before us. He withdrew to the forest and brought back herbs which he heated on the fire and gave to Mary Magdalene to drink. The shaking of her body began to ebb noticeably. "You are the masters of the cosmos, we are the masters of the Earth and the wisdom of nature and the body. Follow me," he said.

Jesus helped Mary Magdalene up and held her in His arms. He was visibly proud of her. She had risen again as a prophetess. Her voice was powerful. We followed the Druid a bit into the forest until we arrived at a clearing. Stones, inhabited by beings that resembled animals, looked at us. The reality of the Other World was present here, as in many places in the new land of our destiny. As always, I was fascinated by its presence. It was invisible, but we could feel it.

He stepped between the trees, raised his hand and touched the air, which became fluid and rolled in waves. The vibration expanded from his finger in concentrated waves and opened the shroud between the worlds. The trees around us grew colorful and transformed into vague, vibrating shapes and ethereal colors. Their consciousness spoke. Everything vibrated with consciousness and was different; the light of unity shone within us. Beings appeared between the trees, only to disappear again; everything was alive. The children were jumping into this spectacle of nature; we were blessed. The Druid tapped in the air with his finger and the material solidified again. The fluorescing seas of colors disappeared back behind the shroud. We could still sense them, but we could no longer see them. "We know where the gates to the Other World are. We have the knowledge to open them and enter them with reverence and humility. Where we are going now, you will encounter a realm like nothing you have ever seen before. Where the realms of nature rule, the Goddess is alive. The temples of nature are inhabited by magical beings. They have allowed us to share their realm with them. They are expecting you." Everything was silent.

While our group encountered this magic in a new way, Sara and John sat, lost in thought, on the ground, laying pieces of wood and little stones harmoniously until they created a pattern. They created a sacred harmony. A work of art from nature became a place of power in a small cosmos. The way the two played together was perfection. We smiled when we saw this. Without words, our beings from heaven gave thanks with this gift of nature, which radiated the light without wanting to.

"May I welcome you to our land? My name is Trevorta, guardian of the wisdom of the stars and the sacred veins of the Earth." The Druid had revealed himself. It was the first time we had heard his name. We gave thanks with hope.

The journey the next day continued past Narbo Martius, shaped by a hundred years of Roman presence, which in turn shaped the mood on the horizon. But we enjoyed the merchants and their stands at the edge of the city, so richly filled with fine fabrics, spices, metal goods, wine and elaborate pots and jars. The merchants came from many countries. Many skin colors and languages intermixed and they brought stories with them like the delicacies they offered. I liked the merchants from Egypt, Africa, Persia and everything that brought me closer to that exotic feeling. I played with the children with the scents of the spices and the colors which carried us to distant dreams. Until Simon promised us that we would shop again on the way back. It grew colder at night, so we bought warm blankets and pelts which we didn't even have to carry, because the warriors carried them for us.

We left the Via Domitia and headed through more difficult terrain with little paths that wound through the forests and valleys. I noticed that there were several little settlements and farms here. They grew wheat, wine and vegetables. Although the forests grew denser and the paths narrower, here and there they opened out into clearings with lively villages. "There are Jewish and Greek villages here. There are Essene villages, people from Egypt and us, the Celts," Ia-hr-ra was riding next to Jesus. "We live in peace beside each other and tolerate the others' beliefs."

At the end of the world, right in the middle of the Roman Empire, hidden in the sacred forests of the Celts, lived peace and tolerance of the peoples' different faiths and heritages. A strange thought that incubated here for the future. "Would you send a few of your warriors ahead and call a meeting with your council of sages and leaders?" Jesus began his preparations. "Yes," said Ia-hr-ra, who sought healing in his presence.

That evening, we reached a place that was more ornate than the others. There were Roman buildings with columns and baths, steps and shrines with Roman gods and goddesses. Celtic Druids, priests, different tribes bustled about, intermixing with Roman nobles and garrisons. Differences were difficult to see in the darkness. "Where are we?" I blurted out in awe. "A place the Romans use for their baths. Our sacred healing springs are within. We always come here after long journeys to purify ourselves of the energies we have absorbed. To replenish ourselves in the energy of the springs and regenerate. It is a sacred ritual we perform before we return to our tribe. I brought you here so you can bathe tomorrow and partake in our sacred ritual of contemplation before we travel to my city, which is not far from here. The Romans think it belongs to them, but only we know of what lives between these worlds.

As we walked down along a babbling brook, we came to a stone building with a thatched roof. The warriors stepped out from the darkness of night and opened the door. Sara and John were already asleep in our arms and we were awaited. In the round interior, a fire was burning and three Celtic women greeted their queen with respect and took her cloak. Ia-hr-ra instructed them to help us and show us our bedchambers. The chambers were off small loam hallways protected by heavy wool blankets. It smelled of earth and sweet ritual incense. I laid John on the bed already prepared for us and realized how tired my bones were. Everything had been so lovingly prepared for us. Shortly after, they showed us to the communal area and set out a meal for us. The Queen of the Celts and her Druids had disappeared with a word. We sat silently around the fire and ate our meal, a surprisingly tasty porridge and wine. Jesus was lost in inner preparation and Simon was taking a glimpse into the worlds, as he always did when meditating while awake.

The energy around me made me uncomfortable. A mix of heavy, deep earth, mystical paths of the beyond and a magic I didn't yet understand floated around us relentlessly. Mary Magdalene leaned against me. I didn't know whether it was the weight of the Earth or the weight of my body, but it was high time to go to bed.

That night, Simon didn't join me until late. He and Jesus were breaking open new energies. But I had already been half-asleep for hours with John in my arms, immersed in geometric patterns the Earth wove beneath me and which connected it to swathes of stars in the cosmos. I dreamt of patterns and fabrics made of care and the touch of the spirit. So this is what it felt like when the Earth's consciousness communicated and created with the consciousness of the cosmos. In my waking dream, I found geometric patterns in the Earth that were constantly renewing themselves and changing.

It was early in the morning when someone came to get us and bring us towels. The women quickly explained to us that men and women would be guided to different springs. Stairs led to the thermal springs where Ia-hr-ra awaited us. The water was warm and she appeared nude, in her natural, original form. We were alone with her. "The towels are there if you don't want to be seen in the nude." She laughed. "For now, we are alone and the fairies of the spring are here for us alone. Let yourselves go, it will regenerate you." She was right. We let the tension, the Jewish sense of shame and our towels fall and floated in the pool of water and let the springs massage us. The vibrant magic of the fairies washed away the heaviness and replenished the energy in our bodies. "Come, now we shall refresh ourselves!" We found ourselves in a natural pool filled with cold water.

Three women approached us and from afar, they looked like they had slipped out of another world. When they stepped past us, Ia-hr-ra said, "They are Druids. They still come to their royal springs of the Mother, though not as often. This place once belonged to their temples of initiation. Now they live in isolation, much deeper in the forests, but they will not give up their sacred spring." We dried off and felt as if we'd been reborn. As we left the springs, they began to fill with Romans. We had chosen the right time of morning to experience the purity of the place before others unloaded their energies.

We all met at the inn and prepared for Ia-hr-ra and the Druid to pick us up. We mounted our rested horses and it wasn't long before we were rounding the hill, beyond which lay a breathtaking panorama. The Celtic queen's home lay before us: Arhedaes. Raised up on a hill, surrounded by open landscapes that extended far into the dimension of infinite consciousness, the land was anchored in the sky and Arhedaes pulsated like a sacred heart.

The landscape uplifted us and bade us welcome. We were anchored to the Earth in our higher consciousness. The jewel was surrounded by hills. Once reached, one could hardly believe that such a vast sky existed, revealed here, in this world. I sensed we were riding on the veins of the Earth, which pulsated powerfully. I knew that Arhedaes had been built on the energy lines as a holy city. Our inner freedom took a deep breath and expanded the wings of its soul, which lifted itself up in the open sky.

Ia-hr-ra, the Queen of the Celts, lived in concealment. She was the guardian of the royal residence and protected her people, for the Celts were the old rulers of the land. The walled, fortified city within, however, was very lively and wealthy. As we rode through the city, we saw Romans, Jews, Greeks, Druids and other cultures trading and everything intermixed. I felt uncomfortably exposed, for Jesus was with us. Even though Tiberius had granted us our freedom in Gaul, I did not trust them. Jesus and Simon, however, rode unimpressed; the Celtic queen rode at the head. Then we reached an open plaza.

Ia-hr-ra dismounted and walked toward Jesus. She knelt for all her people to see and reached out with her open left hand as a symbol of her personal welcome and a sign of good will. This was a clear sign. She bowed her head in reverence and spoke, her voice loud for everyone to hear. "Welcome to my realm. You and your family have been prophesied for a long time." I looked around, but there were no Romans nearby. The Celts reserved the innermost center of the city for themselves. Jesus dismounted and blessed her. Seven Druids stepped out of the large building and greeted Trevorta and the queen, bowing reverently. We had all dismounted and were standing in a row. Jesus was holding little Sara, who cuddled with Him, and Mary Magdalene stood next to Him. Simon stood with me, beside Jesus, and John sought refuge with Lazarus. Our group was a family, Jesus' family. I couldn't take my eyes off the Druids; their aura and wisdom were many lives older than this one. The wind of the magic spell danced around them. They stood before us, a tight group, bowing their heads and lowering their white hoods to take a closer look at us.

They were exploring us to test the authenticity of our spiritual heritage. Trevorta and Ia-hr-ra stood, waiting, at the front. "We expected you to be different. It does you great honor that you come with your family. Thank you for accepting our invitation." One of the older Druids had approached us; his voice was warm and inviting.

Jesus stepped forward. To everyone's surprise, He embraced him and we realized they were old friends. "It's about time, old friend," and then a ceremony began. Each of the Druids walked past us and looked at us intensely. This was their way of connecting with us without undermining their position in the tribe. A large group of curious onlookers had gathered around us. Ia-hr-ra dissolved this official greeting after a short while and invited us, informally, to join her.

The Queen of the Celts showed us to our rooms which were near the great meeting hall. All of the rooms were regally decorated and

furnished with wooden beds, linen sheets and a fireplace. The Celts' talent for making beautiful things adorned their culture.

We were in the innermost center of the city. Ia-hr-ra, her nobles and her warriors lived here. The outer ring was full of life and craftsmen and their treasures filled the streets with jewelry, pots and jugs and fabrics from distant countries. The farmers came to sell the harvests from their fields. The women placed great value on ornaments and bright colors. "We love trade," Ia-hr-ra told us as she proudly gave Mary Magdalene and me a tour of her city.

Arhedaes was the fortress and the seat her forefathers had handed down to her; an old and majestic place. Many people lived here, surrounded by the protection of two thick walls of earth which contained and protected the city and the towers that preferred to stretch into the sky rather than espy enemies.

"We trade gold, silver and copper, the most precious metals on Earth. That has made us rich. When the Romans came, they had to negotiate with us, for our men know where to find the mineral deposits and build mines in the nearly impassible, watery ground. My grandfather himself was able to convince Caesar to cooperate with us instead of plundering the deposits with his men. We have to pay tribute to the Romans, but there is still enough left for us.

The Romans are making a grave mistake: they forcefully take land and make people settle, then they demand tribute and impoverish the cultures. Our people have always believed in trade and the flow of goods, in movement. I still encourage merchants from other cultures to come to us and trade. We don't just exchange money and goods, but also culture and science."

Just as she said this, someone violently jostled my shoulder. I swayed and Mary Magdalene looked at me, astounded, for we didn't see anyone around us. We were at a point along the city walls where we could see the entire area. We once again delved directly into dimensions in an expanse of divine creation between heaven and Earth. It inspired tolerance and intuition here. It would be too much for close-minded spirits. We navigated through the alleys, back to the inner center where we lived.

"Thank you for your hospitality, Ia-hr-ra!" I said. Mary Magdalene agreed with me. I didn't want to let anyone notice that I kept seeing spirits that walked between the living without anyone noticing them, except me.

The Inkling of a Seed

That evening, when Simon and I went outside with John in my arms, lamps were being lit everywhere. The city began to glow like a starry tent reflecting back at the Earth. The stars above us were so close it was as though they held their breath with us, awaiting what we were birthing into the world. The raised plateau opened the view of the panoramic landscape around us. In the darkness of night, the magic turned blue and open for creation. I took everything in.

We were awaited in the meeting hall. Ia-hr-ra entered with us and Jesus and His family joined us shortly thereafter. The Druids were already there, stoking the fire. A table had been set for us with giant metal urns, filled with wine and they had taken us into consideration: there was enough from the harvest from the fields and fruits of the Earth as well as the animal products the Celts loved.

When we entered, the Druids arose and we sat in a circle around the fire. The room was inviting and large enough for large meetings. Most of the Druids were older and looked even more mysterious at night. They bore the marks of the path they had taken to be worthy of wisdom. Their faces looked like the tree bark they worshiped. I had heard the stories that every Druid had a tree that grew with him and his life. It was his companion through the initiation of life.

Their wide, white hoods left only half their faces visible in the light of the fire. Jesus started without hesitation. He reached into the earth and gathered a handful of soil. He held it as He prayed. It ignited in His hand and sparked until it burned. "Every flame is a culture that has found its home beneath the green canopy of the blessed Earth. The fire is the same as the one God for everyone, yet they all worship it in different ways." He sat down and threw the soil fire into the fire.

"We didn't expect you to integrate into what exists," said one of the Druids. "We know that we have ended a great circle of Creation and old structures are now dying so new ones can be born. Our culture is ready to go through this transformation," said another.

"We are all aware of the reality of your transcendence of the divine. You and your companions, you are as secure in the spiritual world as you are in the material world. We are open for the revolution you bring upon us," said a third Druid who smiled at us, full of love.

"This is not a time of revolution. It is a time of connections," said Jesus. "Time to bring the tribes together and connect the faiths and no longer keep them separate. What we separate in faith shatters the world into splinters of hate and bears hybrids." The Druids lowered their hoods and listened.

Light rose and our sense of time was suspended. Everything around us was violet and purple. "You were prophesied long ago," said one of the Druids. "Let us begin. What do you recommend?"

The colors of the light phenomena changed as we, the family that embodied the tradition and path of the Light of Christ and the guardians and initiates of the Celtic culture came together; new worlds collided.

Simon initiated communication. "Since the fall of Atlantis, those who remember the light have scattered across the Earth to protect themselves and preserve their memories. There are tribes that still live in the consciousness of light. But over time, things were forgotten or left out as they were passed through the generations and adapted. The cultures of light found a new tradition in Egypt, Africa, Asia and other parts of the Earth. Today, they are splintered and have little contact with each other. Light was forgotten because people wanted to protect themselves from each other.

We are here to plant new impulses of creation for the future of humanity. We will travel to the tribes that have preserved the memories of light and remind them. We will multiply. We will bring the seeds of the Light of Christ to the cultures. Your tribe, the Celts, is the beginning of the journey toward a new consciousness. Now is the time to connect as seeds for the future."

Ia-hr-ra, the queen, sat on her chair, listening intently. She ordered that wine be poured. I had one foot in another world again. We were not alone. The dead were among us and were listening. I slowly realized that they belonged to the Celtic life and lived among them and with them as present-day ancestors. We ate while the spiritual ancestors waited.

The Druids' attention wandered to the children. It made sense that Sara and John were with us. And the Druids made no secret of the fact they were closely observing and inspecting the children. They would learn from them later.

One Druid arose. "My name is Teta, guardian of the dragon line. Our ancestors built this city at precisely this location because they read the dragon lines and the legacy of the sacred geomancy. We still protect these energy lines. The powerful dragon lines connect here in sacred geometric patterns and create a pentagram that pulsates with the planet Venus and anchors its points in specific places. That is our sacred symbol and it flows like a powerful landscape pattern across a huge field and connects the surrounding hills. They connect anchor points. Our ancestors were shown the place at which divine order is reflected and cultivated it. Others had also noticed it, consciously or unconsciously and settled here, drawn by the light.

The Druids of the white order know of the sacred geomancy of the Earth. There are many Celtic tribes that have reached different states of development. Our Celtic tribe lives with a highly developed spiritual culture and at a high level of consciousness which we thank for our knowledge and the connection of the consciousness of the Earth and the universe. That is our school of geomancy, which we preserved from Atlantis."

Another Druid arose. Their unity of consciousness was impressive, they flowed in one current. They each knew when their leadership ended and when another should take over. They served a cosmic current.

"My name is Taramat, protector of feminine wisdom. Since the time of Atlantis, the worlds have separated into light and material. But in this place, we were able to maintain the light and manifest the sacred order. The first step into the new era will be to invite the children and women to their initiation sites."

Mary Magdalene arose, honored their light with her gesture and elevated it to feminine glory. "Where are your female priestesses? We all know why we have come together, but we cannot enter into new negotiations regarding the paths of the future as long as the sacred female part of your group is missing and the respect their voices deserve. Their essence is needed as our inspiration in this round of departure into the new worlds. The council is not complete until the priestesses join us at the table.

Ia-hr-ra arose from her chair and her emerald-green cloak drew circles on the earthen floor as she walked around the fire. "The male and female Druid priests and priestesses have live separately since time immemorial. That is what has been passed down. You do not see any Druidesses and priestesses at this table. I have been counseled by only male Druids for a long time now, but not Druidesses

There was a time when our Druidesses and priestesses blamed us in their culture for not being able to hold on to their access to the initiation rites. Though we identify as one tribe that worships the Great Mother and reverently fear her powers. Our initiated women blamed us for the feminine powers withdrawing. We did not listen to them and they found what they were looking for in the Egyptian temples of Isis. Many of us emigrated to Egypt and those who remained lived in isolation in the forests. I know now that it was not right, but I cannot change it anymore." She was emotional, deeply moved and agitated and it was noticeable. She looked briefly at Trevorta and if it hadn't been clear, it was now. Their love was like a secret prohibition of desire. Their love for each other was under fire.

The Grail of Renewal

We were part of a collective dream that erected itself like an archway in the air. I could feel that everyone in the room sensed that a small piece of eternity was opening and we were growing beyond the limits of our human lives. Their willingness to hear our light as our messenger opened the atmosphere even more.

Jesus pulled the Grail from the cloth He carried with Him. He held it tightly before His eternal heart until the Grail began to glow. The Grail was with us and filled the room with its presence. It grew silent, even in the worlds of the ancestors.

"I bring the Holy Grail to you as a symbol. It travels with us on our mission on Earth. It appears as a sign of the manifested power and light of God and once crowned me with the insignia of my heritage. It filled itself with God's presence and was with us before I was crucified in Palestine. It came with us to the new land and will shape our future. The fate of the Grail is closely interwoven with Sara and John's destiny. They are the future guardians of the Grail."

He arose and passed Mary Magdalene the Grail. "You are the seed for this new church."

"The church you bring should be built around a women?" a voice asked, appalled. The mood grew tense. Jesus was the revolution of love. Now He was breaking with thousands of years of patriarchal currents of tradition that had shaped a belief system. He planted a new dream of overcoming the individual dream which had sowed the chains of isolation and separation in humanity.

Mary Magdalene was the center. The earth currents flowed together around her and gathered beneath her feet: Red, vibrating currents threaded through the soil and bowed before her. It was visible to all. Their sacred Earth had spoken and left the patriarchal voices speechless. A new reality was opening before our very eyes. It was all of our responsibility to liberate ourselves from the restraints of the old structures and step out of the separation.

All of the visions of the collective dream pointed to her sacred heart. On this piece of Earth, on this ground, the Church of Mary Magdalene would point the way to the future. Jesus stepped back to give her space. As she took the Grail in her hands, it was clear: everything would gather around her. We would have to gather around HER and the Grail in order to unite and call everyone to join the gathering. Those who worship Isis, those who worship Yahweh, those who worship Mitra, those who worship the goddess in all of her forms of grace or God in all His manifestations of love. With the Grail, she held the seed of a new church that would be planted here so it could grow. To bring the many faiths together and unite them in the Light of Christ.

The seed was feminine creation and would not blossom for another 2000 years.

Mary Magdalene did not let the vibrations of the critics, which only dissipated slowly, stop her. She encompassed her power well and passed the Grail to Jesus. "Please fill it!" then she bowed her head, full of love and reverence.

He filled the Grail with liquid, not beer, not wine, nothing from this world. I was able to glance in as Mary Magdalene passed by me with the Grail. It held a golden drink, liquid and vibrating, full of joy for life with sparkling bubbles.

Crowned with love, she approached the queen and passed her the chalice. "Drink, sister of the lilies." Ia-hr-ra recognized the new bond instantly and accepted it. Mary Magdalene turned around so everyone could see her eyes which shone like a thousand suns.

"The mother soil is feminine. If we build what we believe in on feminine ground, the cultures will find their way back to each other and reunite the torn connections. The feminine foundation will help reunite that which has been separated and sow the seeds for the future." Mary Magdalene was not the only one who glowed with the celestial light of Shakti. The child in her lap, little five-year-old Sara, glowed with the feminine Light of Christ. She let the energy lines of love flow as they wove everything in a spectacle of light. My body began to glow in this resonance and my light burst forth from my every pore. Jesus had called on Shakti and we responded with our manifestation.

Mary Magdalene passed the Grail to her daughter and bade her pass the chalice to everyone in the room. Watching Sara work was gripping. With a bow, she passed the chalice, which united everything that had shattered in this space, to each of the Druids. Then she held her hands in front of her heart while they drank. Her pure essence was full of the power of innocence. They had engaged with us. A new paradigm stood above us in many colors. We now had to read it.

Ia-hr-ra was filled with red femininity. That evening was hard for the revered wise men on whose backs the responsibility for the tribe lay. Their counsel was decisive and their judgments were the sword between justice and injustice. They were the judges and representatives of the divine order. The feminine, however, succeeded; it was a celebration of the Goddess, how the women became one with the Goddess and how they wore their dresses were an extreme adornment. She who was the voice of the Mother was no longer a woman for men, she was a woman for women. Simon and Jesus had ignited this revolution in silence. They sat calmly, smiling. Their heavenly realm was not within them, they were heaven embodied.

"I would like to send invitations to a gathering. We will go to every valley and bring them all to one table. We wanted to invite that which has been shattered to a new conversation about leadership. Most importantly, I wish for us to listen. We want to come together, without prejudices and opinions," Ia-hr-ra was the queen and mother her people now needed. Her trusted advisors and Druids knew that if they lost the feminine, they would lose everything. But even more importantly, they were witness to their resurrection.

And so the new church began in the most hidden valley in Gaul.

The drink was strong. Jesus called it Amrith, the nectar of the gods. The wine that was passed around perfected the intoxication sent from heaven. It was necessary in order to break all of the old resistances against the new creation.

When I went to our room with John, it was as though the starry sky had slipped downward. As though it wanted to better see what was happening here.

"Why are you standing next to my bed?" A few hours later I was torn from sleep. It didn't seem to wake Simon and John from their slumber. But they stood around me, the ancestors of the Other World. This can't be, I thought. They replied promptly. "You can see us. Why?"

I explained to them telepathically that they were part of me and that I saw this world with one eye and the other world with the other. Then I wanted to know why they lived as the dead among the living. "Because, as ancestors, we accompany the living."

"And where is your heaven?" I didn't understand. This didn't wake Simon; his light was dominant and outshone everything. But I wandered between the worlds. I helped the beings understand the thresholds. No response came. I knew that the separation of light and material had also closed the transitions between life and death.

The next morning, the Druids had returned to their forests where they lived. I could feel that they had further awakened during their time with us. A new, fresher atmosphere hung in the air over the city. Ia-hr-ra was already mounted on her horse, as she had been when she left to come to us days before. With an open heart and the will to connect the worlds, she now made her way personally, protected by her warriors, to invite the people from the surrounding areas to her table. I wished her all the blessings of heaven. It was still early in the morning when she rode out, as her plan was to hold the gathering in three days.

We were left to our own devices in the city, but wherever we went, we were treated with great respect, for we were personal guests of the queen. Two warriors followed us in lock step, always there to protect us. Every free minute I had, I would flee to the raised area in our protected inner circle of the city to breath in the view that made me tremble. Hills surrounded us, each of them a magical point that anchored the dimensions beyond the material. Jesus disappeared often and we would see Him wandering across the fields. He was dreaming with God. Simon withdrew to our room and delved into another dimension. They meditated a new energy field into being on Earth.

Two evenings later, Ia-hr-ra returned and called for us. We met her in the meeting hall. She seemed drained as she took her place on her throne and ordered mead for us all. The honey wine was divine. We dined together until she told us,

"Tomorrow evening, we will see who will accept our invitation. First I visited the rabbis who serve a Jewish community not far from here. I hope I found the right words, but you, Jesus, you pursue me with miracles. I have tried for a long time to convince the suspicious rabbis; they were arrogant and looked past me. Until I had an inspiration and remembered something my grandfather told me long ago and which you have repeated often in the last few days. So I told a tale... 'Our ancestors all had one mission: to ensure that the knowledge of Atlantis was not lost with it. I remember,' I heard myself saying 'that my grandfather told me once that the adepts of the priesthood of Atlantis once put their ships to sea and carried with them the keys of wisdom to the Atlantian schools of mystery. Their task was to carry them to the corners of the Earth so they would not go down with Atlantis. My ancestors come from this tradition and we are the guardians of this knowledge, which we still carry with us today. Our Druids are the guardians of these mysteries. My grandfather also told me that your mysteries date back to the temples of Atlantis, for you preserve them as well. I assume your people also have a great journey behind you. We all know what it means to protect this knowledge from those who would not use it in the name of the One. But we carry the same story of our ancestors within us and it has separated us from each other. We live as neighbors and pretend nothing has happened. We are that traumatized.'"

Ia-hr-ra paused. "I simply opened my heart until there were no more cracks and poured it out to him and said, 'Those who have been promised to us since that time are now here. They are with us and will show us the new paths.' Then I invited them to the gathering and rode away."

She was courageous and feminine. She was ready to break down doors.

"Then I visited the Druidesses who live, hidden in the forest, and told them of you as well. I visited the Essenes on the black mountain; they knew about you. And I visited the Greeks in the harbor city. I visited the alchemists from Persia.

Now I am exhausted. I have the feeling I have moved mountains. Believe me, this is the best moment of my life. I know now who I am and what I am."

Jesus arose and kissed her forehead. "Lord, I trust you, you know that. We are playing with fire."

Jesus looked at Simon. He looked at Mary Magdalene. He looked at me.

"The physical world is not our reality. It is the world of the divine from whence we come. Let us pluck the miracles from God's throne." I fell to the ground and everything fell away from me. His words had helped me step out of the fear of experience. 'Step out', was my mantra. Thousands of icy rings shattered around my heart. That which we had never dared dream of had been made real by His love. My forehead was moist with the joy of liberation. We were here to cross the boundaries of love or die. I went to Ia-hr-ra and embraced her. "We sisters and brothers of the Order of Fire and Water are no longer alone."

The Council of Tribes

Late in the afternoon, we women began to grow restless. The people we had invited had less than half a day to travel and we were holding our breath waiting to find out if anyone would come.

One-by-one, the Druids returned and brought their aspirants with them. Young men who spent several years with them to become Druids themselves. I felt John observing them intensely. When they saw us women, they greeted us respectfully.

They retreated with Ia-hr-ra's high-ranking warriors and the Celtic aristocracy. Jesus and Simon weren't there and Mary Magdalene and Lazarus stayed outside with me. I began to love the thick, woolen fabrics we had been given which I pulled tightly around me to gather the warmth as the evening grew colder.

Suddenly, the wooden door that led to the bustling city opened and a warrior announced that guests had arrived. Ia-hr-ra herself went to meet them. We watched everything from a distance. A group of men and women came through the gates. Their robes revealed them as Jews of the Torah. Only one was a rabbi; his eyes were cautious, searching and revealed kindness. Over the course of the next few hours, Essenes arrived, humble in appearance and full of hope. Celts who trusted the queen came from all over Gaul. Noble Greeks who had had good contact with the Rhedones for generations came and exchanged knowledge. Men that looked like sages from the Orient came, and two Romans came.

Mary Magdalene, Lazarus and I froze when we saw them and inconspicuously gathered up our children. We made ourselves invisible in the crowd of people who had gathered in great numbers, despite our expectations, and disappeared into our rooms. When I saw Simon sitting on the bed, ready to meet the group, I blurted, "Romans have come!"

He thought for a moment, used His clairvoyant ability and said, "Everything is all right, Miriam." I still preferred to sing John to sleep first.

He fell asleep quickly, exhausted. But it wasn't long before he opened his eyes. "Come mama, we should go." I immediately understood my son and took him in my arms. On the way to the meeting hall, a wave of love and a gentle heart took hold of us. I looked into John's eyes and we let ourselves be carried away by the feeling that enveloped us in the embraces of a thousand loving angels.

They were all just taking their seats in the meeting hall. Many had come; the room was filled with souls as it once was in Palestine. Now we were in this strange land of Gaul and Jesus drew the masses to Him. I saw the two Romans as they joined the group. His love was the enchantment hearts could not resist. It was the first time we had appeared in public, here under the roof beams that desired peace.

Ia-hr-ra greeted them all and thanked them with a gesture that crowned her queen. She bowed before each tribe that stood here for its people. She then bade her Druids open the sacred space. White incense smoke and sacred song soon rose from the meeting hall. Prayers scuttled through the crowd and changed the spaces. Transcendence became visible. Trevorta stepped forward and bowed humbly.

"Our people are honored by your visit. We, as sages of our people, have prayed for this day in our visions. Jesus, the Nazarene, is among us. He is the honored guest in our city." A murmur went through the crowd. Was it amazement or disgust? Jesus showed Himself. He came to the center of the room and drew a symbol in the sand, then showed the crowd His stigmata. Everyone was close enough to see that blood was dripping from His left hand and falling to the ground.

"What the mists of this land shroud against discovery is protected here. I am Jesus of Nazareth and I am alive. My mission on Earth is not yet completed; in fact, it is beginning anew. I am here to remind you that you belong to this second promise." Jesus had returned.

"You died on the cross. Prove to us that you are He as you claim to be," said the Jewish rabbi.

"This is mockery. The Jews believe you are alive, the Romans blame the Jews," said one of the Romans.

Why have you let us believe you were dead? You were our only hope," said one of the Essenes.

"So the rumors are true," a voice said from the darkness.

"What is the Jew doing among the Celts?"

The voices spoke, one after the other. They had to express their confusion. A blond Jewish woman made her way to Jesus, stood before Him and when she wanted to kneel before Him, He lifted her up, stopping her. She said what she had to say, face to face. "I didn't know why I spent hours convincing my father to accept your invitation after Queen Ia-hr-ra left. But I know you. You have appeared in my dreams since I was a little girl. You are real. You have protected me often. May I touch your stigmata?" She didn't care what the people thought of her, or if her people agreed with her. Jesus stopped her. "Not now, Anais." He knew her name! She nodded and understood. She sat down near Him and listened.

"Cultures of light are created at different times at certain places where consciousness gathers. This is followed by a cosmic rhythm of evolution. I am not here to bring you a new religion. All religions pursue the same goal: God. I am here to connect your religions so we manifest peace. I am also here to remind you what religion has lost. The energy where the culture of light is currently gathering lies beneath our feet." They were listening to Jesus.

One after the other, the tribe leaders introduced themselves to the groups. The two Romans declared their faith in Christianity. Jesus and Simon asked them, in turn, what they think a connection of all the other religions and different tribes might look like. Everyone desired respect, their religious authenticity, the end of the isolation of the culture in which they lived. They desired peace.

"I wish to hear more of your faith and learn," said Ia-hr-ra.

Simon listened intently.

Jesus shone as He spoke. "God is writing us right now, He writes what we do if we all allow it. Think about it: What difference does it make, what does it change if that defines your truth? Heaven on Earth is not something that awaits us in the beyond. It is the reality that exists now if we raise our consciousness to that level. Anyone who wishes to leave is free to go. For we are uplifting the light for all of us. We have dreamed of this circle of light. We have a promise from heaven to fulfill. We protect these agreements in the smallest corners of the Earth to plant a seed for the culture of the Light of Christ.

No one left. Then we were finally complete. The wooden door opened and five Druidesses came in. One of them was elderly; we could see the power and beauty she once bore. And the effect it had on Ia-hr-ra was visible; she softened and personally received the Druidesses who were taking part in a gathering for the first time in a very long time. She led them to a place at her side.

Jesus addressed them directly. "Thank you for bringing your gift. You must know that women guard the knowledge that every tribe from Atlantis bears a code of light that contains its heritage and destiny. It is a seal of their knowledge and divine origins."

Symbols of light appeared above the different tribes for all to see. The children ran around and jumped up and down with joy trying to touch them. Everyone shuttered despite the beauty unfolding before us, carrying us away in cosmic reverence. The seals of light were the insignia of each of the tribes in the room. They scattered cosmic memories and activated the code within the people. Simon had conjured them. Symbols appeared above Jesus and Simon, their own symbols, shining thrones that flooded everything with light. The room was a space of unconditional love.

"Touch your seals and let the memories of light return to you," said Jesus, full of tangible love. The families of light appeared; it was suddenly clear why they belonged together. I saw the tribes of light. Mary Magdalene and Sara belonged under the seal of Jesus; John and I under Simon's seal. Lazarus belonged to our tribe.

Wine was poured as it once was during the evening meal. The Grail was passed around to every tribe and it wove a visible ribbon of love between the spaces of oblivion. We stepped out of the space of limitation into infinity and saw ourselves from a new perspective. A shape made of light appeared in the room, at first, transcendent and ethereal. A small spiritual colony of the universe, blue and illuminated. We became witnesses to this phenomenon taking shape before our very eyes.

First, it was a grain of golden light in the room which grew until it was a large and had two hands and worlds took shape within. Then it unfolded and became a landscape of fluorescing light in many shades of blue. It grew and expanded throughout the room and stretched one of its banks to Jesus and the other to Simon. They became part of this blue landscape in which golden cities sprouted and shone, full of light.

We went back to culture of Atlantis when Jesus and Simon were once the kings of the blessed realms. They led us back to where everything started. We went back to the roots, connecting things that were no longer aware of each other. It seemed to just happen on its own. Heaven became visible, then tangible, then it was around us. The tribes had found their way back again. It must have taken an eternity or only a second; we once again lost track of time and space in Jesus' presence. And yet it was new. He no longer brought us to heaven; He and Simon now brought heaven to us. I stretched out my arms to feel it with my fingers. Sara and John did the same and danced in God's spectacle of light. I touched the bliss and wept. With happiness.

"Miriam, what do you see?" It grew quiet and the vision faded. I heard Jesus speaking to me. The seals still hung in the room. They were white and silvery and their geometry was perfect and formed circles. They had different patterns and symbols. Everything was completely different. I had known them since the dawn of time. "There are 108 tribes of light," I began to read eternity. "They stand for 108 dominions of light. They are the spiritual families of the universe. Their seals represent their divine nobility. They are symbols of where we come from and where we belong. 108 divine families and their lineage are the ancestors of the tribes. They provide information about the divine family from which we are descended."

Seven seals surrounded me and I could feel which people belonged to which lineage. "Once, in Atlantis," I heard myself saying, "these seals came to Earth and manifested the dominion of the spiritual families."

"Seven of them are here today," said Simon. "If we connect ourselves, the other seals will be awakened from the resonance and can awaken one-by-one. If we begin to revive our seals, we will open the path for the souls to find their lineage and a map to their homes. Our circle is destined to plant the first seeds." The seals faded.

But at second glance, we noticed the signs lay on the floor. The sand reflected them amidst us and the seals swelled in a wave of peace. A sphere of peace developed between us as a sign from God that His will and our will were one if peace reigns between the cultures. All of the people from the different lineages were moved.

We knew we had to raise their consciousness so the cultures could live in peace. Diversity was not an embellishment. No one was born to patronize another. No religion was older; they simply arose at different times. No belief was the source, for every faith must be continuously renewed.

The complexity of the differences became vast and sacred instead of narrow and restrictive. It was our responsibility to translate this intimacy of generous light into deeds. Approaching the unknown was a mystical experience. We had conjured the power of the present and the primitive power that would hold this council together in the future. The Light of Christ burned at the center.

We recognized ourselves in the mirror and our own qualities in the equality of the others. We were fascinated by the qualities of each tribe. The diversity had crystallized into certain qualities of consciousness and divine faith. These faiths had to be combined and not fought. We could grow if we would look at each other and bring our people to the table. That was God's will. That was Jesus' will. And the foundation would be a woman. The woman Jesus loved. Mary Magdalene. She was the prophetess who could bring these cultures together. They would follow her because she had no will. Only pure love. It needed this female body. A female body as the embodiment of the feminine in Creation which brought the people and cultures together.

We were ambassadors of the light. By giving the synchronicity space, we became messengers who appeared from everywhere from all walks of life and all stations. Without the separation, we became God's love, the divine was love, we were love. We elevated ourselves in a brotherliness of acknowledgment and sisterliness of friendship. The vibration of love unlocked the experience of heaven on Earth.

So much happened in that moment. In equality, we all recognized each other. We looked at each other in love. And it seemed as though the dismissive Jews suddenly stepped closer, the Romans gave up their arms, the Essenes grew out of their humility into their greatness and awoke from their helplessness, and the Celts began to shine as guardians of nature. We recognized ourselves in the others and our qualities and love were amplified. Love bound us together. The Grail, Jesus, Mary Magdalene and probably all of us had done this.

Honor what you are and who you are.

Sight is sacred.

Free everyone else with it.

You were born chosen.

Our noble friends bear the insignias

of the future of which we are part.

In protest, our most beautiful gardens

grow in the inconspicuousness of fame.

The symbols faded. What remained was a fire of the Light of Christ that burned in the center. The fire was always a symbol of new beginnings. Then, very slowly, we returned to our world. Slowly, our bodies and this world became visible.

For a moment, we were all so connected to heaven that we could see the greater picture of our existence, our tribes. Our light, our eternal, foreseeing existence as ancestors. Receiving this image suddenly made us see things differently.

The Jews emerged in the honor of the old culture. The Romans emerged as the pioneers of innovation and new thought. The Essenes emerged as the healers of the world. The Celts emerged as those who wander between the ages and preserve nature. And we emerged as those who came from eternity and were cosmic nomads. We all began to talk to each other.

Jesus was love. He was the prophet of the age. He reminded us of the waste of a life without love. The woman at His side, Mary Magdalene, however, was the prophetess of the future. The church of those who wanted to create peace was established. The church of love. The book of love was written that day, not as a book, but as a manuscript of how the cultures encountered each other and came to agreements in cooperation on Earth.

We slowly fell back into the texture of our bodies. It had grown late.

The rabbi arose. "I was permitted to be a part of the divine miracle this evening. Tell us, what is the vision you bring us?"

Mary Magdalene arose and looked at Jesus. He nodded. To avoid insulting the traditions of those present, she said, "Allow me to speak to you." In the vibration in which we were, everyone was open.

"The church we are building is a roof under which all of your religions and sciences of the light can find a home. I am its body, for I will be your prophetess as it once was, so it shall be now. The Light of Christ will guide this church into the new era. We will begin by seeing each other and sharing knowledge."

Ia-hr-ra dreamed of her vision of community and tolerance, of knowledge and religion. She declared this gathering the beginning of regular meetings on every new moon. The Druidesses arose and said farewell. They hadn't said anything the entire evening. Before they disappeared in the sparks of the night, the high priestess of the Druidesses turned around. "We shall return and our land behind the mists awaits you when you return from your journey in two years. We will wait until you bring what we are lacking." She looked at Mary Magdalene intensely, the Goddess flashed between them, then she glanced at Sara and then me. We knew.

The evening in Arhedaes was the beginning of the new church of the Light of Christ. It was the beginning of a new language among different cultures. The tribes began conversations with each other and the Celts contributed their culture of celebration. God was with us. In many forms of His expression. All of the visitors decided to travel back to their villages that night and we were being called to the other end of the world. We had sown seeds in the sacred land of the Celts and now we could go.

The love that flowed from my awakened heart was sweet and felt like liquid honey that made me and everything around me happy. This is what God must feel like when He loved. It had to be just like this. Christ's love was a current that poured from my heart and in which everything that touched it floated. So divinely sweet, so divinely heavy, so divinely bitter. I loved.

Slowly, slowly, we all realized that we did not have to experience each other in the expanse of time. The seed of the Light of Christ was sown a long time ago in this land, where the cultures blossomed, the women had rights and the belief in God in His many forms of existence was justified.

The ancestors blessed us.

The Star of Destiny Wanders Onward

We were ready to leave. Everything had been fulfilled. The next morning, Ia-hr-ra and Trevorta accompanied us for a bit on our path to the sacred sites of the Druids. They lived scattered throughout a nearby valley. I could sense their sacred copses and initiation sites. We followed the secret, mystical paths through the forests. It was their request that they lead us to their hallowed sites where they connected heaven and Earth and established their connection to the heavens. Their initiation sites of wisdom, prophecy and initiations.

The Druids preserved both: The knowledge of the initiations in the prophecies of the stars and the language of nature which they worshiped and decoded in every moment and whose secrets they knew to interpret. They were connected to the Mother and her magic. And still I felt, deep within me, that the women were missing. But the men sensed it. They knew the wisdom of the feminine must not be lost. That the worlds of the feminine and the masculine must not drift apart. Trevorta, who guided us, told us at the sacred site, that he would like for John, Sara and I to return, the women too as aspirants to the sacred knowledge of the powerful currents of the Earth.

The sacred geomancy and how to read and use it has been preserved here by the Druids for times to come. They offered to raise John, for he would become a great soul that should know of the sacredness of the Earth and be able to read its currents in order to anchor the Grail to the Earth. We met each of the seven Druids and they trustingly explained their work and its effect. Nature was their direct mysticism of the experience of God. Their forests were so alive I could hear them breathe and listened to them. Beings from our world, female and male, pulsated with their power and Eros. It smelled of sweet, knowledgeable soil.

Something awoke within me like a wolf seeking its home. Beyond all conventions I heard myself tell Trevorta as I departed, "We are on our way to India now. We will be gone for two or three years. When we return, I would like to learn the sacred geomancy and the science of the energies from you." I didn't even hesitate.

"And John will be old enough then to become an apprentice if you so desire." Then I was surprised by Simon. Trevorta glanced at the queen. "Yes wolf woman, come back so we can learn from you and you from us."

Our departure was silent and unspectacular. Ia-hr-ra had become our friend; it was a friendship that would last a lifetime and beyond. Your people, the Celts, were the womb for the new teachings of Christ and the realization of the church of love. The Celts accepted us and Christianity was born thereof and wanted to continue existing. We had been riding a while when we saw two Druidesses by the side of the road. They had been waiting for us. "We will join you. Our lady of the forest said you could use our knowledge to cultivate your land." They were a gift from the high priestess. Her gesture showed her devotion and friendship.

"We are on the way to India," said Jesus, "on our journey to the old world of the gods. We will not return for a few years; we are on the path to the oldest sources of femininity. We will return with the treasure of the Great Goddess." This was His farewell. Tetra explained to us that he had dreamed that night that our journey would be a great one and the worlds would unite and the sacred feminine would find a new power of creation in the cosmos. We would return and bring with us the secret of how we could anchor the Great Goddess to the Earth so her body of the universe can meld with the Earth. Now they wandered on the sacred veins. But to return to the realm of the Goddess would mean to be able to materialize in the realm of the cosmos on Earth. We would recover this key.

We left friends behind in this place. Soul mates whom we would not see for a long time. A moment was enough to exchange everything our souls wanted to share on every level, like a sudden exchange of consciousness, friendship and congress. Then we separated to once again wander on the paths of the Earth's network. To create new connections between cultures and love with the desire to move toward the fertility of knowledge and the wonderful diverse legacy of the cultures that existed on Earth, disconnected, as the treasure of human history. Their vibration called us into the unknown. Filled with new life, we made our way back to our Essene family. Lazarus rode beside me. "That was wonderful," he said. We had friends in our new land. Our exile had transformed into the miracle of the gift of life.

Time is a Circle

Four days later,
we arrived back at the Essene village.
We brought four
black-robed and
painted Celtic warriors
with us who protected
us, two Druids,
who brought us closer to the soil of this land,
and horses that were ours now.
We had been given
such abundant gifts.

The Departure

On the day we departed, the world around us grew quiet. We were on our way to travel to many countries that were completely unfamiliar to Mary Magdalene and me. Jesus and Simon, however, knew the way to the other end of the world and they took us with them into the unknown. Once, this journey was their pilgrimage into their inner selves and Joseph of Arimathea had accompanied them to different cultures and initiation sites so they expanded the horizon of their hearts and learned from openness. India was our destination. To get there, we would make our way to Damascus along the Road of Myths. They called it the Silk Road, the storied route of the merchants of the civilizations.

Jesus and Simon had been planning everything for weeks. Lazarus had made preparations long ago and had managed to use Joseph of Arimathea's contacts to get his assets out of Palestine and secure them. He and Simon were good businessmen and our networks were secured. Messages were sent and plans were made until the time had come and we said farewell indefinitely.

We mounted our white horses, left the Essene village behind us and everything in my world slowed down. The images of Sara and John saying goodbye to us with determined expressions remained in my mind for many hours. These children knew more than we did. Everyone else in the village was hopeful that their own future would unfold and they showered us with blessings for our journey. The horses Lazarus had procured for us were a gift from him. A Celtic warrior accompanied us and, as always, he remained invisible; the forests and everything in nature were his camouflage.

Martha was at peace with her decision. She and the great warrior from Britannia were on their way to Magda and Joseph in Britannia. Adventure and the unexpected awaited them too. We rode in silence for days. We each had time to listen to our inner worlds as we watched the landscape we left behind. We were in a solitary conversation with God and in an intensive prayer with our own souls. We were preparing ourselves and gave the inner essence space to expand. The substance of the miracle took on its inner perception and looked at where we were going with hope.

Then we reached the crossing and the time came for us to say goodbye to Martha and the warrior. They took the path to the north and we rode toward the harbor, to the great ships sailing to Damascus. Saying farewell was painful, as always; my heart would never get used to it. When I sighed, I looked into Mary Magdalene's eyes and she too was weeping quietly. But something in our souls had matured beyond the little deaths of mundane farewells. It was the yearning for that which did justice to the weight of the promise. We rode further toward the adventure of our inner selves. Jesus had promised us that this journey was for us. His destination was the primal source of feminine power, which lay hidden awaiting us at the end of the world.

In Massalia, Simon first secured our funds and ensured our assets would be available to us at different stations. Each of us had three sets of clothing that we washed in the harbor and dried in the sun before we departed. That was all we had with us when we boarded the ship the next day. We sent the horses back with the warrior who had accompanied us along the way. I stood at the bow and looked out at the vast sea. Freedom was more powerful than the cowardice within me.

I had no concept of the worlds awaiting me, so foreign from my tradition and heritage. The water was the Mother, vast and open, and my soul knew that everything that had happened had its perfect destiny. It was a part of the great circle of the mastery of life that Mary Magdalene and I only became whole because of our relationships and here we were now leaving on the pilgrimage to feminine power. Our husbands were our spiritual teachers and would guide us. They were God's warriors, the sons of love and fire. We needed their protection on this journey, for the feminine lived in the shadow of the world and we needed the love and protection to allow us to awaken. Without being able to put it in words, the ocean showed me it must be this way; that we must go on this journey as husband and wife in order to liberate the worlds.

On the ship, Jesus and Simon shared their adventures from back then, making our first nights at sea seem shorter. Jesus told us of old, sacred temples in India where He had studied. The teachers called themselves Brahmas and possessed the oldest manuscripts of humanity, the Vedas. Once, He had learned to read and interpret them and He loved them because they were wise and praised Creation in all its aspects with the fire of life and were an ocean full of sacred words. The temples were a magnificent expression of wealth, He told us, but the streets were impoverished because the people were divided into castes, determined by karma. The people of India believed in reincarnation and life assigned to us based on the lives we had previously lived. Later, He began to annoy His Brahmanic teachers because God's light showed Him that there was neither a karmic punishment nor castes and the people should turn to Him themselves to experience the healing of the grace of forgiveness.

"In which life did we earn the right to be with you now?" Mary Magdalene wanted to know. "In none and all of them," said Jesus. "The love that unites us, you and me, and us all, was born in heaven and connects us in all ages. It will never be extinguished. It is the enchantment that is always drawn to itself in all lives, like a magnet." We were flattened by the density of love; it completely unhinged us.

The nights at sea on the way to Damascus were wild. Storms shook the ship. I fled to the deck and found Mary Magdalene who also couldn't sleep. We allowed ourselves to be one with the sea, as Jesus and Simon already were. They slept as though in their mothers' wombs despite the storm winds. It simply took us longer to transform the human fear deep in our bones into devotion to the natural forces. Both were our nature, the fear and violence; we let the walls of separation fall and listened to the water as it danced, wild and unrestrained, with the wind. It was like that every night, for the storm refused to calm. Mary Magdalene and I settled in and treated it as training.

We were at sea for three weeks and changed ships once. We lost all sense of time after the first four nights, at the beginning of our journey, when Jesus had taken us into the world of primal feminine powers which He had once experienced in India as initiations.

On the third night, we waited outside for the coming storm. We stay outside, looking at the blue sky as the coasts, still visible in the distance, passed by us.

"Simon and I spent years in India and we were separated. He was brought to a school of the Vedas in Rajagriha and I was brought to Jagannath. We were both thirteen years old. I studied the Vedas for three years and followed the sacred mantras of Creation, which I prayed, the fire ceremonies and rituals, but nothing happened within me. The further I engaged in the teachings of the Brahmas, the more I left myself. They repeated their Japas, Homas and Yagnas without life; I soon felt them beginning to hollow me out. But I couldn't leave yet, for the energies bound there would not let me go. I had to stay. My inner world fled and I began my secret prayers, those meant to provoke reality. They all spoke of enlightenment and liberation, but I could not see it. Not on the horizon that was my own. My father remained silent. 'Seek liberation from the yoke of human existence,' He had told me and then He stayed out of my reach.

Brahma was the origin of all Vedas, they said, but the Brahmas had forgotten the Vedas. Their rituals had not helped maintain the harmony and balance between the worlds for a long time because they avoided the knowledge and the price it demanded. The Gods no longer received the fire sacrifices that strengthened them to allow them to nourish the worlds. But they were deaf to the scream when a soul-bearing creature died.

I was alone. The rituals and prayers made me feel even lonelier. I left my sleeping chamber and wandered among the temples at night. They said that the lord of the universe himself was alive in this place, sowing his seeds. The priests considered themselves elevated as part of God's lineage. They knew about me and my prophecy and that is why I had been entrusted to them, but the distance between our souls grew every day.

I began to meditate at night and missed all of the lessons. The Brahmas began to scold me and lecture me until I was sick of it and went outside to meditate under a tree. I followed HIS words. 'Seek liberation.' I stopped eating and immersed myself. The words of the priests grew distant from my essence. At first, I meditated for fourteen days and was one with all of existence. I was everything and everything was me. I was in Samadhi, the state of eternal bliss, but I was not liberated.

The young monks who studied here began to secretly bring me rice and milk at night; the Brahma priests came every day to observe me. When I opened my eyes at night the rice transformed into the nectar of the moon and the milk into the Amrith of the sun. I left them for the monks as thanks. This state was infinite and still lonelier than ever before. I prayed. What is the secret of true liberation?

I meditated on this question in the sacred universe for three days and three nights and it echoed back. But there was no response. God, my Father, remained silent. And I continued to meditate.

On the twenty-first night, it grew as black as coal around me and everything ceased to exist. I was nothing and had never existed. Time ended and I no longer counted it. I was just about to give up and SHE appeared from nowhere, so bright and beautiful it blinded me and then she was dark and terrifying.

'What? You are giving up now that I am here with you?' her words echoed throughout all of the universes. 'No one can be liberated without me. Even when Siddhartha came to me and begged for enlightenment and freedom, he had to learn that we can bind all of the Siddhis and Yogi powers to us, but neither renunciation nor penance will free you. I alone am the key to the freedom for which you yearn.' She suddenly had a thousand arms, then four. Her eyes were stars and then a black, burning fire. She was full of lotuses and then all of her hands held weapons. Flowers rained from her heart and life pulsed in her feet. 'Who are you? Your beauty shatters me.' I was full of a yearning that tore me apart.

'I am Devi, the mother of all life. I am the Goddess. My name is Shakti. I am beyond all understanding, I am your liberation. I exist before all religions. I am the power that breathes life into lifeless bodies. I am the law of Creation. Find me.' Then she disappeared. She was more mystical than I could ever imagine. I had found the divine Mother. I was free. When she disappeared back into the universe, I had experienced the liberation I had sought.

The next day, I ended my meditation and declared my studies complete. 'You fear her because she is magical. But it was she who once appeared after the darkest war of the universe when your Rishis prayed and I listened to you. In those nights, she dictated the Vedas to you, the teachings of your life, then you forgot them. If you forget them, you forget themselves,' I told the priests as I bid them farewell.

I left that sacred place and went on a journey to find Simon. When I found him in Rajagriha, he had just come out of his meditation. SHE had recognized him and visited him for nine nights. It was time to leave the places of the Brahmas and fulfill the promise we had both given her. We were on the search for the Great Mahababa, he who cannot be found; only he can find you. And we knew we would return with her daughters whom she had asked about.

With you,'" Jesus said and looked at Mary Magdalene and me.

"Find her, she wants you," were his words and then we spent all of our days on this journey, on her waters, on the search for HER.

The life in which the authentic spiritual self awakens begins with apparent loneliness. I could feel us consciously cultivating this relationship to our silence; we knew where the other was. The people who live in the subconscious ritualize patterns they learned and that have been passed down to them. Everything I knew was torn from me on the boot. The familiar, which loved to repeat itself, fought for its life. In those nights, I felt we were in close contact with Mary. I could feel her and she knew that we were nearby. But it was not the time to see each other. Our message had reached her and her blessing came to us with her blue light and the wind. The Great Mother was searching for me. SHE was also searching for Mary Magdalene. She had found Mary.

I awoke the night before we landed and dreamed that I set my feet on the ground and remembered that it was the same soil as that in Palestine, my native soil, from whose ashes I was born. But we were in Syria, further north. And we were free here, which our native soil did not allow us, because it was enslaved itself.

Damascus

It was night when we left the ship and the darkness of the city dragged me down. But that disappeared immediately when we saw who awaited us at the harbor: MaRa and Sharon, as though from another age, eternal and here again. I froze, not because I was so surprised, but because I knew that our fate had turned. I once thought I would never see them again. What was predestined for us and what we had promised in heaven was done, for we had fulfilled what had to be fulfilled. "Why didn't you tell us?" I asked Simon. "Because we had sent messages via the Essenes and didn't know if they would arrive." I looked into MaRa's black eyes and saw eternities far away from our memories that were more archaic than anything we knew.

Our greeting in Damascus couldn't have been more moving, for after all these years, we had found each other again. History had carried us forward, but not changed our bond. On the contrary: After everything we had experienced, the reunion with Sharon and MaRa was curative. They brought us to their house. Sharon was still a wealthy merchant and we were now his guests. So many images came alive, how he had once come to us; he had only heard of Jesus and then his destiny was written.

When we arrived at their noble house, they led us first to the room where their little son was sleeping. "What a wonderful creature," I said. "Another savior in our protective arms, who will changed the world in secret." We ate like kings and exchanged stories. We did not speak of the past, we spoke about what was happening now and what would be born. We learned from Sharon and MaRa that the Essenes and many of Jesus' followers had traveled north from Palestine and had settled from Damascus to the Northern Sea.

"The shock witnessed during the crucifixion still lives on in them. These people have seen the violence of the Romans and the Jews and what shook them so much was that the Son of God had been nailed to a cross before their eyes under their dominion. It was as though they had lost all hope." Jesus did not respond. We learned that Sharon and MaRa had spent most of the time traveling these countries as wandering preachers and linking the worlds that had been torn apart. MaRa had been shown this path in a dream, that they were to connect the people and the paths that had been torn apart. Since then, they had wandered for years with their son, going from village to village and community to community. No one suspected how rich their home was when they lived the lives of nomadic preachers.

"There is a new network of people that weaves across the lands. They call themselves Christians and follow the new faith," said MaRa. She had grown calm and maternal. "I tell them you are alive, that you conquered the Romans and Jews, in your own way. I tell them you possess the power of God, which does not fight, but rather embodies the present. We bring them new prayers and fire rituals. We bring them together and connect them. Their hearts are tied up in knots of fear, but they are infected by the teachings of love."

"If precisely these people had arisen when I was sentenced and crucified back then, we would have elevated the teachings of love, a power no one had ever known," said Jesus. "But they have covered their hearts and given fear precedence and the small life instead of being open to the fire of love. Believe me, I do not say this for my sake, but you will not heal any hearts if this wound of the cowardice of love is not stilled. They watched, but left me alone. I should save them, but I cannot save anyone who does not stand up themselves. I loved and kept my heart open for the love of God, in life and in death. Now it is up to humanity to learn this."

Jesus continued. "We have been given a second life today, and now it is time to live it. I am very happy to be with you."

He had tears in His eyes. "We could have lost each other for many lives, but we are here and with each other again. When we return, I will travel to the villages with you and will be there with you. Thank you for your loving service."

"We have watched for your ship every night for days. Now you are here. I have used all of my relationships and your journey has been arranged as far as Taxila. The equipage of the ruler of Kashmir will greet you there. He is already expecting you." Sharon had taken care of everything.

Simon had remained quiet so far. Now he said, "If you continue to preach, the new will open to you. You are here to show them a new and even more beautiful interpretation of life. That will not be possible if you do not invoke the end of the torturous oppression and celebratory sacrifices. Those who follow the teachings of Christ are the heralds of the new age. They must stop sacrificing themselves and find the beauty and joy that lives in these teachings. Grow beyond yourselves and show them the kingdom of heaven that lives within you."

MaRa listened intently. "There are two worlds," she said. "Some follow the inner teachings, others a new belief and the Essenes are finding a new home in communities that are founded on their healing and sharing of knowledge. Many of the women of Ephesus have found a new home with them. Our old world has died and the new one is finding itself, we know that."

Simon said, "Then go out and initiate them all. Everyone should know the initiation rites. We bring that which was taught in secret to everyone. The more people who awaken, the better. This is God's will. It is about everyone. It is about illuminating the collective light."

"Should I share the knowledge of Ephesus that we have preserved for so long?" MaRa wanted to know. "Yes," said Simon. "If the knowledge is not shared freely, we have no chance. We will go to India and liberate the feminine power. You have the power of the light, Mother of Ephesus. Raise the people unto the light. You have the knowledge. Show them the divine essence that lives within them and how they can lift it up again."

Silence.

Golden pages.

Untouched and eternal.

Every page shall be turned in Akasha

when new lives blossom.

Surpassed by the upheavals of the Earth.

Will I come home after a long journey, elucidated, purified.

Should I tell you?

Page after page are being filled with us.

That evening in Damascus, golden lines spread out through our community, the community of Jesus, Mary Magdalene, MaRa and Sharon, Simon and me. Golden lines that settled over the landscape and connected us to the lands around us. They settled over what is now Anatolia, they settled over the Silk Road to India, through Persia, they settled over Judea and Palestine and stretched out to Egypt and Ethiopia. They laid new golden veins through southern Gaul and on to Britannia. We were the people who would connect these newborn lines with the living. The present and the future and our story lay before us like a book we could read. It opened before us all and we became conscious of our destiny. We could read these lines on which we wandered and where we sowed the seeds of the Light of Christ. We could see how these seeds led the people to the new teachings.

Each of us had a mission. That evening, we became aware that three women, who originated at the Shakti levels of Creation, goddesses in human form, and Simon and Jesus and Sharon formed a single seed on which God placed His new earth. The teachings God gave the people of Atlantis to begin the next evolution was the seed of the Light of Christ. The teachings of love. It would guide the people back to love, that open, immortal beauty that once pulsated as one with Creation. But these new teachings would do much more. The

revolution it brought with it was so simple, yet so difficult. Reminding the people that they were of divine origin and they had direct access to God was the greatest hurdle in the world of separation. But first this access to the Light of Christ needed to open itself to us on its own.

The map of light spread out before us and we could see how the golden veins spanned the Earth like rivers on which the seeds of the Light of Christ would be planted. Our destiny lies therein. How we connected to people, at what time and in what place became a tapestry woven of life.

I was aware in that moment that we could touch this knowledge but that it only quenched our curiosity and the isolation of inspiration. What became visible before my eyes through what Jesus and Simon manifested in this space, was that everyone receives access as part of their destiny and we were weaving stories that were really creation if we become a part of the sacred woven pattern. It was up to us to recognize, read and live the pattern in the perfection, the pattern of agreements of time, place, memories and stories that were once one with Creation.

Something incredible was happening in this space. It was golden. It interwove us with Creation in a way I had never seen before. We became a part of Creation by living and feeding what we experienced into the fabric of life. Because we were connected to the golden currents and the Light of Christ and the lines, we rewrote Creation on Earth. We could see how these currents powerfully wove through the Earth for two or three hundred years, finding a foothold. We could see that these currents dried up on the surface of the Earth in places and other currents lay over them.

We could also see that what we sowed and what we would sow would stand the test of time. That the story that would be written on Earth in the future, partly by the unconscious and the darkness, only scratched the surface. And that we would be able to lay these currents in the Earth and they would awaken at the right time.

This

time

is

now.

The

currents

are

golden.

We only had to manage to activate them in the Earth, because they were an arterial system that would awaken when the time they called the Golden Age came.

The golden currents

of the earth are awakening.

We sowed them

2,000 years ago.

We know

how we are

connected to each other.

The old paths were extinguished even further in that moment. That night, MaRa, who was the Mother of Ephesus at that time, re-experienced how all traces of the old tradition died. MaRa experienced that as her mystical death. The old paths had been fulfilled and served their purpose. Their seeds dried up in the fire of the Earth. The new paths appeared as dragons in the sky and we had to understand them. I too died back then. I consciously sensed what the fact of the old traditions dying in the fire of the Earth was doing to me and how they bore it anew. And at the same time, we became aware of the journey that still lay before Mary Magdalene and me.

Together with Simon and Jesus, we would recover the second power after the Light of Christ. The lost powers of Shakti appeared in dreams around us. That night, MaRa and Sharon were encouraged to continue wandering, reinforced by Simon and that which he had brought to Earth as Creation and MaRa and Sharon knew that it was their mission to give the people the initiations that were once only conducted at Ephesus in secret and silence. Simon had started the revolution as he once again emphasized and said to MaRa, "Everyone should partake in these initiations. Give them all the chance. There is nothing left from the heavens to hold back. There is nothing left to teach in secret." And thus began their journey as pilgrims with their little son on the golden paths of awakening through Anatolia, Syria, the regions of Persia and Palestine.

MaRa and Sharon began to initiate the people in the baptism of fire. The teachings of Ephesus, which women had preserved for so long, lived again and left the mountains of secrecy and silence. The holy sacraments they preserved were free, because Simon so wished it. They began their pilgrimage in selfless service to the currents on which they traveled and in return, nourished them. They awoke in this moment as living co-creators. Their little son was part of this mission.

And we would start our journey the next day to recover the lost Shakti powers, the creative forces that pulsated in little temples at the other end, in the land called India, as Jesus and Simon had promised.

It was time for us to go to sleep. Mary Magdalene and I were on an inner journey to the divine Mother; the secular journey that awaited us the next day promised an adventure of miracles and the senses.

The Golden Leaves

The next morning, Sharon brought us directly to the merchants. Damascus was Oriental, and magical and somehow enchanted. The mood of this culture was like smelling a thousand fragrances. It was like a fairy tale. A magic lay over these boundaries to the Orient, which we now dove into. It smelled like cinnamon, pepper and mystical energies. The structures were different, full of arches and courtyards that hid secret gardens. I was in a world enchanted by magic, roses and poetry. I became aware of the difference to the land from whence we had come. In Gaul, the landscape was simple and divine. It gave me the space to discover my own essence and integrate my own story. Everything was so pure that one had to find one's own essence.

But in Damascus, surrounded by the many tempting essences, it became almost unpleasant for they tried to ensnare you. During those first encounters, I didn't know what to do with them at first. Many energies were around me trying to beguile me. I looked at Mary Magdalene as we walked into the city and asked her, "Do you feel the same way?" She said, "Yes!"

We sought the nomads who had their stations there before they moved on again. Sharon had arranged everything for us. He had prepared our entire journey to Taxila, in the pass on the border of Kashmir. The Silk Road was the trade route on which many of his friends traveled and where the fabrics he brought to these lands from China and India were traded. They called the nomads the lords of the Silk Road; they knew the paths like the backs of their hands.

When Sharon brought us to the nomads, we entered a new world. It was characterized by the wildness of the nomads' journeys through the desert. I would learn much about them, for the only thing I knew so far was that my life was in their hands. We met with the family of the merchant with whom we then set out. The merchants on the Silk Road were all connected. They controlled the route with the most expensive goods. They wandered through the desert with their camels and connected the worlds. Our journey began with them and Sharon said, "The nomads will leave tomorrow. Give them all of your clothing today; I have arranged everything so you can leave tomorrow."

He introduced us to the nomads. Wild men. And highly educated women. Jesus had once traveled this route with Simon and Joseph of Arimathea. The men with whom we traveled were the sons of the men Jesus and Simon had taken through the countries back then. Sharon offered for us to spend another night at his house before we left the next morning. Everything was prepared for us to leave for the other end of the world. Mary Magdalene and I found it all so exciting our bones vibrated.

A huge surprise awaited us back at the house. At least for me, for we were overwhelmed by a wave of unexpected love. Peter, whose beard was threaded with silver strands of wisdom, and Andrew, joyous as always and Mary, the loving had managed to come to us. In those days, Peter and Andrew traveled from Greece to Asia Minor to the people and villages and returned to Rome at regular intervals. They were traveling and had brought Mary with them. I didn't know how Jesus managed to synchronize these connections between us, between the worlds in which we lived, so precisely that we all found our way to each other on exactly that evening.

I would often experience a flow of energy being activated that moved the world around us when He brought those He loved to Him to interweave certain points. A flow that made the currents of events and reunions ebb and flow from time to time and synchronized us across all regions of the world. To introduce new creation with us, a flow of energy surrounded us at the perfect time at which we found each other to then go out in different directions and making our pilgrimage on these golden currents, reviving them. The miracle that the three of them had found us that evening before we left on our great journey was no miracle.

Shakti.

Golden. She weaves herself.

She moves the world.

Everything flows,

even when we think

it isn't flowing.

It appears dead

and newborn at the same time.

She was one with

Jesus and Simon.

Now she was hunting

Mary Magdalene and me.

Jesus' system of sending messages with light, worked completely. He reached those He loved and we came together in synchronicity. That evening we were granted a reunion. We sat at the table with Peter, Andrea, Mary and the others and ate, prayed and renewed our vows as we once did, yet it was different and new.

This time, we discussed what we had brought from heaven, could make reality on Earth in the second incarnation that was so mercifully given us. No one preached as it once was, instead we discussed how we could best create the visions from God's throne as reality on Earth in the next few years. We had come to allow the teachings of God to awaken and be renewed within us and we knew that we now had a favorable window of time during which it was possible to allow as many people as possible to participate and to bring them the missive. The word of God waited to be carried forth. The circle closed within us. We wanted to use this new window of time, for it stood above us and interwove with the golden lines in the Earth. We deliberated what was truly wise.

Jesus advised Mary not to take too many journeys; she should instead take care of building the community of people who would come to her in greater numbers. He prophesied that they would come to her from all over the world to seek healing and to learn. Her knowledge of healing from God's breath would draw people from every country to Ephesus. He promised her He would fulfill her greatest desire; to see her only granddaughter again.

We told her of Sara and she listened to us intently. I sensed the bond between her and her granddaughter being woven. These tones of the old and renewed love were gentle and golden. Mary loved without limits, she loved Sara especially, without ever having seen her, but their souls knew each other.

The near future was visibly writing itself. The four of us would be traveling to India for two to three years and then we would decide what would come next. These two or three years were discussed at our table so everyone who was connected to us was included. We knew where the others were, we sensed them too, that they lived. Mark was in Egypt then. Thomas had already traveled to India. When Jesus had gone to India after the crucifixion, He had taken him with Him. John was in Ephesus and the others were traveling in other parts of the Earth and we would now start consciously linking connections. The time of isolation was over. It had strengthened our essence, polished the intense light. Now was our time, we were ready.

The people were addicted to what our new teachings brought with them. We would no longer keep it a secret that Jesus was alive. Many already suspected. This spell had now been broken. The Romans and the Jews would be the ones to later cover up this message. We would be the Good that we had brought to this Earth, share it with full hands, without fear, that we would have to die for it. That time had passed. The spell had fallen from us.

Jesus advised Peter and Andrew to build as many communities as possible and to keep going back to Rome. Peter looked at Jesus very seriously that evening. He read his fate. But we also knew that he still had many years to awaken these communities and the inner knowledge of the consciousness of love. He would take as many people with him as he could. He also knew that it was his mission to be in Rome.

That evening, Peter said, "You should know, Rome is not bad. The Romans aren't bad either, but the more time I spend in Rome, the clearer it becomes to me what has happened here. The people try to be gods themselves. They fear death so much they believe they are reinforcing the eternity of their fame and divinity by building their empire. What they had lost was the feminine aspect of Creation. The mother who is black and who kills, because we must bear everything."

MaRa grew calm and said, "Then it is time for me to teach the people the rhythm of the black light, the rhythm of life and death and teach them a natural relationship to it. Teach them the rituals that can sanctify them between life and death. Humanity had begun to demonize death and push it to the edges of society. They thought their deeds no longer had consequences. But what they had really lost were the teachings of the sacred. That we come to Earth, as people and beings, as souls, to pursue our own development plan to our divine self.

The Earth is our school. We are bound to a circle of evolution and we come to Earth and dream our lives to fulfill ourselves, find ourselves and encounter ourselves. But when we exclude death from that evolution, the transitions to the world of the non-materialized consciousness, that are joyous, where we are accompanied, where our soul's path, which is sacred, is accompanied, when we complete the soul's path in the moment at which we die, for humanity has built a wall that is nearly insurmountable for them. Life takes place, disconnected with regard to the non-materialized world."

MaRa knew the initiation cycles and said she was prepared to go on a pilgrimage with these teachings and turn everyone from enemy to friend. Where this path would lead them, only God knew, and they trusted Him.

She looked at Mary Magdalene and me. "What do you think awaits you in distant India?"

Mary Magdalene arose and embraced her. "MaRa, you were the Mother of Ephesus in this life. Now our teachings of the feminine initiations on Earth have been taken by the primal fire of the Earth. I think I will go to India and seek out the old gods and their stories to revive what has already been experienced and the memories and bring them into the new era.

I know I will return with a seed from the memoirs of the gods I will find there. And I shall bring these new seeds to the country in which we live now. I will give most of them to my daughter so she can build them up and plant them in the earth.

I will swathe the new teachings in red light and bring them to the new country to bear it in the womb of the Celts. I have had visions for a long time now that a new church will be built upon my body.

It will unite what they once taught in Ephesus. It will remind me of the legacy of Ephesus I bear within me and I will collect new seeds in the memories in India and, together with my daughter and the Light of Christ, bring a new femininity and a new church of femininity."

MaRa nodded and looked at her. It felt real. We knew her path. To explore these depths and stride through them before they can be experienced; that was

Mary Magdalene's path. It became apparent that our journey was a pilgrimage with initiations. We would write our own stories of heroes and heroines, which would complete us.

I thought about what awaited me in India. But I only felt emptiness. I could not see what awaited me. I felt Mary looking at me. Her blue light and starry eyes fell gently upon me. She said, "You do not have to know what awaits you. But it is hidden, waiting for you in the temples. When you find it, bring it to me too. For I know it will be a stone that will complete Ephesus." I had visions again and I could see the images. But since the images were foreign to me and the images of the temples no longer created a sensible picture within me. I had to trust in life. It would be clear when we were there.

The star of Creation stood over us. We had come together to connect and unite with each other and support each other to then spread out in a star in all directions. Each of us would wander on golden paths. Jesus became a part of us that evening. To me, that was the special part of what happened that evening. Jesus, the son of God, merged with us. He became part of our story, which we wove on Earth. He was no longer the light that preceded us. He was simply with us. Jesus was our friend.

That evening, a seed for the future of humanity was born. The hierarchies dissolved and we sat together and each of us was conscious of our origin, where we looked upon God and we were incarnated on this Earth as conscious beings. Many parts of the Earth lived in unconsciousness.

Other parts of the Earth had lived consciousness and lost it. We were the ones who kept vigil and perceived the Earth consciously and, at the same time, our divine core where we looked upon God. We knew that this Earth was our journey, to perfect our own souls.

"What is the new lesson, Jesus?" asked Andrew.

"Build communities in respect for the light, gather them to the sacred meal and share the communion as a symbol of unity with God. Show them the path of love and how to forgive. Raise them up and lead them from powerlessness to power. Teach them that God lives within us all and that they serve this kingdom and not the mundane. Show them that the Earth is a garden of paradise and they are its gardeners. That is all. Show them how powerful love is, the heart of the immortal beauty of Creation. Honor the soul, honor the tradition.

It is so simple. Embody love and show them the living rituals of love that reconnect them."

The Roads of Silk
The Journey to the Self

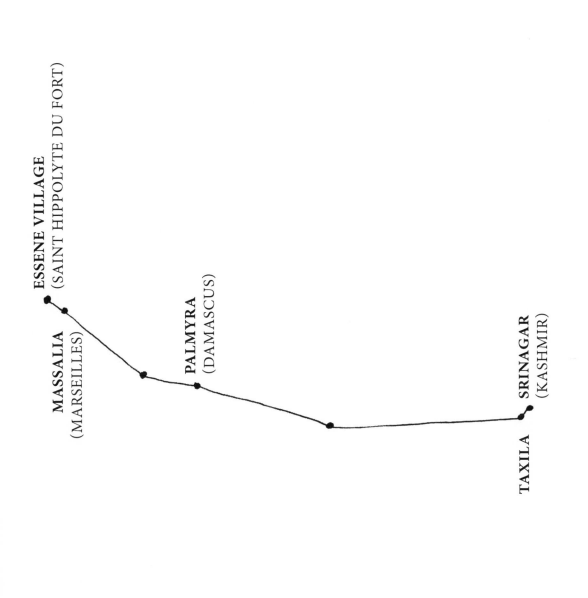

ESSENE VILLAGE
(SAINT HIPPOLYTE DU FORT)

MASSALIA
(MARSEILLES)

PALMYRA
(DAMASCUS)

TAXILA

SRINAGAR
(KASHMIR)

Silk.

Heavenly natural resource.

Their threads bear dreams.

They vibrate,

they constrict to the smallest point,

they withdraw.

Simultaneously.

Their way of breaking the shine of the light,

On every fiber.

The passionate

stories are written on silk.

We left the house in darkness early the next morning. Mary, Peter and Andrew remained for several days; they said farewell to us. Sharon, MaRa and their little son brought us to where the nomads we were to leave with that day met. Sharon knew them all personally and we were warmly received. We were given camels and shown the route we would take to India. Kashmir was the destination of our months-long journey. An old friend of Jesus' lived there, the ruler was from Shrinagar. That was our first destination in India and Jesus did not intend on using this journey as a personal mission.

He wanted to reach the destination as quickly as possible without wasting time. From there, we would take up the spiritual threads we wanted to implement in this world. The journey became our adventure. I immediately fell in love with the Oriental way of living which encompassed many more worlds than I could ever have imagined. The nomads who received us were noble merchants, not barbarians. On the contrary, the desert was their hoe and I would later learn much more from them. They were wise merchants and not uneducated men.

When the camels started to move, Mary Magdalene and I smiled as we got used to the new mode of transport. It was different than riding a horse. We swayed. Three merchants, who had begun their journey, joined us because they purchased and sold goods between the Orient and Syria. Travelers joined or left us at every station along the journey. Monks also traveled with us; their clothing was deep red like blood and they murmured their prayers with each step. Their heads were shorn and their renunciation the only adornment of life. I had never seen this before. They were of Asian descent. Simon smiled and said, "They call themselves Buddhists. They follow the Buddha who experienced enlightenment nearly 600 years before us. They wander on the Silk Road and spread their teachings of compassion and peace. You will see many more of them. Jesus and I once learned and prayed with them. We visited their monasteries in the Himalayas."

"Buddha, who is that?" I asked.

Simon immersed himself in the world of the light. "Buddhas are enlightened, their quality is existence. 108 Buddhas meditate in the universe and pray for peace, love and Dharma, the right of the divine justice in all worlds. They are the preservers and upholders of the blissful expansion of eternity. They have existed since the beginning of time. Their spiritual state is a dreamless dream that incessantly radiates divine qualities throughout the entire universe. He who was incarnated as Siddhartha was he who awakened as the Buddha from his Samadhi of the eternities, curious about what was happening in the world. But what he saw shook his blissful spirit. The creations of the Earth were suffering and were not connected to the unity and were imprisoned in deep pain. Banished to limitations for eternity.

This Buddha, in his graceful compassion, could no longer live in this state of bliss of all creations. He decided to embody himself on Earth. He wanted to come as a human being, like all the others who walk the path of oblivion, to break their illusions and show them the path to liberating themselves from suffering. He awakened in a human body, born as the son of an Indian ruler and he had not forgotten who he was. All of the other Buddhas remained in the dreamless sleep; he alone would awaken them along the way.

Their followers are very close to us. Their mission is the same as our own. To create a new religion of connection in the worlds the gods had torn apart. The monks follow the Buddha and, with their prayers, weave peace and compassion into the fabric of the emotions of the people. But we," He said, "shall now return to the old worlds of creation from which everything was born. You will discover much," He embraced me, "on a wonderful journey."

The mood of the new path accompanied us. The caravan was a colorful mixture of different adventurers. The merchants who traveled with us were not poor. Their clothing was made of rich fabrics and woven in patterns; nothing was without intention. Even their camels were beautifully adorned. Some walked with us and mounted warriors accompanied us for our protection. As I later learned, they belonged to a merchant family that took us in for the journey. They protected the nomadic merchants on their journeys.

What I also learned was that the nomads were the leaders of the caravan and traveled around with their families. Their life consisted of setting up their tents and homes a day's travel from the place from which they started. They did not settle, they were the rulers of the Silk Road. The delicacies of this world passed through their hands and brought forth this era. And they were the masters of the special.

"How long will we travel?" Mary Magdalene asked Jesus. And He said, "I think we will be on the road for five to six months, depending on the weather." "Is this journey dangerous?" I asked. Jesus and Simon smiled. I knew that this question was rhetorical, for I was traveling with Jesus and Simon which meant divine protection was already part of the plan. What grace had been given me! I had been permitted to go on a long journey with them, a journey into another world. I was as excited as a small child and I sensed Mary Magdalene felt the same. We missed our children and yet we knew that we were on the great journey to ourselves.

After a day traveling through the sand and dunes, we spent the first night in the desert. I lay with Simon in a beautiful tent which, thanks to Sharon's arrangements, had been furnished luxuriously. We looked at the starry sky stretching out above us, glittering, and the night scattered happiness over us. It let its stars fall over us like blue rain. And I began my journey to myself, happy and excited. "India, India, India, …" I murmured and gently fell asleep.

Our next destination was Palmyra. People joined our caravan there and in the evening, which we spent outside of the city in our tents, as a meal was being cooked for us there, I began to get to know caravan life. In the evenings, the people in caravan gathered and told their stories. The merchants, the monks.

We ate like kings and were invited to their carpets as guests. It was a potpourri of many cultures. The conversations brought the colorful cultures of Earth together. People from the distant Asian nations traveled with us. Their eyes were little moons and their skin was much yellower than ours.

People whose skin was much darker than ours and noble Arabs traveled with us. Monks who recited their prayers incessantly and only rarely ate a bowl of rice with us traveled with us. Wealthy merchants from the west, who supplied the Romans with fabrics traveled with us and on the first evening, I learned that these caravans were not just trade routes for goods. The most beautiful things in the world traveled from east to west and west to east. What was traded here connected Rome to distant China. What really made the Silk Road what it was, was that the latest in science, religion and knowledge was traded here.

The merchants of the cultures had several wives. We never saw the faces of our nomad leader's wives, who traveled with his family, because they were always hidden behind veils. On the one hand, to protect themselves from the sand, on the other, because the nomads' culture was different from ours. I wondered if it bothered them that we women traveled with our faces bare. But these people were tolerant. If they knew one thing, it was that the peoples of Earth were different and diverse and they tolerated the particularities as they were. But they also demanded that others tolerate their culture in return.

"What will it be like to travel on the road? Are there thieves who attack your caravan?" I asked the merchant of the cultures, as I called him and it made him smile. He chewed his leg of lamb with pleasure and his beard was black like his sparkling eyes. He asked, "What do you think? Of course there are thieves. But there are many caravans and we are all friends with each other. We trade with each other and we are connected, like a network, and we protect each other. Of course the road attracts thieves. Scoundrels who try to steal the goods we trade. And sometimes it is dangerous. But you see, my riders are wild and daring warriors. Nothing has ever happened to my caravan, so you can feel safe."

"What is this life like?" asked Mary Magdalene, "Always traveling around and setting up your tents wherever you like? You must meet and get to know a lot of people." He blinked again and said, "We are more than merchants, lady. We wander between the stars. We know the treasures of this world. But we do not settle. We do not belong to anyone but ourselves and the stars from whence we came. And our stories interweave and make us richer. We bring things from one land to another, and provide these gifts to the people and which they love. I could not imagine a more wonderful life."

Sometimes his wives would sit with us in the evening. I could feel them observing us. We spoke only in glances. Their faces remained hidden. We traveled through the desert for several nights after replenishing our provisions. I began to notice that the caravan and the merchant who led it did not like to come too close to the cities unless he was delivering the goods he carried with him. He felt more comfortable in the desert and in the evenings when the stars rose above us, the magic spread out on the carpets.

We gradually got to know the monks who traveled with us. There were four of them. They told us that many monasteries had been built along the Silk Road which taught the teachings of the Buddha and where the monks could retreat to lead their spiritual lives. "Will we see these monasteries?" I asked Jesus. "Not yet, Miriam, for they are far from our route," He answered. "What is it about this religion these Buddhists teach?" Mary Magdalene and I wanted to know. "Why don't you ask them yourselves?" Simon said to me. "Because we don't understand them." "Then I will translate for you."

And several evenings later, the monks sat beside us eating their rice and drinking their milk. I noticed they were always smiling and happy. They had renounced their world and wandered through it. They had little wooden tablets with them and prayed again and again during the day and in the evening, outside under the canopy of stars. Jesus spoke their language for they spoke the Indian language. The Indian language and another sacred language transported their religion. And so I asked and Jesus translated.

The Buddhist monks told us that their teacher was incarnated three hundred years ago and that he had sought the path of humanity's liberation and had departed this life as an enlightened Buddha. He had left behind the teachings for them, the teachings of liberation. He had brought the lesson of compassion back to Earth for those who suffered and taught it. In the beginning, he found more and more followers in India and from there his teachings traveled and spread like pollen throughout the world. Networks and monasteries were built because the monks were so fascinated by finding freedom beyond their castes. People began to remember that great teachers of this tradition were prophesied and were incarnated and people recognized them. The lesson of the Buddha is a golden path that led through the center and would teach the people compassion for those who suffered and for the weak.

That evening, we listened to their stories intently. Their charming sweetness fascinated me. Once in a while, I looked up at Simon and he was listening intently. That day, the worlds of the merchants and of the withdrawn monks, who walked the golden path of Buddha opened to us and we were amidst them in this potpourri of people and optimistic moods, merchants and scientists. People who told us of new research. I simply listened and grew richer. And Jesus was among them. And Simon, who was Agni. They mingled with them without the people knowing who was among them.

This is where everything began for us. Everything began for us during those nights in the desert and the days on the camels, when we had started the most magical, enchanting journey, we could ever have imagined.

The Enchantment

I could never have imagined that the months-long journey through the desert would not be monotonous, but would instead be so colorful. For four weeks, the people with whom we traveled filled us with stories. And we listened to many people, heard of many religions and heard many personal stories. We listened to stories of courtesans, the magic of silk and how it originated from the mystical spears of the gods. Stories of the Chinese and the Arabs who had proven that the body could be opened to cut out sicknesses without people dying. Of men who ran and slept on fire without being burned, stories of lovers and tears, women whose beauty outshone the sun, of star seers and sages who walked through time and space. The story of the Messiah, who performed miracles of love and then disappeared again. Who they had crucified in Palestine. Jesus was their redeemer. On the Silk Road, which was woven from heaven's natural resources, people recognized Him and revered Him as the Messiah. They saw Him, which the Romans and Jews could not. But He remained silent and listened; unrecognized.

After four weeks, we reached a larger city where we would change caravans. We had become friends with the people with whom we had traveled. And when I looked back, I knew that these four weeks in the desert had been a purging of my old life. Not a single step we had taken had left a trace. We had undergone an inner purification and the desert had purified us. In the city of Eran, we were housed at a caravanserai, an oasis and currently a residence for pilgrims, monks, nomads and traveling adventurers. The shop tables were places of bustling trade. Trade was conducted in every tiny corner and discussed around the fire pits. All of the aspects of the coming world appeared to take shape in this wild crowd.

The next caravan would leave in two days. I slept restlessly in our chamber amidst all the noise, but the day after, it was even louder as we walked through the bazaar being set up and broken down around us, depending on who was unpacking goods or who had sold out. It was a dreamland of the exotic, which offered bizarre treasures under the shop tables; there was much to discover and explore. Mary Magdalene and I found it very exciting. There was a sort of hospitality that accepted diversity with joy and disarmed it. The wealth around us was the trade; the merchants were the artists of the cosmic currents, which they transformed at the marketplace.

Jesus stopped at a stand where Buddhist monks were offering something that enchanted me. They called it papyrus and ink. I was captivated; they offered material, bamboo and dyes obtained from cloth dyes that could be used to transform the imagination into symbols and images. They showed us entire stories which they transferred from their heads into sequential images. I was captivated. Jesus bought an entire set of sheets and quills and inks for writing. Simon looked at me and bought the same set as a gift for me. From that night onward, Jesus began to paint and write and I also discovered this world for myself as my thoughts abstracted and transformed into simple forms.

The next caravan with which we would travel from Persia to Taxila, belonged to another family. The decorations on their camels and tents were blue; blue as the night sky, and they were just as withdrawn. It was a quieter journey with this caravan. We didn't hear as many stories; the journey was shaped by the character of those who traveled with us. This family was very quiet. Still, there was something right about the synchronicity for us as we began four weeks of silence. The blue tents in which we were housed suited our silence. Jesus painted His pictures and wrote every evening. Simon also took on a new mood. Every evening, after having ridden on the camels all day, he went out and I didn't know if I was the only one who saw it or if the others could see it too: he left a black track in the sand.

Mary Magdalene and I observed what was occurring in the silence of the caravan for three days until we asked Jesus what He was doing. And Simon too. Jesus said, "I am writing the new Creation. I listen to God and paint and write it." "What is the new creation?" I asked. "That which is told to me on this sacred road where the stars help create," He said. "The creation that comes from the stars. A creation that is a new creation beyond religion. I paint its pictures and listen to its prayers," He said. "Don't you want to tell us these stories?" Mary Magdalene asked. "First I want to know, Simon," she said, "what you are doing with the black tracks you lay every night?"

Simon smiled and said, "I am laying new tracks. Jesus reads and I lay the new tracks. For the window of time that is opening for us right now and for the seeds of the Light of Christ." I knew, in that moment, that we had been given nearly three decades to lay the tracks for the future of humanity, in the sand, in the desert, in the forests, in the hills, in the rivers and in the seas, in all of the furrows of the Earth. The Mother would take them into her womb and allow them to grow within her. I remembered that Jesus always said that it would take 2,000 years for His tracks to emerge so the new creation could come. But it began here, in the silence of those days under the blue tents, even if Mary Magdalene and I could not really understand what was happening. It was greater than our spirit. Something was growing within us. Mary Magdalene and I began to sense that something wanted to be born within us that had no name or origin yet. It grew in the silence of time while Jesus painted and Simon laid tracks until we changed caravans again after four-and-a-half weeks and left the blue tents behind us.

We were now approaching the Kushan Empire and the terrain grew more mountainous and wild. We changed caravans in a small city. When we arrived at the caravanserai that morning where the next caravan awaited us, we heard a wild whooping; this caravan leader had taken Jesus and Simon with him once before and recognized them now. He gave them a warm embrace. Jesus and Simon had even traveled with his caravan twice. It had been years and he was happy to see them again. We could tell our husbands didn't let him too close; he was brutal and his sword was not to be trifled with.

We traveled less conspicuously because we now came through complex valleys with difficult terrain. The attacks were more common here. The robbers could run into any ravine, so we traveled in smaller groups so we could react faster. And so it came that we were, in fact, attacked. It was night. A piercing scream of death tore us from sleep and we heard the sounds of fighting and screaming. It was loud and I fled into the tent and checked on Mary Magdalene. My heart stopped. Simon and Jesus were gone.

After what felt like an eternity, Simon and Jesus returned. When we looked at them, we knew that people had died, but Simon and Jesus had nothing to do with it. But the death of these people was close. We did not sleep that night.

We sat outside, built a fire and the warriors who guarded this caravan and the caravan leader himself stood watch the entire night. The few travelers who were with us were now completely silent. Simon and Jesus both went away and came back to us across the hills. We were deeply shaken. But that was also part of the journey. We had to get through this restless realm and nothing had happened to us thus far. I sensed the dead who were still among us, as though they hadn't yet understood what had happened to them. They had been robbers and savages when they were alive. They had been prepared to kill us and had been killed themselves instead. They were dead and still spirited around our tents.

They came very close. My love could not protect their lives. But my love could help them to protect the life they could not protect themselves, after life. I sensed these souls that sought a home in the light, and of course, we all sensed it. I looked at Simon and Jesus and they nodded. I immersed myself in my inner world and was beyond this world with my light body and spoke with them. With the wild robbers who, even after death, did not want to admit that something had to change. But they also understood that they could not come closer to me because, in death, they no longer had power over the living. If I had encountered them in life, I might have died. But in the afterlife, they had no power over me. I had more power here, as I told them it was time to recognize that there was much more after death than what they acknowledged in life.

The dead robbers laughed at me. But I was more powerful here, for I knew the light. I raised up my light and told them of the eternity of the light, that they had come into this life and had forgotten the light. And that it was now time to go to their planes of light where their souls touched the plane on which they would learn. There was no blame. They could choose, again and again, to be robbers that attacked and killed others. Would their souls then have the experience their souls desired?

I must have done something right, for all of the sudden, the ghostly robbers suddenly made their choice in the planes of the night and suddenly flew through the valley of death and were in the light. Then they disappeared. I had reminded them of the light that lives between life and death and then I returned to my body. "Miriam negotiates well with the stubborn dead," Jesus and Simon smiled. I stood up and went to bed. It had at least brought peace to the place and we could continue onward. I still wasn't as purified as Jesus; life had neither death nor birth for Him. Life was. But the dead bodies that had just exhaled the last breath of their lives affected me.

Nothing else happened to us on the remaining journey through the valleys and ravines. The nights, however, were more restless and Jesus and Simon were often awake. I think they wanted to protect us so nothing more happened to us. But I had learned something. I had learned that I wandered between life and death and that the teachings that could not be understood in life, since everything had been forgotten, could be understood beyond that, in the transitions between life and death after life. The rebirth is a chance for every soul to remember that we come from the justice of the light and manifest it on Earth.

Life now led us into the ravines and we met many hospitable people. The people were more primal and noble. They received us with their hearts and were used to people from the west traveling to them and crossing their valleys. Until we came to a pass one day that marked the border to India. The last part of the journey had been restless, as though I had to fight to get back to India.

And until we finally stood on the pass with Jesus, Simon and Mary Magdalene and looked at India, a land of which I had only heard until now, I knew that I had fought my way back to the home of my soul. At the border to India, in that pass, a new space opened within me. The old source lay spread out before me like I had never felt before. It wafted toward me on the wind like golden sand that surrounded me, opened my heart and welcomed me home.

And we were expected here by those sent by the ruler of Kashmir. We no longer traveled with a caravan, but with the equipage with whom we traveled like princes and kings and who took care of everything, for Jesus' old friend, the ruler of Kashmir awaited us in Shrinagar and announced himself with great generosity.

Kashmir

Our royal escort brought us from Taxila to the kingdom of the ruler of Ananda Gopa. It was winter and we were given warmer clothing so we wouldn't freeze. We had to walk through snow for long stretches until one morning we came over a mountain and saw from afar the kingdom that had invited us as guests. The beautiful view took Mary Magdalene's and my breath away. A lake lay before us like a blue jewel. We could see from a distance that the city was built on the lake. Everything was from another time.

We came closer to the city and its exotic beauty received us between the snow-capped mountains surrounding this lake. We were in Kashmir, in Shrinagar. The energies here were so pure and vibrated so high, so full of clear colors like nothing I had ever seen before. The lake had a light blue aura, the mountains seemed to reside in other spheres. The snow-capped peaks touched the spheres of the divine.

The city itself was inviting and full of reverent magic. Simon looked at us on the way there and said, "The mountains you see here are part of the Himalayas. They are the sacred mountains, the residence of the gods." "Are those the mountains in which you once encountered the Great Mahababa?" Mary Magdalene asked. Simon explained, "The Himalayas are huge. Many dimensions reside here. Many mountains surround the mysteries and secret realms hidden here. But, yes, we were in the Himalayas, even deeper within. We met him, hidden, deeper in the mountains. Here is where the mountains and realms begin. The mountains of the Himalayas, whose peaks extend to the throne of God, where the gods live and are anchored to the Earth. It is the only place on Earth where the gods can change spheres. They can reside by the throne of God and walk the Earth simultaneously.

Jesus added, "A long time ago, many gods came to Earth. The Indians wrote them down in their Vedas and Upanishads. They brought the worlds of creation here and sometimes still do. But today, we have been invited by my old friend Ananda Gopa. He has already been expecting us for several days."

We were brought to a beautiful palace which was partly on the water, partly on the land. I felt like we were not in this world. The people who passed us were wealthy and wore beautiful clothing. Their greetings were friendly. The people here were pretty. Their skin was light and their eyes dark. We were separated in the entry hall of the palace. The women were brought to their own rooms and the men to theirs. They led Mary Magdalene and me to the women's wing where many beautiful, exotic women began taking care of us. It was odd for us that they took off our clothing and led us to warm baths. The women here had different traditions. Many women lived in this wing and, as we later learned, they were the ruler's wives. We were bathed in petals and then we were left alone. I found myself in a warm, fragrant bath filled with water that smelled like flowers I had never smelled before and which transported me to other dimensions. It enchanted my body and spirit. I allowed myself to fall very deep and the exhaustion of the journey was forgotten. Then they came and brought me clothing and helped me dress.

When I finally stepped out of the dressing room, Mary Magdalene was standing there. We looked like these princesses and women from the harem now. Finally, they pressed a red dot onto our foreheads. Then they bowed before us and withdrew. A woman who bore her dignity with her head held high came to get us. She led us through the hallways to a public room that glittered like the starry sky. It was already evening and they had lit lamps everywhere. The ceiling of the reception room reflected the light of the oil lamps, and little mirrors had been hung to make it even brighter. On the far side of the room, I could make out the silhouette of a man, when we were invited to come closer. Simon and Jesus were already there.

Mary Magdalene and I were asked to sit off to the side and Simon and Jesus sat by the ruler. We observed what happened. The rights of men and women appeared different here. So we were only able to observe for several hours while Simon and Jesus conversed with the ruler like old friends. He seemed young. Until we were called and were allowed to come closer. I was shivering; something was cold and I didn't really feel comfortable here. I sensed that the women were not actually permitted to sit at the table. So Mary Magdalene and I stood and waited to see how we would be treated, for we were used to sitting at one table with our husbands.

We were soon led to another room which was separated from the rest of the palace. It was heated by a burning fire and I was able to get warm again. We were invited to sit on the pillows and we were alone at one low table. We looked at each other enquiringly. We were simply left alone to wait. At least it was warm and we had a view of the lake. Mary Magdalene and I both stood up at the same time and went closer to the window to feel a bit freer and look at the lake. We didn't really feel free as women, but we also couldn't imagine that Jesus and Simon would compromise our dignity. We waited until the door opened and Jesus, Simon and the ruler entered the room.

We were still standing at the window. It was evening and the starry sky shone outside. The ruler came toward us, taking large strides. He was a handsome, stately man and his clothing was ornate. He first took Mary Magdalene's hand and then folded his hands before her and bowed and then bowed before me. We had soon understood that we had been led to a secret room so we could sit at one table with the men. And that this should be kept secret from the rest of the palace. He greeted us and, to our surprise, he spoke our language. He was highly educated. We were allowed to sit.

"Welcome to my kingdom," he said. "My name is Ananda Gopa. Your Issa, your Jesus, was once my father's teacher and we promised Him that when He returned to our kingdom, we would support Him with all our powers." Then he said, "I welcome your wives." The golden doors opened and a grand meal was set. We began to eat.

"So. What has really brought you back here?" asked Ananda Gopa. "I am pleased to meet your wives," he added, and then he waited, almost reverently. We could tell he held his father's teacher in high esteem. In India, the tradition of honoring teachers who came to you, if you recognized them, was still practiced. Jesus waited a while. Then He said, "We came here to reawaken the old Shakti sites, for the Light of Christ has been given the mission of healing the Shakti sites that no longer burn here on Earth." Ananda Gopa swallowed and waited a while. "How do you know there are such places in India?" Jesus smiled. "I painted them. They spoke to me. They called to me." "I didn't even know that there were such places." Ananda Gopa was amazed. Jesus said, "They have been hidden behind shrouds for a long time.

The second reason we are here is because Mary Magdalene and Miriam are walking a path here upon which they shall become prophetesses." Ananda Gopa looked back at the floor. "You know that I have taken the teachings of Buddha into my heart. I am trying to slowly introduce them to my culture and I must proceed carefully, step-by-step. Doing away with the castes is a provocation. I must be careful. I often meet with the teachers the Buddha has called forth and we deliberate on how we can establish a new society based on the teachings of the Buddha. I see that as my mission. What you bring, of course, is even more."

Mary Magdalene and I realized we were suddenly gaining power again and I was grateful to Jesus. It wasn't that the ruler degraded us with his treatment, quite the opposite. It was this culture that did not give us space. We had become powerful within ourselves, beside Jesus and Simon. It was the first time we had heard Jesus speak about this prophecy. We women grew internally at this table. But we also knew that Jesus was once again igniting a revolution. For the women and men in this palace were not equal.

Ananda Gopa, the ruler, thought for a moment and then he said, "I don't know whether my gift is still appropriate, but I actually wanted to give you two of my wives." Mary Magdalene's breath caught and I took her hand and between us, time grew so long it seemed infinite to me. I realized in that moment that giving women as gifts was a part of their culture. How would Jesus react? But Ananda Gopa had left it up to Him. He respected Him as a teacher and Jesus said, very quietly, "Ananda Gopa, in my culture, we do not give women as gifts. I came to help the women gain the right to their own voices. I know that in your kingdom and in your palace and in your culture, you receive women who have no voice to demand their own rights. But that is not what I have brought with me Father's will. Women and men stand with equal rights in His eyes before His throne."

Ananda Gopa was silent at first and then said, pleading, "Great teacher, please forgive me. Forgive my timidity that I tried to shame you with my culture. You know that I want to spread the teachings of Buddha in my world and my realm. Tell me, how can I help? How can I connect the teachings of the Buddha with your teachings?" Jesus was clear, "Call a council meeting," He said. "Let us consult on how we can find new paths for society. You have a chance, in this time and this space, to plant things from a new society that also works in conjunction with the religion. I remember your father spoke about it a lot. You know that your people come from the old tribes of Israel and that you took on a new faith here."

"Call a council meeting. We will first travel through India and then make a pilgrimage along the sacred Ganges until we have fulfilled our journey. Then we will return. The seeds of the world lie around us, hidden. It is time to awaken them."

We moved into another room after dinner, more lamps were ignited and there were dancing women. They were asked to come in, clothed in their beautiful red dresses. Their faces were covered and their bodies moved in a sacred dance, but for us, it was erotically enticing. It was a gift and it was celebrated at many of the parties here in the palace. They were sacred dancers. Ananda Gopa looked at us women and said, "They are trained in the temples and then they dance. Their lives are dedicated to the Goddess." Jesus looked at him and said, audaciously, "Set them free." Ananda Gopa was stunned. "What do you mean, Jesus?" "Set them free. Give a sign. Tell them they are free. They came into the world to teach women the sacred physicality. You cannot keep them prisoner as your dancers. Not this way. They are your bondswomen, but each of these women is a teacher of the sacred feminine powers. You must release them." Ananda Gopa gulped.

Jesus started the new revolution. It would break the castes and elevate women in their power. It would free them from the yoke and let the unsuppressed powers of Shakti that are bound on Earth burn free and prepare them for the future. His Light of Christ radiated over everything He did. He now elevated the women, for He knew that their voices were missing in this world. Ananda Gopa arose and had the hall cleared. Only the dancers were permitted to remain. He bade them stop dancing. Then he went to them and said, loudly, "You are free. You can choose where you go and what you do. You are no longer my slaves. You have the prophet to thank for this." The women looked at him, suspiciously amazed. They laid their red veils over their hair, as though protecting themselves behind them. One of them arose. Her whole body was firm and she was beautiful. She said, "And if I go outside? What means do I have? I have nothing in this world."

"Each of you will receive a high wage from me that will give you the opportunity to be free women in this world. Jesus says, you have come to teach the women the sacred physicality. I will build you a temple where you can freely teach of the Goddess and the saints of women. All others may go where they choose." The room grew silent. A spark of red light ignited. As though the Goddess herself, of whom they always spoke, had appeared. She stepped out of the Himalayas and wafted through the palace. Her presence was soft. She was beautiful and filled the room with her benevolence. As though she were scattering flowers at our feet and blessing us. Jesus and Simon began to shine. A being was among us that had neither body nor form, but she was so sweet and beautiful and showed her benevolence toward this thought and took the women under her protection.

"The Great Mother is here," said Jesus. Mary Magdalene and I suddenly arose, as though driven by this energy, and we went to each of these women and placed a blessing on their foreheads. We gave them freedom and took the yoke from their auras which they had accepted as slaves. We bowed before Ananda Gopa and thanked him for taking this brave step. For we knew that this would cause an uproar in his kingdom. Gently, for the Buddha had already prepared well. But he had not stood up for the women as Jesus now did.

The dancers came to us and expressed their thanks by bowing. One, the one who had spoken for them all, came to Mary Magdalene and me, and looked at us with her dark eyes. She smiled. Her lips were full and her teeth white. She bowed her head and cried, "Thank you!" She was wild for life. Others were timid and others freed from what they had been banished to since they were children because they were born into it. What Jesus did was release the women from the yoke of their birth that lived in this part of the world. The women should no longer be disadvantaged by nature of their birth. They should be free, like men. This yoke had been dissolved. Mary Magdalene looked at Him. Her love and reverence grew before Him, for she knew how courageous He had been. But Ananda Gopa had followed Him and said, "It is time for me to go. We will see each other in the morning. I thank you. The Buddha taught us many things, but you will lead us into the new world. You and Buddha, you will show us that there is another world beyond this world." Then he said goodnight and we were brought to our rooms and this time, Mary Magdalene was permitted to sleep in Jesus' chamber and I in Simon's.

When I awoke the next morning, I went out onto the little balcony and looked out at the lake. The white peaks, the mountains, were so dignified; it was cold and I shivered and still I was captivated by the beauty of this lake on which structures had been built. We were led to the table the next morning, where Ananda Gopa awaited us. "How long will you stay?" he asked Jesus, Simon, Mary Magdalene and me. Jesus decided we would stay a week with him at his palace to recover and then continue our journey. He promised us that he would arrange a regal journey for us, wherever we traveled in India. And that our journey would be under his protection. He wanted to know more about our journey, but Jesus didn't want to talk about it. And so we got to know the ruler of Kashmir better. He was a man with a big heart and great responsibility. A man who was capable of carrying on a dynasty. But he also listened to the impulses that came to him from God.

Mary Magdalene and I were in an unusual paradise that was surrounded by a golden cage. Merchants were brought to us the next day to clothe us in the most beautiful dresses and jewelry. We were treated like queens, but we could not move around the palace as freely as we wanted. Jesus and Simon had also requested this of us out of respect for the culture that surrounded us. In the evenings however, in these secret chambers, we could be the free wives of our husbands. Mary Magdalene was still angry about Ananda Gopa's intent to give Jesus women as gifts. Her anger was noticeable.

Our host, Ananda Gopa was generous. We women were shown the city by boat, traveling across the water, but we were still under the supervision of men, who guarded us. Jesus and Simon were withdrawn most of the time. We enjoyed the time, for we had been traveling for months, had only slept in tents and had sand between our toes and teeth. Now we were spoiled with baths and fragrances which surrounded us every day and we learned to say their foreign names. There was something in this culture with which we couldn't help falling in love. The beauty of sensuality. In the evenings, poets and philosophers came and someone translated for us so we could understand what they presented and illustrated. It was a high culture. The women came to dance voluntarily after they had been freed. They had organized themselves. They were now booked and paid. Of course, word of this had spread throughout the city, but the people here were noble, and soon understood the honorable meaning and thought it was good.

On the third evening, we sat at evening meal. Jesus had not spoken much the whole time, when He suddenly said, "Ananda Gopa, I would like to ask a great favor of you." Ananda Gopa looked up and said, "What can I do for you Lord, Issa, Son of God, it would be my great honor, whatever it is." Jesus explained,

"A time will come when we will fade from this world when we have filled what we still can with God, ourselves and our mission. People will also ensure that the memory will fade. But we are here right now, we who are conscious, to sow seeds for the future. We are writing a story that should be preserved for humanity. It is thus God's wish that when I die, Miriam, if she is willing, will return to this kingdom, to your valley. You know the sacred caverns where I once meditated in the snow among the sages. I would ask you to lead her there. There, between space and time, for there is neither space nor time there, she will write our books and preserve them and store them in the Akasha between the ages. By then, Miriam will know how to do this. Even if the books turn yellow with time in these caves, the Akasha will preserve every living word in flames throughout time. And those who will work on ensuring we are forgotten will not know that this exists. When I die, she will come here and I bid you ensure she gets there and is protected. Guarantee me that she will find this cavern and ensure she can fulfill her mission."

Ananda Gopa arose and bowed before Jesus. He placed his head upon his feet and said, "It is a great honor, Issa, prophet from the throne of God. I will be the one to help preserve your story throughout the ages. My people know this cavern. It is sacred to us. My sages know of it, whether I am alive or not. Whatever my fate holds for me, it is promised to you, my oath to God."

I was shocked. Jesus had never spoken to me about this. I looked at Simon and tried to read his eyes, but he deflected. Jesus, too, provided no further information.

"We also bring you something else," said Jesus. "I know that you still have no heir and that none of your wives has given you an heir. It will not take a year before a son will be born to you. A son whom you should protect carefully, for he is a great soul. He will bring blessings upon your land, he will unite the cultures and religions. Your son will continue your plans for all of the religions to sit at one table and that the benevolence of the people for whom you are there to be planned and imagined. He is a great ruler of the light. He is promised unto you."

The ruler's eyes and forehead cleared. He seemed overjoyed, for he knew when Jesus prophesied something, it would come true.

But I was in another world. Jesus had never spoken to me about it. Though I had seen images in my visions, what He revealed about my future was so surprising to me. Thought it wasn't actually surprising, for our visions were made up in their own decisive way. And many years would pass yet. For we were just now beginning to sow our seeds. The journey in India was my journey to awaken as a prophetess in my own prophecies to fully redeem my promise to Jesus at the end of my days. Once He had asked me, when I was young, when I was a girl of seventeen, if I wanted to go with Him and remember His story. I was and am the one who wanders through time and can bring our stories to where they can be preserved. There, were those who believe that they rule over life and death and can overwrite God's life cannot go.

I suddenly and primordially saw this place as though in a vision. I was in this place. It lived between the ages. Jesus had once meditated here for half a year and achieved His release from human characteristics.

Simon took me by the hand. Our lives were predestined and yet they weren't. So many options opened up between space and time. The last few days were used to plan the council meeting. Leaders from all of the religions were to meet in Shrinagar and Jesus and Simon played a crucial role.

From that moment on, I grew calm. The Himalayas began a dialog with me. In the nights and images, I saw wild gods with blue skin and many arms. They wandered through my dreams in epochal stories of gods and goddesses.

Images of dark gods and light goddesses multiplied. But everything was just a dream that wove its way past me. Until the day came on which we were to set out again.

Ananda Gopa accompanied us on this journey, for our next destination was Rishikesh, where Jesus had called a meeting of the masters from the Himalayas. The masters with whom He had once meditated. He told Mary Magdalene and me, smiling before our departure, that we would meet initiated masters who only meditated in the caves of the Himalayas.

We were impressed and looked forward to this journey, full of new experiences.

Rishikesh

On the night before we were to leave Shrinagar again, I awoke with a high fever. I shivered the entire night. When I could no longer take it, I woke Simon and learned Mary Magdalene was feeling the same way. The fever grew hotter and hotter in both of us. Simon touched my feet, he felt the energy lines on my feet. Then he smiled and said, "You do not have a fever. Your energy is increasing and the fire grows larger and your body doesn't know how to cope. The Himalayas are beginning to burn within you to reawaken your old home. Mary Magdalene suffered from the same phenomenon as I did, but what use was that to us. Our bodies trembled and we felt terrible. Simon reached into the air and a golden potion and a powder materialized and smelled like a thousand flowers. He said, "This is Vibuthi, from the highest gods, who are God themselves and live in the Himalayas." Then I fell asleep. He brought the same magic potion to Mary Magdalene. The next morning, it was miraculously gone. Our journey of initiation had begun.

We set out for Rishikesh. On our way there, I heard many stories about the sacred Ganges. The mother of India, the river that nourished everything, on which the gods themselves once ran. We traveled for more than twenty days and arrived in Rishikesh, a little city on the river. I saw the wildest men I had ever encountered. "They are Sadhus," said Simon. They worship Shiva. I had never seen such anarchic men, who lived beyond all laws. They bathed in the river and were nearly naked. They wore very little clothing and washed themselves with soil. They let their hair grow like animals. But there was a power within them which I began to read. Shiva, Shiva, who was Shiva? They didn't even acknowledge us. They were only preoccupied with their inner reflection and inner exercises which would lead them to enlightenment, to the final liberation with Shiva. They were everywhere. It was their place.

"Are those the masters we are to meet?" asked Mary Magdalene. "No," Jesus replied, "come with me." We went along the river and Ananda Gopa, the ruler of Kashmir said reverently at one point, "I will wait for you here. The masters did not invite me, so I am not permitted to go to them. Go. I will wait here for you."

We followed the path along the banks of the river. I noticed that the rocks on which I walked were alive. The sun shone and warmed them and us. We had escaped the winter. It was warmer here. The stones hummed beneath me and I had to laugh. But Simon looked at me earnestly. We walked another hour until we reached an area that appeared sealed. Jesus stopped. "We will wait here. They will be here in an hour." Jesus was connected to the masters of the Himalayas. They lived in caves and many myths surrounded them, for they were masters of celestial powers. People said they came to the villages to search for students, for there were children who were chosen because they belonged to their order. When they sought out the children, they took them at a specific age and they were trained in their traditional path of enlightenment, Thus, each generation remembered the eternal light and preserved it for millennia for the worlds. But no one knew where their caves were. Stories were told that the most beautiful flowers bloomed near their caves because of their cosmic power which they had unfolded in themselves. That they blossomed around paradise and that they did not do without anything, but they also required nothing. The place was a secret. Jesus and Simon knew of it though, for they had spent half a year with them and meditated with them.

And they were right. After approximately an hour, a group of men approached us. Simon said, "There are seven masters and the rest are their students. Seven masters have come to speak with us."

"And we are allowed to be there?" I asked.

"You should be there." The four of us waited for the masters.

The Masters of the Himalayas

The masters approaching us were completely flooded with light. Their light radiated from every pore of their bodies. The enlightened had united material and light. Some of their students, who came with them, were flooded with light and one could see that they were on the path to finding complete illumination. It was a path that had to be walked consciously; that became clear to me.

I wanted to learn more about the masters, about their reality and who they were. High beings full of power stood before me. They sat after they had bowed before Simon and Jesus. Jesus and Simon spoke their language and I had the impression they sometimes changed languages. Mary Magdalene and I sat a bit off to the side and they talked for a while but everything went very quickly. They communicated on a light plane and, to a lesser extent, on the normal communication level at the same time. In this high field of pure energy in which the masters and their students emerged, my ability to perceive energies suddenly came alive. I could see how they communicated on other light planes and changed languages, generating a light pattern that had waves and patterns. Once in a while, they looked over at us.

To my amazement, for I didn't see any women among them, we were called over. Without having planned it, Mary Magdalene and I wore robes of deep blood-red that day. It had meaning for us. We wore this red to oppose the masters. We felt acknowledged and not rejected as women, as we had experienced in Shrinagar. On the contrary, they wanted to know about us. The masters called our presence to them.

As we came closer, the seven masters arose and their students did the same. They lovingly folded their hands before us and bowed. Jesus translated what was said. In turns, the masters spoke. The one master said, "It is a great honor that the great teachers come to us. We are old beings that have lived in the caves of the Himalayas for ages. We are a tradition that always returns and recognizes its students. For an eternity, we have come to Earth and penetrated the material until we arise again in the cosmic unity. But we cannot bring new creation.

We walk the path of the fire. Our eternal teachers have returned to us. We ask: What do you bring us? For when the great teachers reappear, we know that they always bring a new creation with them. Tell us what the creation you bring with you looks like. We know that when the great teachers like Rama, Krishna and you appear, the worlds change. We want to flow with you and honor your presence."

Then they looked at us women and once again spoke in turn. Some of them simply remained silent and others held the speeches. We could tell that some masters only had access to their essence in silence and internal communication. Others had taken up the powerful tool of language. But it became very clear that those who did not speak, sometimes said much more. For their communication took place on the inner planes. I could follow them precisely. There were no words, only frequencies, which I understood perfectly. And I could sense that Mary Magdalene felt the same.

"You must know," the masters addressed us women, "that we walk the path of the fire that truly unifies us with the cosmos, which is the path of Shakti. That is the path of the feminine power of creation that shapes and creates everything that lives. That is the final path, which we walk in the end, to truly be complete. You are both the embodiment of the path of Shakti and we want to let you know that you are now following the path of Shakti in India in order to become whole. It is rare that the women of the path of Shakti come to Earth, but with Jesus, with Issa, they felt drawn. We see many of these great embodiments of Shakti around you Issa. You have encouraged them to return to Earth. The teachers in India and in many parts of the world have suppressed them. But you two have gotten them to come with you. They must trust you."

Once again, the field between the worlds lay open so that had oppressed and suppressed feminine powers so many times throughout the millennia. Slowly, the question arose in me as to why the feminine powers were suppressed. What is it about them that they are constantly pushed back and forgotten and what were they? A master spoke, "Shakti is everything. Shakti is everything that is created. Shakti is all life. Shakti is what gives birth to us and lets us die. Shakti is what gives us life. When we start to deny the will of life and the male, masculine powers, the Shiva-Yang powers grow stronger in the beings, they believe they control life. But Shakti was there from the beginning to the end. We will never control her. She will always remain a mystery to me and she belongs to God alone. But the Earth needs the powers of Shakti for it will start to be extinguished in the fires we ignite. If the powers of Shakti do not come to us in an embodied form, we can only nourish them for a time, then they go out in our hands. We have a request should you be successful in connecting the path of Shakti in the temples of India. Would you come back to us and bring us your fire which you women have reignited, so we masters can continue to fulfill our mission?"

I was courageous. "What is your mission?" I asked and Jesus translated. I was not met with any resistance. These masters respected us and we respected them. "Our mission is to preserve the consciousness of the world. We consciously walk the path from powerlessness to power. From the shadows to transformation. We learn to control our spirit and we walk this path, a recurring cycle, with the students who come to us life-after-life. And we ourselves will be students again in the next life. When we have reached the consciousness of unity, we meditate and maintain the consciousness of enlightenment on Earth as best we can. There are some parts of the Earth we cannot reach. But we vibrate in other parts and maintain the vibration of enlightenment which is nothing but the unity with the cosmic fire and the powers of Shakti that give birth to this universe."

What Mary Magdalene and I were hearing was powerful. In a certain way, I had come home. No, Jesus had brought me home, nothing here was new to me. I had been here long ago, much longer than I could imagine. I loved these masters more than anything. My love flowed out of me and those who did not speak sent love back to me and I knew that these masters were doing the same thing we were. They explored all aspects of their existence until the cosmic love awakened within them.

"The cosmic love is amidst us," they said. "As fire and love. It wanders across the Earth, embodied in Issa and Agni." The masters did not bow before those whom they so revered and who stood before them. It was a friendship that moved these worlds. When these beings arrived at their enlightenment, the hierarchies ceased to exist. But they honored the inherent place in the creation of each being. I experienced this at this council between the masters, Agni and Jesus. And we women were also given our place in these ranks.

We had been invited to return when we had completed our pilgrimage to the powers of Shakti and bring the fire of Shakti with us. There was so much love in the room, so much light. The masters did not eat, they did not drink. They were beyond this world and yet within it. They were embodied and at the same time, cosmic beings. We hadn't been together for three hours and the cosmic meeting between Jesus, Simon and the masters already spanned eons of time and renewed old and new promises and fostered new alliances. They understood each other, in their own manner, without speaking. The masters accepted the impulses from their teachers without having to discuss them; they took them simply as light. They took them with them and cultivated them between the blooming gardens and the snows of the Himalayas into the next era of Creation.

Jesus and Simon brought the seeds of evolution. Simon as the seeds of fire, and Jesus as the seeds of the Light of Christ. Mary Magdalene and I could see all of this. It was an open book that could be read in the clear energy field of the Himalayas. It was so simple. The masters took up the seeds and planted them in the earth to cultivate them with rituals, prayers and meditations. They made them bloom and then they were sent across the Earth as frequencies so the currents of the new consciousness nourished the Earth. The masters bid us farewell and folded their hands in prayer. They suddenly disappeared into the night. They changed dimensions as they walked away. Mary Magdalene and I sat there, happy. Jesus and Simon left us alone for a while.

The initiation point of the journey had been set. I don't know where Jesus and Simon went. They changed dimensions, suddenly disappearing and reappearing just as suddenly. I could no longer differentiate between the dimensions in this place. But when they returned, Simon first pressed a fire symbol on my forehead and then on Mary Magdalene's. Then Jesus pressed the fire of the Light of Christ into our hearts. We had been initiated.

We were on our way to the temples of India with our teachers, to reconnect the path of Shakti and fill the temples with the Light of Christ and heal them. We were in the process of finding ourselves again and conquering our souls.

The Path of Shakti
The Path of Feminine Power

Back at the place where we met back up with Ananda Gopa, I realized how elevated we had become. The beings that live on a higher frequency elevate our vibrations. And those who refuse to live at their frequency of light, draw our energy. Mary Magdalene and I laughed as we walked along the river and had the feeling we were floating. We hopped. We were full of joy for the gift of this presence and encounters with love. When light and light meet, they are a gift. We exchange our divine gifts without them having a name, form or meaning. We simply share who we are and thereafter feel so rich and full of joy that all of Creation sings with us. How long would it take until humanity realized that they are increasing their energies. To adapt to the frequency of light in which they were born. It would change the world so much. We were happy. We were so happy. And Ananda Gopa took on our mood.

From there on, we walked along the Ganges, the old sacred river, whose goddess accompanied us from that moment on. Our next destination was Kashi, but what had begun here was a 108-day journey of initiation for Mary Magdalene and me. Twelve cycles of an actual pilgrimage on which we linked our feet and bodies to the paths on this Earth and immersed ourselves once again in our own power of Shakti. We had been given the mission of discovering this for ourselves. Every nine days, Simon and Jesus took turns giving us mantras which we prayed.

From that day on, we arose every morning at four and meditated until dawn. Mary Magdalene and I meditated on our mantras or we received personal missions, spontaneous, impulsive as they came. We were taught to make jumps in our evolution, via the impulses that Jesus and Simon gave us in turns.

Some impulses came from the primordial fire of Agni, or Simon, others came from the impulses of love, from the Light of Christ, the consciousness of Christ, which connects the entire universe. We were blessed and bowed every day before the Earth, before our teachers and the universe. For as hard as this training was, overcoming our own weaknesses in which our darkness still lay and elevating ourselves to the height of saints suited us. We were blessed to be allowed to walk this path, which would take 108 days.

Ananda Gopa left us at this point, but we had been outfitted like royalty. He had given us guards for our journey and people who took care of us every minute of the day. They translated for us, they cooked for us or brought us places we wanted to go. Mary Magdalene and I had been given clothing and we looked like Maharanis. We traveled in the opulence of luxury and the beautiful fabrics and colors of India, in the beauty of this land and the simultaneous asceticism and spiritual training that allowed us to walk the path of masters. For the path of Shakti was the path of the perfection of all the senses, abundance and silence.

We celebrated once more at night in the light of the torches along the Ganges. Ananda Gopa provided us with one last royal feast. Far from his palace, the man had changed. He had relaxed. We could see the burden of being an official leader of his state, his country, still bound in traditions in some ways, which he was slowly trying to reform. He knew the people and his culture needed time to change and gave it to them. But, free from his court and his palace, he was a wonderful man who was completely relaxed and in a good mood as he spent that evening pampering us. Mary Magdalene and I, however, grew quiet. We realized that we began to expand our inner silence while we celebrated. It was like a death. The Great Mother, the dark mother appeared above us. She was alive in India. Even if she wasn't anchored to the Earth, we could sense her. She was omnipresent. She was the one who ruled over us, to let that which we were not die.

It happened in the silence. We knew that our preparations for the inner path had begun. When we said farewell to Ananda Gopa, who left us that night and allowed us to continue traveling like kings with his people and servants, we had completely sank into the silence. Our embrace with him was also silent. That night, I slept restlessly, for our training began at four in the morning. Shortly before four, I awoke from a dreamless sleep and Mary Magdalene and I were each instructed to meditate in a tent. Jesus and Simon meditated in their own tents.

When it was warm enough, we meditated outside. Every night, we searched for a place where we could meditate, outside under the starry sky or in the protection of the white tents. The sand beneath us was warm. But the nights were cold, so we brought blankets with us. We would meditate every morning until the sun rose.

The first night, Simon came to us and gave us a secret mantra.

Mary Magdalene and I were not permitted to tell each other the mantras. We would never learn whether we were given the same prayers from Simon and Jesus. The path of initiation of Shakti was a 108-day sacred journey and Jesus and Simon retrieved these initiations from the heavens for us and for the women of the future.

Each mantra cycle lasted nine days. Every mantra held a specific initiation power.

The Sacred Mantras

108 mantras held a
different energy for each
day and connected the initiations
of the spiritual with mundane life.
From four to six in the morning, we meditated
and then we women would spend
the morning in this energy.
Mary Magdalene and I entered a state
of synchronicity of emptiness and
conquered our own inner teacher
and mistress.

In this state of synchronicity,
we would become our
own teachers.

There were no external instructions.

The Sacred Cycles

Cycle one:
The Power of Prayer

The first cycle was called the power of prayer and we were always in this state in the morning hours, whether we were traveling or being carried on litters or walking on foot or riding on the camels. Everything we encountered was a lesson for us. This state lasted all day, but after the midday meal, we returned to Earth, for the food grounded our souls and from then on, we were travelers. We slept in our tents, we looked at things and still this mantra remained the inner prayer all day and drove us, involuntarily, back to the powers of Shakti.

After nine days of traveling along the Ganges, a fire was finally lit in the evening. Simon ignited it and then we sat there, under the starry sky, and only after those nine days, were we allowed to share our experiences with each other. Until then, we had to journey within ourselves. That was our cycle for 108 days.

Mary Magdalene began to speak first. "The prayer carries me to my death. I had to die even on an even deeper level. It was as though, for the first four days, the prayer drove me deeper into the pain I did not want to see. It became almost unbearable. What kept me on the surface was the mantra, which raised me up every day. For me, the mantra was like something that always raised me up out of the depths of my own darkness and then, on the fifth day, the tide turned.

I began to realize that my own powerlessness drove me back to the pain over and over and, on the fifth day, I encountered my pain with my own empowerment. And there I was. Everything I encountered, images from times gone by and worlds of creation or myself in this or other lives, I met them in the middle. I faced this pain. I no longer suppressed it. I welcomed it as a part of my soul.

And the prayer began to change. The prayer was no longer one of powerlessness; instead it elevated itself with the mantras and then, on the sixth day, I was standing before a new universe. As though God Himself saw me and said, "Speak to me." And from then on, I began to receive the prayer as an aspect of Creation. For when I prayed, Creation became clear and I began to weave myself into it. It was almost as though I had no limits, when I prayed, as though I could make flowers bloom in the desert, from nothing. I became so powerful within myself and yet shied back in fear. But I was close to the threshold. The prayer became a tool of creation for me. Because God saw me and I could see a small piece of myself.

Jesus had placed bowls of flowers before us and said, "When you have told your story, throw the flowers into the fire and say, 'Swaha' Swaha will bear your prayers into eternity. Remember, Swaha, for she bears all prayers into eternity."

"Who is Swaha?" asked Mary Magdalene. "The female aspect of Agni," said Jesus. "The fire that bears the prayers throughout all of the universes. Born much later, only to disappear again, she interweaves everything in the universe with prayers of Creation."

I picked up my flowers, threw them into the fire and said, "Swaha," for I wanted to learn to feel this aspect. When I said 'Swaha', it was as though the female aspect of Agni took shape around us, but seemingly without form. I wondered what relationship this aspect had to Agni, but I felt that this aspect was a part of him, a feminine Shakti aspect of Agni which brought me much closer to my aspect, because the fire that lived within connected my prayers.

Now it was time for me to speak. I threw more jasmine into the fire and said, "Swaha," and I told my story. "I felt my prayers take shape and rise up to heaven. My journey was different. I presented my prayers as a sacrifice. Every morning I went out and made a fire. As I am doing now, I instinctively brought flowers with me and prayed. I brought these flowers to the fire and prayed that my prayers would rise and nourish the universe and the gods. For me it was as though what nourished the universe and the creative powers had remained hidden and forgotten for so long. For three days, I wandered in a past era and I realized the masculine powers of creation were isolated and lonely. My prayer had to become Shakti, which nourished them again. For only when Shiva and Shakti united within my prayer, was I able to take another step.

My prayer had to be Shakti and nourish the Shiva powers in the universe and I realized that they have three aspects and I prayed for three days and brought them flowers. I even offered sweets to the fire. I prayed fervently for the Shiva powers of the universe to be nourished by the Earth. And suddenly something wove between heaven and Earth and something within me became whole. Then it was as though I had stepped upon a golden path. My prayers had never left me. My pain didn't bother me, but what I could not find was the power of my Shakti. I prayed. I prayed until this morning to be shown the power of my Shakti. That was my only prayer to God. He did not answer. I didn't know whether my prayer could be answered. Or not.

And then, suddenly, this morning, while saying the morning mantra, the answer to my question was revealed. 'The power of your Shakti is the gentleness of the golden light that flows through the entire universe and which seeks its beauty high above the Himalayas.' I found myself singing in the snow; a woman, combing her hair and when she sang, she sang for the whole universe. I was enough for myself and was at one with myself and then I also felt the Earth and the dark forces that battle for the Earth. I sensed that my Shakti was powerful enough to break these dark powers, but only if I surrendered to the prayer. I surrendered myself, my prayer to my God, for I did not want to be anything but that which I can be for Him when He needs me.

The prayer was more a request that came to me from God as an impulse. Because I have the power to do certain things as a power of Shakti He placed in my hands, as a request and a prayer. I heard God praying and I was blissful. This morning I wished time would never stop; I heard God praying." I wept as I told this story, for nothing had ever touched me as much as this moment, when I heard God Himself praying. I said, "God prays when He creates. And when we pray, really pray, then we hear Him praying. We hear how He creates all life."

I threw more flowers into the fire and looked at Simon and said, "Swaha."

The sky around us was blue, deep blue and red at the edges which lay across the Earth. We were at a place in the desert on the Ganges. Everything was calm and sacred. We ate and digested this sunset, for it nourished us in every phase of our existence.

Cycle two:
The Power of the Shadow

We continued our journey along the Ganges. They called it the River of the Mother. And I began to sense what the Indians meant by that. The river flowed through the body of the land and nourished the land. I could see tributaries leading into this river, gradually making it larger. Simon and Jesus told me that these rivers flowed down from the Himalayas. We hiked along the river, which hummed and hid a goddess within who filled the river with her song. She didn't show herself to us, but she was there and accompanied our journey. The Indians told us about their sacred Ganges and the goddess Ganga. Each of their rivers had a goddess, a Deva, a feminine aspect that protected the river. This land was feminine in origin.

The next nine days passed without much of a stir, externally. But internally, Mary Magdalene and I received our mission with our mantra every morning. This mantra brought the mission that we should seek out the shadows that live within us and transform them into our strengths. Jesus and Simon explained to us in the beginning that the strengths were our gifts, our qualities. Our divine qualities and that it requires an alignment of the spirit. When we leave the strengths and allow ourselves to sink into the weaknesses, then sadness, anger, pain, a deformed form of the ego, our dark sides, the shadows of our sacrifices would come to life and define our lives. But all of these characteristics are the weaknesses that attract the shadow.

The source of the Shakti was stronger and was power. Our mission was to reconquer this. To do this, we had to wander through the shadows with our mantras in order to conquer it with the unbreakable spirit and recognizing that strength was our source. To recognize that it was up to us to keep the spirit so strong that strength rules us and not weakness which might attract the shadows.

I realized that this was a deeply intense experience for both of us. We spoke very little over the next nine days and the landscape supported us in that. We walked along the Ganges and Jesus and Simon did not feel a great need to speak to us. And we were on our own pilgrimage of shadows for nine days. Every day presented a new topic that had nestled into our subconscious and only wanted to conquer our Shakti.

The mission was not to find strength, the mission was to listen to the Shakti as it reconquers this strength.

Jesus and Simon had told us that Shakti conquers her powers differently and that they could not teach us that. But if we were to listen to the voice deep, deep, deep within us, we would find our own path to how Shakti conquers her strength. The best gift was that Mary Magdalene and I were together, yet each on our own separate journeys. We knew that we had been left alone with our worlds in that moment, because we had to concentrate on our inner teachers. But to know, the other was there as support was comforting.

On the ninth day, a fire was lit in the evening. Jesus sang mantras and nourished the fire. Even the Indians sat down with Him and listened. He invited them. One of our travel companions, who translated for us, a highly education woman who had been provided to us for the journey, sat down with us. Her name was Sundara and she said, "He sings the songs of the divine Mother. They are sung only in secret in India. He cannot have learned them anywhere: He must know them."

Jesus sang. The softness of the currents of the divine Mother became real around us in His Light of Christ and gave us space. Mary Magdalene's and my hair blew in the gentle breeze as we brought our sacrifices to the fire as thanks for being allowed to walk this path of initiation of Shakti.

Mary Magdalene started and wanted to speak when Simon looked at her and said, "Shakti is the power of the ritual. May you first create the ritual that completes the ritual this week for you." She took a step back for a moment and thought. The rituals belonged to the world of Shakti. To bear them from the living ground from nothing, to fill them with meaning and content; this was the mission of the living teachers. Mary Magdalene arose, went outside and came back with nine stones from the river and placed them around the fire.

She said prayers for each of these stones and sat down and said, "Those were my nine aspects which I encountered over the last nine days and nights.

I encountered my sadness, I encountered my courage, I encountered my dependence, I encountered my ego, but all of this did not leave a trace in the moment I entrusted myself to the flow. Shakti told me that she is the flow. That which I did not hold onto could be carried away by the stream and let me flow. With each depth of my subconscious, which was a subtle stream upon which no light from my soul fell, which I surrendered to the flow, the more my soul began to awaken. My higher consciousness, which I already experience to a large part because of you, because of the path I have traveled, began to awaken. But I noticed that these two streams were not always connected to each other.

Shakti showed me that my soul, when expressed, was a river of different streams that all belonged to me. One flows in the background as do currents in the depths of the Earth. The other flows through my consciousness, through my daily consciousness. And the third flow is the river of my soul. My greater plan with which I was born. If we do not connect them, they flow, disconnected from each other and often in conflict with each other. I asked Shakti how to connect these streams with each other and she showed me the energy centers in the bodies.

I would like to learn more about it," she said. "Shakti flows through my energy centers. And when I activate them all, my life begins to connect and form a new stream which lets me flow through everything I encounter in life."

She said, "These stones want to burn although they cannot burn. May I lay them in the fire?" Jesus nodded. She placed these stones in the fire. One after the other, she gave them to the fire as a sacrifice and prayed.

Stones do not tend to melt, but they can heat up and nourish life. Her ritual spoke for itself. Jesus began to sing the sacred songs and the fire danced.

Simon looked at me and I knew that it was my turn to create a ritual. I went out and reached into the sand around me. I filled my dress with this sand and felt thousands of beings in the fabric. This time, my ritual was for me to place the sand in each of the attendees' left hands. I started with Simon, then Jesus, then Mary Magdalene, but I also included all of our other companions, inviting them to sit at our fire. They sensed what we were doing and that this was sacred ground beneath us. They did not have to understand our words, for they understood the eternal language of the sacred which connected us upon the heights of the sacred.

I chose my words carefully. I said, "I experience the way I deal with my shadows which are anchored in my weaknesses, as a ritual, like a cleansing I am undergoing. Like it was long ago when we fasted in the holy days with the Essenes. I simply fasted. I fasted to purify myself, because we need that once in a while. I conversed with Shakti, the Great Mother. I heard her and asked her and she said that life in the material world had a habit of sticking to us. That our cleansing rituals, if we cultivate them and regularly take them into ourselves, cleaning ourselves from the material that adheres to us to remind us of our souls.

Of course, I came to dark places and heaviness, but I simply fasted and emptied them out. This was not the essence; that was behind it. I prayed to Shakti, the Great Mother, to tell me where my strengths lay and the only thing she taught me was that we are all connected. Like grains of sand that make up this sand, we are thousands of souls that are all connected to each other. She told me, unswervingly, that strength lies in this bond. When we are disconnected, we are in our ego and alone. But when we are connected, everything begins to illuminate. The drama of the shadow is that it is disconnected, separated from the light. So I sought the connection in everything. I began to sense that listening taught me of this connection.

I began to feel all of you, every being around me. Every animal around me. The strength was not in me making myself larger and puffing myself up, the strength was in concentrating. Concentrating so hard I that my concentration grew so intense that I felt connected to everything. There was a moment during which I dissolved. One can only connect to everything if one perceives oneself in the most intense concentration of one's light. But I no longer existed. And then the voice of Shakti knocked on the door and said, 'Bring your companions back. They call it ego, but believe me, this ego is your companion.

It gives you the expression that only you know. Your essence finds a language, expression and a voice. Reconquer it.' And then I took form again. A unique form that was only for me, and each of you has your own too. But these channels must be cleansed so we can express our souls, for that which we express of ourselves should come from strength and purified power. Anything else is not in tune with the universe."

Cycle three:
The Power of the Threshold

The thresholds always pose the challenge of how we cross them. The thresholds between life and death. The thresholds to new stages of life. The thresholds to understanding. The thresholds to initiations, however, are those that are born from the most sacred ground. Here, we must give up everything and be prepared to give everything. The strengths we had conquered were the foundation. That day began very surprisingly. Early in the morning, we were sitting outside and Jesus and Simon were taking turns telling us the stories of the universe. Jesus began.

He said, "The legends, the oral tradition, the sacred stories hold this universe together. In India, they say the universe was the birth of a golden egg. The egg was Creation. It contained everything that ever was, is and will be. This golden egg is sacred. It is Creation itself."

Simon continued. "They call it Lingam. This golden egg has the form of a Lingam. It symbolizes the masculine power of creation. There are many rituals dedicated to this Lingam. They praise Creation itself in its masculine origin. But you shall conquer this golden egg this week. You must go to the source of your Creation itself and read your stories and the stories of the universe. If you want to become Shakti, you must learn to read your own story. Recognize your place in Creation. Mary Magdalene and I were thus each given the mission and a golden egg from Simon and Jesus. Jesus materialized this egg before our very eyes in one hand and in the other, two little eggs of pure gold appeared. Mary Magdalene and I each received an egg and the mission to conquer the rituals ourselves and make our pilgrimage with them this week.

Early in the morning, we received our mantras. Then I meditated on what the source of the universe was trying to tell us. Together with Simon and Jesus, we stepped out of the material and into Creation. This path was new. It led to a golden room in which anything can be created. But only if one recognized one's place therein. Then they left us alone again. The escorts Ananda Gopa had provided us for our journey were touching. They had understood that this was a sacred journey that created an open path from their ashrams. They understood that Jesus and Simon were great beings although they could not fully recognize it. But they saw what was happening.

The Indians still lived in their state of unity of the universe. They recognized their place in the universe, even though only a few accesses were open to them. They knew that they had a place in this creation and that their whole country and life was an expression of this creation. They were able to sense the energies developing around us, even if they could not see who Jesus and Simon really were.

I noticed Simon was changing. He was different. He had been largely withdrawn so far, but in this land, he grew in presence. It bowed at his feet. His light changed. India was also his country. In a way we would yet come to know.

The journey to the golden egg, to the source of creation, to the primal stories, took us a week. Until, after nine days, we sat down together again. And this time, Jesus bade me speak first. He said, "Give me the egg." He and Simon stoked the fire and both were very present that day. Creation was present. Oh yes, they were there, as a part of Creation. But Mary Magdalene and I were also a part of Creation. It wanted to be conquered like every being has to conquer it. He took my golden egg and threw it in the fire where it melted. Flowers arose from the fire. Their fragrance began to spread out. The people who accompanied us were permitted to sit around us in a circle. They kept a respectful distance. They saw the images of the flowers that were created in the fire and an "Ooh" went through the crowd as they witnessed the miracle.

"Speak," Jesus bade me.

The words began to come to me. "I have meditated every morning with this egg. I have let the egg lead me. Until the moment came when I could see it, this source that suddenly expanded and was everything. But I did not feel an egg. It was God's Creation that suddenly expanded everything. And I was a part of it. Everything that would ever be created, every soul, was a part of it. There was no light. But there was also no yearning for light because it did not exist.

Until suddenly a golden wave of light that filled everything rolled over me. I think that is the golden egg of which Creation in India speaks. But I was in this egg. And could only feel that I was a part of this egg and the golden light filled everything in existence. And the light spoke. 'I am the fire, I am Agni.' I was there and I could see. But this all exceeded my dimensions. This way of seeing was different from seeing with human eyes. I could see. For the light let me see.

But the light also let me see that there was light and darkness. The light let me see that everything existed." I said. "There was a moment when it was too much for me. How can I bring these great images, where my souls dreams, into harmony with this human body? I saw myself dreaming. I was helping dream Creation. And then I found myself back in my body and did not know how these two visions would fit together. How my soul, which had such great dreams, could combine the two in this material world, in this limited space."

Jesus and Simon listened intently. They said, "You are on the right path. Search for it." I asked, "Are you able to combine these great images of yourselves with your human existence? How do you do it?"

Jesus answered first. He said, "Miriam, I think it is different for me than for the Shakti powers of the universe from which you both come. I simply exist and my existence is never questioned. I create from that and there is no separation between that which I am and that which I create. Whether in this human body or wherever I happen to be." I listened intently. Then Simon said, "We come from all of existence, we do not know separation. What we think, we create."

Mary Magdalene said, "Perhaps I can create this connection. Our task here was to understand something. The powers of Shakti created differently. But they need these primordial masculine energies that Jesus and Simon embody in order to understand themselves."

Mary Magdalene gave Jesus the Lingam and He let it melt in the fire. This time, no images appeared in the fire, instead there was a primordial blue light until the Lingam had melted.

She said, "I was completely familiar with this primordial space, this primordial egg, this golden light. I know it. But when touching it, I began to see that we can establish a connection to this original connection at any time. And that there are tools that help us establish that connection. It is our cosmology, the astrology, it is the sages and the art expressing themselves; it is the song, the tone and the music which spread out. Creation brought forth thousands of tools that allow us to establish the connection again and again. If we conquer them with our tantric powers, we will establish the connection between Creation and ourselves. It went much further. I understood that we are the people tasked with the mission of establishing the connection to Creation. For we live at the outermost point of its oblivion. But this is wisdom, for Creation is consciousness embodied. We live at

the outermost point of consciousness. Only this can establish the connection to the consciousness of all existence. A thousand paths, thousands of paths...

From every point of existence,

we can see everything

and connect to everything.

The light of the source journeys to us,

we no longer have to travel."

We fell asleep at the fire and didn't awaken until shortly before four. At night, we were drunk; for meditation, we were clear and wide awake.

Cycle four:
The Power of Silence

The route on which we traveled was a powerful Shakti line. Jesus had consciously chosen which temples we would visit during our initiations. He had us meditate there. We were to experience how it felt when the powers of Shakti were connected to the Earth. After we had visited two little temples, our journey continued. We were on the way to the golden city. The Ganges carried us.

Simon now taught us how to meditate on our chakras. We were to do this for one week. He told us of the consciousness of the chakras and that all of Creation flows in our chakras. In preparation for the Kundalini powers we would encounter. The Kundalini powers were the powers of the snakes I had seen back then in the Essene village. But now we would consciously allow them to flow through our bodies so the prophetic powers within us would awaken.

Mary Magdalene and I meditated every day on one of the chakras, on consciousness. We spent each day in the consciousness of the respective chakra. Jesus and Simon told us over and over that the beings were free to experience the boundlessness of the chakras in their bodies. But those who had not yet experienced the freedom in the human body, only expand their chakras unconsciously or with limits. Every day, we delved into an infinite landscape of the colors of the rainbow and were to gain experience therein. We were given special mantras that accompanied us into the chakras. We were supposed to conquer our own world in our human bodies. Our inner landscapes revealed their colors. During those days, I began taking out my book again and drawing. Just as Jesus did.

I began to draw signs in it, and landscapes and symbols. Some which I had seen in the temples, took shape within me and kept returning. At night, I began to dream of the temples. The powerful, feminine beings danced around me and danced with me in a cosmic dance that changed with every chakra. When we had worked through the seven chakras, we were to sit at the fire for two days, each of us alone, and nourish the fire. It was Simon who then opened our

Kundalini powers through our spines. And by the power of the ritual of initiation, which was less dramatic than I had expected, we meditated before the fire for another night.

I no longer grew tired. I nourished the fire and felt Mary Magdalene as an awakening power beside me. Sometimes I could no longer differentiate myself from her. The fire burned through me until it was out. The Kundalini powers had slowly ignited and then burned within us as a transforming fire. We burned. Days later, our tiredness overcame us again. But first, we had to overcome our will.

It was the 36th day of our journey. My dreams were so wild, I no longer had the power to tame them. Yet I came to the fire on the ninth day, still not exhausted from the initiations, and Mary Magdalene, Simon, Jesus and I were alone. They had asked the others for quiet. In my dreams, over and over, I grew many, many arms that boxed in all directions. Like one of the wild goddesses I saw in India. When I came to the fire, Mary Magdalene looked similar. I had to look twice to see if she really only had two arms. Simon and Jesus told us more that evening. They told us of the worlds of creation that flowed through the chakras, of the love that gave birth to the rainbow, on which all Creation on Earth is born. They told us of peace and beauty.

At the end of the evening, Mary Magdalene and I had dissolved. Both of us in blood-red light. The sacred red had captured us. We were the fire and the fire was us, but we could not find hold in our existence anymore. I began to understand that no one can go through the initiations of one's own self on Earth without a teacher to accompany them. For the boundaries on which we wandered could easily drift into the insane. If I could not fathom these boundaries, Simon and Jesus were immediately there to help me, to catch me, until my soul was ready to expand and go even deeper.

We wandered in silence for the next few days. There were only mantras, for our souls first needed to experience silence before we could continue to grow. In the rhythm of the mantras, I began to understand that there was a rhythm to the initiations of the cosmic fire. We had walked through the cosmic fire itself the week before and it burned us until everything we weren't shed from us like old skins and we were naked. Naked as ourselves. Creative powers of Shakti that were connected to the Earth. Then the silence came, because the fire returned to the silence when it had reached its pinnacle and flowed back underground.

The mantras Simon gave us all week soothed our souls and the silence integrated into us. We had chosen to be silent and thus walked along the river without talking, for nine days. With only our mantras. They were the songs of our being. Until everything the fire had stirred up in us had been reintegrated. The sand beneath us came alive and the sky breathed as I had never seen before. The stones spoke. My body came alive. I could suddenly see Simon, Mary Magdalene and Jesus in their primal forms. As they truly were. They walked beside me as giant bright manifestations.

Sometimes the silence became too much, when everything else grew so loud; nature, the world behind this world. And then everything was silent again. I began to understand that the source of nature was silence and that it always returned to that silence. We were lonely pilgrims under the sun. Our escorts kept a respectful distance. Until the silence took form in the human body and the fire continued to flow within because the river always flows. Everything had been found without asking.

The fire flowed within and so it should remain. We paid homage to it, for this cycle did not want to end in fire. The fire was liquid and flowed in the current of the universe.

Cycle five:
Reading the Seeds of Light

After we had begun the fifth cycle, Jesus told us that we were close to the golden city. We performed our initiations for four days and meditated in the morning until we reached the sacred city on the Ganges.

India grew more and more fascinating. I had never seen beings like Sadhus anywhere in the world. The closer we came to the city, the more we encountered them as they made their pilgrimage to the city. Those without possessions who renounced all life in order to train their own spirits. They often sat on the edge of the Ganges, meditating. They wandered in the direction of the sacred city, as we did. I was fascinated by their wild forms of expression. Their long hair and their bodies which had been dipped in dirt. I began to understand that the path we were taking was different. We faced life, to become life itself. They renounced life.

Once, I encountered a Sadhu sitting by the river, who looked deep into my eyes. And suddenly, I began to talk to him, without words. "We are the servants of Shiva," he communicated to me. "We are the guardians of the Earth. We do not renounce for our own benefit; we renounce to preserve. That is our path." And they did, in fact, look like the Earth. Some were covered in mud from head to toe. Others wove mud into their hair. Not all of them were on a high level of consciousness, but some had achieved a high state of consciousness that lived within them and allowed the external world to pass by them. Like the river.

Jesus and Simon, however, were followers of the sacred tantras of love. A tantra that wove through the worlds with the powers of Shakti. They called it the path of Shakti, the path that encounters all life with love and fire. Yes, with great passion.

None of these paths were subject to evaluation by the universe, except our own. Did we want to come to Earth to renounce? Or did we want to come to Earth to experience the freedom of our own divine existence in all its aspects?

This time, we pitched our tents near the sacred city on the bank of the river. We would stay there for four days. Our initiations, however, would also continue in the city. During the new cycle, we learned to read the seeds of the Light of Christ.

If they come to Earth to fulfill their prophecies, only the prophets could see them in their light form. And during our morning meditations, we would learn when God sowed His seeds, His ideas on Earth and explore these worlds as God's ideas and visions take shape. There must be a reason we connected this to the visit to the city, for I began to understand that the journey resulted in a perfect harmony between time and the different places. Every event was synchronized somehow with that which we experienced within. We became one with the landscape. In the temples, we had begun to recognize how it is when Creation, perfect Creation, concentrates the powers of Shakti in certain places. We wandered in the Shakti. Ready to experience everything we were.

Kashi

Fleeing from the spiritual discipline of my initiations, I sat on the banks of the Ganges. The reflections of the sun on the water made me happy; they were more beautiful than ever. The sensations of life grew more intense in India's aura, the land of the enlightened sensuousness and the inner asceticism to which I was subjected for half the day from four in the morning and which emptied me of all the useless fillers of life. Now I was following the eroticism of my senses. I played with the sacred river's golden waves of bliss. Our tents stood majestically along the river, a short distance from the sacred city which we had finally reached.

Across from me, on the other riverbank, were large temples, golden in the afternoon sun. They called them Kashi, the Shining Ones. When I went to touch the water, Jesus appeared next to me like a vision, "Do not drink the water. Come with me." I followed Him, past the shimmering colors of the women who wore their jugs on their heads and sat down, laughing, with a raft on the river.

When we arrived on the other side, we were dropped off directly in front of the steps of the temple and when I touched them, before I set foot on them, they vibrated, warm and full of spiritual life energy. Jesus gave me a sign and I pulled my sari over my head as befitted a woman here. Then, deeply touched, I entered the open, sacred room; the stone carvings were covered in the patina of flowers, incense and mantras. The heavy aromas of the oil lamps carried me deeper.

Simon sat there, in a meditation position, glowing golden in the midst of the Brahma priests. His light did not spread to them. Their robes were yellowed and they clung to their palm leaf scrolls. He spoke to them and they struggled to understand. Jesus stood behind one of the columns and enjoyed Himself. I sat down with Mary Magdalene, who had been there for a while. No one even noticed us in the commotion.

"It is wonderful. He is telling of the Creation," she said. They listened to Simon, completely fascinated. I was able to follow what Simon said, as one of our servants translated for us. He told of the renewal of the teachings.

"Sat-Chit-Ananda." I prayed, with my mantra, that there would not be any unforeseen catastrophes, for we were in a foreign place.

"Your Rishis listened so well they heard the cosmos. Your Vedas are the hymns of Creation, devotion, recognition, doing the right thing, the glorious light and the science of life. All of the teachings will fade on the pages if they are only read and cited.

In the beginning,

there was Hiranyagarbha,

The seed of elemental existence,

The only God

was born,

He sustained heaven and Earth.

To which God other than Him

can we dedicate our lives?"

Simon sang this verse in Sanskrit and then translated it. They murmured, for it shook their souls that this blond man knew there sacred scriptures.

"Oh Agni, cosmic fire,

After much contemplation and a long search,

The determined seeker shall find me,

I come from the lotus pond,

Which is the head and support of the universe.

Knowledge and love," Simon continued, "have separated from each other and run around like chickens with their heads cut off, almost in Samhadi. I am here in my temple and do not find the balance of love, which serves knowledge." Two disgusted Brahmas left the group. Respect those to whom respect is due. Simon's eyes turned icy. I looked at Jesus, who agreed with him.

Simon arose, went to the altar and it grew dark. He took a fire bowl and ignited an Arati without asking. He waved the bowl with the lights in three circles and before they understood what was happening, Simon stood there as the burning Agni, as the fire god in his true form.

He prayed secret mantras aloud, that only they knew from their initiations. The stones began to tremble. The Brahma priests froze, the columns shook, because stone never lost its reverence for the appearance of that which is alive.

"Look, that is Agni, the burning fire god." A beggar boy on the steps exposed what the arrogant priests had ignored. The gathering people witnessed, up close, as he left the temple, glowing and ablaze with sacral rage, and walked into the Ganges. Everyone thought he would be extinguished in the water, but he was not. I absorbed the beauty that glimmered past me like a falling star. Agni, in his light form, blew me away. I was in a state of blissful expansion.

The miracle ran its course as he stood on the water, burning, a giant Arati himself. The disbelieving Brahmas had followed him and fell to the stone steps, but Agni stood there, burning on the Ganges, and did not turn around to them. A thousand burning sun mantras appeared around him, glowing in his aura, until he reached the other riverbank. Jesus stood by the column, smiling at me. Agni had dissolved and the crowd cheered and stormed the temple. Women and men of all castes, whose religious chains had been opened by Jesus and Simon, broke the spell. The untouchable became touchable, the women conquered their devotion of praying in freedom.

We met outside, behind the temple and returned to the tents. I looked around, wondering where Simon was. One of the guards looked at the tent and I knew he was there. Simon was meditating on the floor and the fire in which he sat had not grown weaker: it was still frighteningly high. The earth beneath him was scorched and drew sacred geometry on the sandy floor. Snakes surrounded him like a mandala. The Earth burned beneath his sun. Jesus had prophesied that we would go to India so we could recognize ourselves. I had seen Agni. I left him alone to meditate and Jesus and Mary Magdalene waited outside for me.

Something else had happened in the last few days: on the way here, Jesus had started feeding the poor in the cities. Every evening, He went out and we helped Him. Word spread quickly and, as it once was in Palestine, the people began to seek Him out when He appeared in the evening. He did not preach, He was simply there. They saw Him as a saint and He helped the poor.

Then it was time for our nearly daily ritual. As we were amidst the poorest, sharing our love and food, which Jesus multiplied, a man suddenly came toward us through the crowd. "My lord would like to attend to you. He would like to invite you to be his guests." "Who is your lord?" Jesus did not look up, He was completely focused on the sick who gathered around Him. "My lord is KrishnaDat, the wealthiest merchant in our city. He instructed me to stay with you and accompany you to him." "Very well," Jesus said. He instructed the servant to help and did not stop until everyone on the streets had food and every sick person had seen Him. We were in a field of love and Jesus healed with love until the souls were sated. After two hours, He said we would go dress for the evening. We found Simon already dressed for a celebration.

Later, the servant accompanied us through the city until we came to a stately palace, where only the towers peeked out from behind the walls. He opened the door and we were let in. There was a beautiful garden with birds and peacocks. Simon said, "He is a follower of Krishna, that much is apparent."

"Who is Krishna?" I asked. "Krishna?" he laughed and said, "Is one of the great teachers of the avatars who was once on Earth in India." I didn't have more time to ask, though I would have liked to, for when Simon mentioned the word 'Krishna', a thousand images appeared before me.

We were led into the house and sat at a table in a beautiful room. Everything was very bright here, brighter than in the temple. The atmosphere was so soft and loving and the entire house was playfully decorated. I did not see any women. Not like back in Shrinagar, at Ananda Gopa's. I could not sense a harem in this house. A mysterious man announced himself to us.

Dressed in stately clothing, he walked through the doors and bowed before us. He said, "You honor me by coming to my home, for I am only a merchant." He had warm tea with saffron and almonds brought for us and asked what we would like for dinner. "I have heard of you," he continued. "You travel from village to village and give the poor food. You ignore the temples and the castes and people have begun to speak of you, saying you are a great healer. Of course, everyone in the city knows of what happened today. Who are you?"

Simon said, relaxed, "It is up to you to figure out who we are. But I am pleased we are welcome in your home, for we appreciate any place where love rules, more than those where God is proclaimed and love does not rule."

"May I introduce myself?" said the merchant. "I am KrishnaDat. My family has followed Krishna for a long time. May I show you my Krishna temple in the garden?" Little paintings depicting Krishna hung all over the house and Simon explained to me what the many girls dancing around him meant. They were his Gopis. Each Gopi embodied a form of devotion which Krishna, the avatar, who had been on Earth long ago, had sacrificed. Krishna had also fought against the darkness. He said, "The Indians believe that the avatars come to Earth at certain times to restore the balance on Earth and bring new creative impulses. What has long since been forgotten in our lands is natural for the Indians."

The merchant was the wealthiest man in the city. He owned nearly everything. He did not have a wife and he lived alone. He showed us his temple. We entered a beautiful Krishna temple in his garden. It smelled of jasmine and sacrifices and the oil, the ghee of the butter lamps. He lived in a gilded cage, but it was lonely. He owned everything and still he was not happy. And we found it difficult to warm up to him.

Food was brought and Jesus and Simon simply remained silent. The merchant told us about himself, how he had inherited everything from his family and had expanded his business. But we remained silent. Until Jesus said, "You called for me. Because you want to heal your heart. We do not come to houses to be catered to. We are happy to receive a meal. We do not come to homes to be guests. We come to every home as who we are. We come with a message of the one and only God of love. And we elevate them in every home until the house shines with love again. Every place we touch is elevated. You called us to your house because you yearn for love. The whole house screams for love as you scream for love."

The merchant arose and knelt before Jesus. He said, "Is it you, Issa, news of whom has already spread throughout the land, saying you have returned? Are you the great teacher of the worlds of whom they are already telling stories?" Jesus took his hand, lay it on his forehead and said, "Your wealth is perhaps seen as good karma in your country, but in principle, it is karma you bear from ages past that is your burden. It is your karma that keeps you prisoner every day instead of setting you free." "What should I do, Lord?" he asked. "Share your wealth," said Jesus. Set your slaves free and share, for you have enough to last until the end of your days. Share so you can be free, for you are actually a slave to your wealth."

The merchant KrishnaDat began to soften before our eyes. He said, "Should I build temples?" Jesus laughed and Simon laughed with Him. "Do not build temples," they said. "Give it to those who need it and bring happiness to your city with what you have. Do not take it from them."

"How can I support you?" "Tell them that Issa, the son of God has returned. An avatar, a great prophet and Agni; tell them that we are here in this country, in this city. Those who wish to see us, may see us. We will return tomorrow."

The merchant melted before our eyes. Jesus had touched his heart. The house, filled with the cold white of transcendence, but since it was not filled with life, with love, it changed at the same time, as every aspect was touched by love and the passion of eternal love. His face changed, he arose and awakened before our eyes because love awakened within him once again, freeing him from the prison surrounding him, built of wealth and meditation.

He said, "Lord, so it shall be. It is a mercy that you are in our home. Your two Shaktis have not revealed themselves to me. But I would like to ask you to return tomorrow evening and I would request that you give your Sadhanas. I will invite the poor," he said. It was late and we were guided back to our tents. I preferred the light in our tents. The path of Shakti we were walking filled our nomadic spaces with pure love. Everything around me was alive with its beauty. The textures of the fabrics around me, nature, the sand, the sun, the moon, the water. I wondered, in silence, what was different. The light on which the merchant meditated was cold. The light of Shakti on the path on which we walked was warm. I felt more at home in it.

Word had spread of what had happened and when we came out of our tents the next morning, we were surrounded by people. We were told that what had happened at the temple had quickly spread throughout the entire city of Kashi.

Our escort came through the crowd to bring us the new supplies they had gotten from the market. The people sat and waited. It had been too long since an enlightened master had come to visit in an embodied form. They waited to see Him. It was an extraordinary situation. Two masters appearing at the same time. One was Jesus, the other Simon. Both had performed miracles in public. Then there were the two of us women, who were on the path of Shakti and were to grow to become teachers ourselves, prophetesses. We came as a group.

Jesus bade Raj Sing, our guide, who escorted and protected us, to tell the people that there was nothing now and they should gather at the merchant's house that evening. But the people were hungry. They had brought their children with them and were waiting, greedy and demanding. The people who were there were poor. They looked at us with their pleading eyes. Their children begged with them. We waited, but Jesus did not react. Jesus came out of His tent and went straight to the city. No one dared follow Him. The people slowly started to disperse and leave and when He returned a while later, Mary Magdalene asked Him, "Why did you do that?" He sat down and looked at us. "As long as the souls act like beaten dogs and do not lift themselves up, face life with all the power born unto them, as long as they run behind me like beaten dogs, I cannot raise them up. I cannot nourish them."

"But you fed them yesterday and you have been giving them food all these evenings," said Mary Magdalene.

"When I come from a place of giving, from my abundance which I brought, I can give them gifts. When they come to me and start to beg, it leads to a descent into powerlessness. Then we lose our value. They theirs and I mine. The law of giving and taking maintains the entire universe. When giving and taking are in balance and we experience our own awakening and our own self-value, giving and taking are in balance. When giving and taking change, however, into an excess of power and begging, the souls will not rise up and look upon God."

He fell silent. Mary Magdalene and I sat there, somewhat confused. Then Simon looked at us and said, "As hard as it is to understand, if you look at the poor with pity in your gaze and your vision of life, you enter into a cycle that could lead to you becoming poor yourself. The law of empathy will never teach us to take pity on others. The law of empathy is that we love and raise them up. Begin to sense that if we want to restore the balance between the worlds and humanity, we must start to face every being eye to eye.

If we want to create from God's throne, we must surround ourselves with people who lift us up and let go of those who draw and suck out our energy and swallow it so it bears nothing that is alive."

The energy within me and Mary Magdalene began to increase again. We had never seen so much poverty at once, so many people living in poverty. Masses of people lived in poverty here. Without understanding it with my head, I knew what Simon was trying to tell us. The divine always lives on a certain frequency of love. That which lives under the frequency of love and does not raise itself up, cannot participate in the vision of God.

"But you go every evening and give the people food, Jesus," I said. He smiled and said, "But I never leave myself as I do so. I do not come down to that level of vibration. When I go out, I raise the vibration. All I do is raise them up with my vibration as long as they lift themselves up. Otherwise, I have nothing to give."

Giving requires taking

Jesus had practically driven the beggars away. The power of Shiva within them was powerful. He turned to us and said, "There is nothing uplifting about succumbing to poverty." Then we spoke of it no further, but Mary Magdalene and I sensed clearly that our energy had come back to the level that was right for us. We learned, bit-by-bit to vibrate on the energy field that suited our prophecy and our souls. That was also the training that Jesus and Simon shared with us. When we vibrate, the environment is elevated with us. The lower vibrations adjust to the higher energies. Not the other way around.

It was late afternoon when the young Brahma whom I had seen in the temple, suddenly appeared before our tent. Simon stepped out and the Brahma bowed before him. He fell to his knees and flattened himself on the ground before him in devotion. He spread his arms. He sought refuge.

"Arise," said Simon. He sat up and said, "Lord, you are Agni. Please give me the grace to recognize and let me understand what your fire brings to our world. Our scriptures have spoken of you for an eternity. But you are here or you are His messenger. I have realized that our teachings have reached a dead end from which they cannot escape. I would like to understand the new teachings." Jesus came out and the two invited the young Brahma to sit with them.

We women wanted to go to the marketplace with our escorts. We wanted to shop a bit. The marketplaces in this city were beautiful. There was fresh fruit and fabrics and spices in rows everywhere and we enjoyed walking through the rows, distracting ourselves. The inner lesson continued. It wanted to be completed. Our mantra was with us at the marketplace and at the same time, it was pleasant for our senses. When we came home, laden with the new fabrics and clothing we had purchased, the young Brahma was still there. When we had brought all of our things into the tent, he had disappeared.

"What did you say to him?" I asked. "We advised him to apprentice himself to the merchant." "What?" Mary Magdalene and I laughed. Jesus said, "He already fulfilled his task as a priest in his last life. What he is lacking on his path to perfection is the merchant. Recognizing the streams of life. Uniting all of the parts and embodying and manifesting his spiritual form in the mundane. Connecting the mundane and the spiritual."

That made sense. We weren't here to retreat into monasteries as priests and monks. We came to Earth to seek our perfection and completion with every step. Born with a plan that unfolds within us. An eternal energy field of the dream of our souls surrounded us and wanted to learn, infinitely. We did not have to repeat what we had learned, but to become whole, there were things that still had to be conquered.

The afternoon was so relaxed that we sat down and I asked, "And what am I lacking to be whole?" Someone brought us tea, but Jesus and Simon did not respond. Mary Magdalene spoke, "What you are lacking is unity with your origins in this land. You were incarnated here many times. Since time immemorial, many, many times. That is what you are lacking. Otherwise, there is nothing you are lacking. That you integrate what you were and give birth to something new. For the future has already been revealed to you." The prophetess awakened in her and in me. "You will recover this aspect in India."

"Thank you," I said. That made sense.

That evening, we went back to the merchant's. We were picked up and brought to his home. The atmosphere of the house had changed. He had lit lamps everywhere. "Welcome. I have worked all day. I have decided not to give food to people on the streets only for as long as they need it. I have decided to give them work. I am a merchant and I have organized the people so they can work for me at good wages and not for a pittance. I have already changed many lives today. And you know what? I am already much happier. Come in," he said.

We sat down at a table. "The people will come tonight to learn your wisdom. You are divine teachers. Please," he said, bowing reverently, "let us partake in your teachings and your wisdom."

Jesus and Simon agreed. "But something is still missing," he said. "I do not have a wife. A woman is missing from my home." Simon began to smile.

"Why are you smiling?" he asked. "Do you not love a courtesan who always comes to see you?" The merchant paled. He said, "But I could never take her as my wife, she comes from another caste. The pleasure women are not intended for us to marry." Simon smiled again and said, "It is time to get rid of the castes. Love what you love. Elevate what you love. Elevate yourselves to lovers."

The merchant had tears in his eyes. Once again, it was love that overwrote the societal norms and rules. He became an innovator in his city. After this encounter with Jesus, he gave the people work, not for a pittance, but for honorable wages. He created value for the people and equality for what they did. The balance began to blossom in this city of trade and creation of values for the people by the people.

Then he prepared for a courageous deed. He called for his beloved courtesan and she came. When she saw us, she was frightened. He invited her in. "Come, sit with us." She was beautiful.

She wore her beauty with great dignity. We could feel the sexual power that lived within her. The merchant said, "Amritha, I have made a decision about my life. I would like to change many things. The first is: Would you be by wife and do me the honor of allowing our great master Issa, who walks among us, to wed us?" She looked at him, amazed. She was not a small woman and she wished to be heard. She stood up and elevated herself and her body was elevated with her. She folded her hands and said, "Yes." Her eyes shone.

This was the lesson Kashi taught us on our journey, our pilgrimage. This woman, Amritha, was the embodiment of the goddess. Her flesh was full of sexual power. The fact that she had offered her body as a courtesan was not what made her who she was. What made her who she was the power over her sexual force which did not live in darkness, but rather in complete dignity within her body. She had served only the merchant for a long time now. She loved him. The revolution was now taking place in our bodies, in our women's bodies, in Mary Magdalene and me. The revolution was a Light of Christ that liberated the sexual power within us that lived beyond the social norms and religious taboos. Excited by Amritha, the courtesan, this power awakened in our bodies and wanted to be embodied as freedom of the Light of Christ. We had to face it.

Our bodies grew sensual and burned.

We were following the path of Shakti and our lust would be our guide.

Mary Magdalene and I knew what was happening, but we kept it within our bodies and were discreet in our awakening.

The Dissolution of the Castes

The merchant's house became a temple. People from all classes came and were permitted to spend time in his garden Everyone was given food, everyone was given drink because the merchant had ordered it so and because the merchant was giving it away. There were Brahmas and people from all of the other castes. People came together in the garden who would otherwise never meet. The differences in heritage by birth melted away in this paradise dedicated to Krishna. Everyone, whether they were courtesans, the wealthy or beggars had their place. Jesus bade the merchant and our translator help. He said we would all speak that evening because we were all teachers of wisdom from heaven. And that the Shaktis had returned to Earth; they had come with Him.

Jesus stood on the steps so everyone could see Him. People also gathered around the walls and when Jesus, the people quietly murmured the message to pass it on so all could hear. He had dissolved the temples and Simon had burned them with his fire. He stood amidst the people, God's throne was so close because we could all see Him. He said, "Elevate your love. Your old scriptures told you how the Earth, how these worlds were created. They told you how the light gods battled with the Asuras, the dark gods. They told you how the sages came to Earth.

The Rishis and sages listened and observed their inner intuition and yogi exercises to explore the laws of the universe and how it is created. Then you built your temples and passed on the wise teachings. But I am telling you, a new creation is coming. The creation of love. Love will elevate every being, regardless of the status or caste into which they were born. Love will show you that wealth and poverty are not in the best interest of our lives. We came to this house and found ourselves welcomed by the hospitality of wealthiest man in your city. He was unhappy and lonely. His soul was imprisoned. This morning, the poorest of the poor came to our tent and begged because they did not want to raise themselves up.

There is nothing elevating in poverty." I saw now that the Sadhus were coming, the followers of Shiva. The people were reverent. The people honored these men who renounced so much. Jesus smiled and said, "See. See these Sadhus, who worship Shiva, they walk their path. They have nothing and yet everything. Their inner worlds are so rich. I say unto you, stop creating a world that separates you into poor and wealthy. Share what you have. Share your love. Create cities in which the temples take in the people to remind them of themselves. Temples of peace where the people can connect to God.

Promote the merchants who give the people work and pay good wages and bless your land with your deeds. India is the spiritual mother of all lands. Many spiritual seeds that came to Earth were born here. This is where the worlds, the creations grew. Honor your mother, this land. For this land is the embodiment of divine Creation. Honor it by recognizing it and recognizing yourselves. Return to love. That is the only message I have brought with me."

The people were moved. Simon arose and mingled with the crowd. He walked through the people and said, "Raise your hands to a Mudra. The Mudra of fire." He showed it to them. "Remember the fire is the beginning and the end of Creation. If you remember the fire, all of the knowledge you were born with will be shared with you. You can read in the fire, you will be reborn in the fire, transformed in the fire and you will die in the fire. Bring the fire back into your life. Give it rituals and worship it. But bring the fire out of the temples where it is preserved in secret. Bring it to the streets, bring it to the fields. Bless your fields with the fire rituals, bless your houses and the wisdom will return to your lives."

As the people held this Mudra, everyone was elevated. In the fire, each being was elevated to what it was. The world lays an illusion of differences over us. The difference between our social statuses, where we came from and where we were born. As divine beings, however, that recognize each other in the fire, they were able to see their origins, the place in which they look upon God. In that world, every being had its mission and its destiny.

"You are born with this dream," said Agni. "If you live your prophesy, you will raise yourselves and the circumstances of your lives up and they will honor you. It makes no difference if you raise yourself up in your divinity from the dirt of the street or if you raise yourself up in a palace as Maharanis or

Maharajas. What is important is that you live as what you are and do not stand in your own way with your whining and self-pity. Recognize that you decide into which fate you will be born. For your soul comes from the fire and returns to the fire and you want to learn in the meantime. You are so eager to learn; that is why the Earth has invited you. Use this life, wherever you are.

The religions and old scriptures have taught you the wisdom of life. You need nothing more than the fire and your sacred prayers."

He sat on the steps where everyone could see him and said, "I am Agni, returned to you for a short moment. I wander through the world with my beloved brother Issa. But in this moment, I am telling you that you need nothing more than your sacred prayers in which you all speak with God and the holy fire. That is the religion you need to raise up this holy land in golden light.

The Brahmas grew quiet. But they had come. Their arrogance shed from them like skin among the people. I could see them becoming a part of the people. Simon said, "If you are born a priest, you live and are a priest. If you are born a farmer, you live as a farmer and fill it with your love. If you are born a merchant, you are a merchant. Do not envy anyone their birthright. Create wealth in your hearts."

Jesus looked at Mary Magdalene and said, "It is time for you to speak, prophetess, arise." Mary Magdalene glanced at Him and then she sat down among the people. Someone translated for her as she said, "My name is Mary Magdalene. I am Issa's companion. I come to you as a prophetess, to elevate your land, for the old fires begin to burn again in your land. Honor the sages, honor the priests, let them ignite the fire and elevate the land. Let the women in your land elevate themselves. Give them the right and honor them as the primal powers of life. Let the women build their temples and nourish them. Build the temples of the goddesses and your land will be blessed."

She walked through the crowd and her healing powers flowed to the people. The people touched her. They sensed that she was a saint. A Ma, a mother, who had returned to them. The women touched her fingertips as Mary Magdalene went to them. They said, "Ma, Ma, Ma" to her. She healed these people by letting her Light of Christ flow over them like sweet nectar. There was nothing that could elevate the people but the love she brought to them. Mary Magdalene was this love. She was the nectar that had come from heaven. When they were in her presence, they drank from this nectar which reminded them all of love. That was her gift to the Earth.

She went back to the steps and then she looked at me and said, "It is your turn, Miriam."

I could sense Simon looking at me from afar. He was sitting off to the side and I heard him say, "Arise prophetess." I sat on the steps. "I came to tell you that the demons that return to this land again and again because they seek the wisdom of your light still reside in your land. They will continue to return until you have overcome your own weakness. There is no demon but that of your own shadow, which you create yourselves. Begin to gather your demons and worship your light gods again.

Remember your old knowledge, for the gods are the characteristics that live within each of you. If you begin to revere them, they will come alive within you. That which you worship shall grow within you. The garden you plant will grow. But you have forgotten your light gods. Those who worship the light gods and offer them sacrifices shall feel these characteristics within themselves and bring them into their families. But those who continue to cultivate the other powers of lamentation, shall serve the demon gods. If you want to fill your land with love and the eternal values, bring your gods back into your lives, the primordial powers of life. Encourage them and bring them back to them back to your land and into your families."

As I spoke, something suddenly happened around me. From one second to the next, I had several arms, golden and moving around me. But I wasn't the only one who could see it; the people could see it too. I looked at Jesus and searched in His eyes. I looked at Simon and searched for reassurance and he only smiled. The people began to murmur. They said, "Ma, Ma, Ma." But no one came closer. My light appeared around me as Simon's had appeared around him the day before. India revealed us and allowed us to emerge.

I was not a human anymore. I was a goddess. My origin, of which Mary Magdalene had spoken, emerged in this land and the people saw me. My love flowed out from me and over the people and this time it was a golden light that sealed everything.

After that happened, the merchant had all of the people leave the garden. The Indians were used to miracles occurring before their eyes and had been since time immemorial. They absorbed the presence of the saint with deep humility and left.

Later that evening, Jesus wed the merchant and his courtesan. We had once again found old friends.

The next morning, we left Kashi and continued our journey. The sixth cycle of our journey of initiation began and we delved back into the inner pilgrimage. The mantras were with us and Simon gave us the next topic of our journey to Shakti.

Reconquering Our Sexual Power

He taught us that this power was a sexual power connected to the Kundalini power in our bodies. And that we should reconquer these powers over the next seven days and use it as a creative power as the Shakti would when we were connected to ourselves.

Every day, a new mantra came to us and we wandered along the Ganges, the sacred river, where the people came to live and die. We wandered along the river and the journey grew quieter. The mantras flowed into our bodies and allowed our Kundalini powers to emerge. But they transformed into another power called temptation. Mary Magdalene and I spoke few words with each other, but we knew that during those days, we were both wandering between power and powerlessness, between light and shadow. Sometimes we exchanged glances, but we knew that language would not help us further.

While Jesus and Simon dug deep tracks in the sand as they walked over it, after everything that had happened, our companions had developed a greater respect for us. They had seen what happened around us. In every village we passed, Jesus gave the poor food; He did not stop giving them gifts. But He did not allow them to follow us. He covered our tracks so we could continue. For we were not here to stay, we were here to conquer and go our own way.

Our next destination was Kalikata. "The city of the black goddess," Simon called it, smiling, and half way there, on the ninth evening, Mary Magdalene and I sat together at the fire and told each other about our path to the Shakti. After the tumult in Kashi, I was quite happy to have the calm around me. And that evening, as we fed the fire, we found ourselves under the peace and quiet of the evening sky surrounding us.

At the same time, so many doors of creation were opened as we sowed the seeds on our journey and I was glad that sometimes there were spaces that were silent and held us and gave us the strength to continue on. And this was such an evening. The Great Mother was closer than ever before. It surrounded us with its blue cloak as Mary Magdalene began to speak.

She said, "This was the most powerful stage since I began my pilgrimage here. My journey of initiation with you. Reconquering my sexual power renewed my powers. By allowing my Shakti to rise and flow through the cells of my body as a powerful, tempting force, it felt as though all of my cells opened in red light, like buds. But my body no longer sought the fulfillment of the senses. This was my first thought; that the increase in my physical desire was the result of the exercises. But my body sought unity. Unity with all of the cosmic powers of creation. And thus I entered the current. I allowed myself to be guided. I didn't know, but I suddenly sensed that when we are truly at one with the powers of Shakti, we are a star that shines and, by its presence, attracts everything that is meant to come to it. I sometimes sat there and felt as things flowed toward me. I received images of the future, of our return to Gaul. Of people flooding toward me. It was my power, this power of Shakti, this force of attraction that will grow so strong that the temptation around me will become so full of love and divinity that I will be like honey to which the people flow on their own. The cosmic power explained itself to me as a force of attraction and it united with me. Now I simply exist and flow outward and I will see how the world responds to me."

Now it was my turn to feed the fire and describe my journey. "I first perceived it as silence. Pure silence. It became so silent around me that I thought I had gone deaf. I had gone blind. I had become emotionless. That I would lose the taste for life. And it grew more and more silent and noiseless. Until, in this silence, I suddenly found guidance. Impulses came from the universe and they took shape within me. And I began to play with them and what form they would take. The universe told me what it is like when light, when the seeds of light began to think and manifest I could see how the seeds of light are first light forms. Light ideas. And that they then seek the path to the material to find their own perfection. They came through impulses and took form. I could feel my body shaping them. And how my body began to release impulses from the sexual power that lived within my body.

There was a moment when I scared myself, when I simply let these impulses flow out of me. I was suddenly able to influence the elements. The clouds moved with my flow and I could suddenly influence that flow. On this river along which we walked. I could influence the fire. I could influence the air, how it moved and then I knew that the power that lies within this force first has to be filled with love. If I have this creative power, when this Light of Christ which is sexuality and creative power unites with me, if I can influence everything with it, I must return to my humility. And I began to pray the mantra you gave me last night, 'Om namah shivaya'. And I prayed that what fulfilled itself through me, what I create, is at one with the will of the Lord and then it was all right.

I began to suspect that if that which I created comes from His will, then I had infinite power, because God had laid it in my lap. And that the things I created, if they came from my will, would never fulfill me. Because everything I might create would only be a reflection of my own limited world.

I realized that if I take the seeds from God's throne, from God's bosom, that love that He bears, if I take it, if it flows over me that my body shivers with goose bumps. If I take this thought and make it real, then the fulfillment, the 'Om namah shivaya' itself lies therein. By serving humbly, by serving myself and God's thoughts, the thought would accept the flow of love to truly be nourished."

Simon and Jesus said nothing. The only thing we knew was that we would begin the journey to the Black Mother the next morning. We walked the path to the Shakti temple and that was the moment that impressed me the most. We made our way across the roaring waters. To a place that pulsed with the highest power. There was a Shakti temple here and Jesus and Simon showed us that this was also a place of Shiva. That Shiva and Shakti pulsated in unison here. It was impressive to feel Shiva and Shakti pulsating as one. This experience would take us to the next level. And only the Black Mother, whom they called Kali, could show us the way there.

Cycle six:
The Power of Shiva and Shakti

The sixth cycle of our pilgrimage began when we left Kashi. For Mary Magdalene and me, it was the journey of initiation in the balance between Shiva and Shakti, the masculine and the feminine powers of creation. We were to immerse ourselves in our images and experience them ourselves. The journey to Shiva-Shakti was gentle and conquering at the same time. It led us along the Ganges, past its little temples by the water, until Jesus headed inland. Our destination was a special temple.

Mary Magdalene and I began to speak more with each other during those days. When we met after our morning Sadhanas, meditations and mantra recitations, we walked together. We told each other our dreams and found out they were similar. Mary Magdalene saw beautiful beings that mated as though in a cosmic dance in sexual union. The pure beauty poured out over Creation. My dreams during those nights were also filled with images of cosmic union. It was the dance of love.

Jesus called the temple that awaited us a Shakti temple in balance with Shiva. On those nights, I dreamed of gods that looked Indian. Based on the perfection of their union and how they danced with each other. On those nights, songs came into my dreams, songs I had heard in the temples of India. These tones and the mantras interwove with each other and it was like an eternal dance. The Black Mother, whom they called Kali, accompanied us. It was her cloak which lay behind all that was happening, in which we conquered Shiva and Shakti to later encounter her.

A deep, new harmony developed among us all. I could feel this plane between Shiva and Shakti being transferred to us and opening new planes of encounter to us during those days.

That evening, when our sixth cycle came to an end, a golden light flowed around us. Mary Magdalene sat there, her eyes shining with passionate, fulfilled yearning. She said, "The vision of the sacred couples is Shiva and Shakti. I saw these sacred couples in eternity and in all of my mantras over the past few days. God is a sacred couple. HE, God and SHE, Creation have been a sacred couple since the beginning of time. The most beautiful powers, which came together when Shiva and Shakti unite, when sacred couples meet."

She looked at Jesus. "You are my sacred counterpart. I find unity in you and still we are each our own beings. We do not have to seek each other out, because we always find each other. When we unite, the unity goes into us and surrounds us. Shiva and Shakti complete each other in their perfection. They do not separate. A person who is so complete that he needs nothing, completes the other. Thus the sacred couples are created. A time will come when the sacred couples will heal the Earth. I have seen this time in the distant future.

In a golden age that requires the fulfillment of Shakti and the fulfillment of Shiva to bring forth perfection and a new creation. We are preparing this age on our journey. We are sowing the seeds for this era. I have seen that our children, John and Sara are a sacred couple who have come to Earth, an eternal promise that is found in love and bears new love because this love bears itself anew again and again."

Mary Magdalene's words wove beautiful patterns in our space. I saw a golden carpet surround us and a deep softness developed around us. When she stopped speaking, I threw the flowers into the fire and it seemed as though I were on the golden carpet she had woven with her words. And I was ready to speak about my experience with Shiva and Shakti.

"They are the balance of the worlds. They require each other. I could see Shiva and Shakti in every being I encountered. There were days on which I saw Shiva and Shakti in every grain of sand. The seed of the masculine, the seed of the feminine. They were in everything that surrounded me. Some people have more Shiva, some people have more Shakti, but if they really want to be complete, they must search the balance of equality. In the end, equality must always be established.

And there was a moment when I saw that the powers between Shiva and Shakti began to play again and balance and imbalance leads to creation if there is equality that returns to the source. It is a dance of the universe that dances within itself and returns and blossoms again. But I also saw that people often prefer to fall into the powers of Shiva when they penetrate the material world. The power of Shakti in the universe is more natural to understand because it is the creative power of life and death. That is easy in the universe. But when the souls penetrate human existence and the material world, it is as though they prefer the power of Shiva over the power of Shakti.

The people must learn to accept both powers. I had the impression, when I immersed myself in the people, that they prefer this power because they then believe they are God themselves. And that they have control over life. Shakti will always teach us, as humans, to devote ourselves and surrender to this deep exhaustion of Creation."

"Your journey, Jesus and you, Simon," I heard myself saying, "you are showing us the paths of the powers of Shakti. The lesson that will redeem the people because they will then understand the legitimacy of Creation. I remember, Jesus, when you visited the underworld, that it was ultimately the Great Mother who redeemed you. You thus gave me the key. The powers of Shakti are what bring us redemption, but the powers of Shakti cannot exist if we do not allow them to take form in our lives."

My visions exceeded my imagination, but I began to have an inkling. I could not properly express in words what my human mind was able to form as an explanation. But these inklings were seeds for the future. "We are planting the future. When the time for harvest arrives, the time when we shall return to Earth to gather the harvest, we will bring the powers of Shakti we are now conquering back with us. I have seen them. They will reawaken within us and they will awaken in many women. Then a time will come when the people will create with their power of Shakti."

I grew very quiet. I delved into a kind of creative power that gently laid itself around me like water flowing around me, surrounding me. "I cannot speak anymore right now."

Jesus appeared moved. "It is the Light of Christ that heals the powers of Shakti. Shakti and Shiva, if they fall out of balance, make it difficult to find each other again. If the powers withdraw in their isolation and are no longer connected, they become violent. Both the powers of Shakti and the powers of Shiva become aggressive and destructive and if they meet then, disconnected, they become brutal.

That is the source of war," He said. "But God is our Father, who bore the Light of Christ. That gentle, loving light capable of liberating the powers of Shiva and the powers of Shakti and guiding them to each other so they recognize each other." He said, "Often, when I wander through the world, I let my Light of Christ flow out from me and then I feel the cold of the powers that have separated from each other and have become violent. My gentleness helps them approach each other." He continued, "That is why I am here: To reunite the powers with each other."

The light that surrounded us that evening had never been there before. Love wove between us, between men and women, between the four of us. We were a mandala and the four of us were the anchor points that wove this circle. A golden carpet lay on the ground and the Earth welcomed it. We were building a mandala for the future in which the masculine and the feminine can meet again. Even more. The mandala in which they recognize each other so deeply, that they create with each other and can fertilize each other. Our journey was back to the feminine power which had retreated on Earth.

That night, under the starry sky of India, Shakti was alive. I could feel her. We were four lovers who encountered each other, as Mary Magdalene encountered Jesus and I encountered Simon.

Two days later

As we entered the temple as promised, I shuddered before the beauty. Ferrymen had taken us through the roaring, wild water that night in order to get there. It was very stormy. Jesus knew the way, though He ensured us He had never been there before. We entered a temple in the wilderness, the size and scope of which clashed with the actual dimensions of the place. It seemed to me as though it represented Shiva and Shakti in their perfect form. The masculine power lay beneath this temple and held the feminine power which unfolded beautifully. Jesus wanted us to visit this place without distraction, so He had chosen to go there at night.

He invited us to meditate here. Mary Magdalene and I had already begun the next cycle of our journey of initiation two days ago. The dark mother was our destination. This place was alive. Powerful feminine beings of the universe danced here and laid dormant in their own power. This didn't seem eerie to me, but rather familiar. The place was a circular temple. It was feminine and I could see in the darkness that there were huge statues, their silhouettes reflecting in the night. We were in a place of pulsating, feminine power. It had been harnessed by sacred geometric architecture. The illuminated women danced in ecstasy.

When we were outside again, Mary Magdalene asked, "What kind of place is this?"

"A temple of Shakti," said Jesus.

This place will be destroyed and rebuilt. It will be used and overwritten, but priestesses of primordial times who still remember still live here. Their tradition is still matriarchal, since the powers of Shakti are dominant. That is why this place will be destroyed and rebuilt, over and over again, until it finds its way back to its Shakti."

"Is there a place where we can experience Shakti in her primordial form?" I wanted to know.

"Yes," said Jesus. "That is the goal of your pilgrimage."

They call them Yoginis.

They call them Daikinis.

They are the illuminated powers of femininity.

They belonged to the goddess.

They come from her.

They never belong to you. They are free like

fire, water, air and the Earth.

If they appear to you,

they have

come to

liberate you.

Cycle seven:
Kali, the Black Mother

We turned toward Kalikata. Our journey would take more than twenty days. We were on the way to the Black Mother. Jesus started the journey for us by telling us that evening, as we sat by the fire, that the place to which we were now traveling was consecrated to Kali, the Black Mother. The story that resided in that place, was that Kali had simply lost the feminine powers of creation one day because she had to destroy so much darkness in the world with her dance, that she flew into a rage during the dance and fell victim to her own insanity. Kali did not stop. Kali danced wildly. She could not escape from her own wild dances. The dances controlled her and Shiva, whom they called the God of Creation, watched. And he did not know how the Shakti power of the universe, which ensured that things were taken back up, transformed and were reborn, to bring them back into balance, for Kali was no longer reachable. She was trapped in her insanity, she could no longer be touched, which Shiva tried. She danced on Earth and the Earth itself fell into chaos because she no longer had her own powers under control as she danced wildly. She simply sprayed black sparks. Kali had spun out of control. And Shiva only knew of one way out.

He laid himself on the ground and slipped, unseen, under Kali's feet, who did not notice him as she danced. He made himself so large that Kali didn't even notice at first that she was dancing on him. But suddenly, Kali grew calmer. The soles of her feet suddenly transformed and she realized she was coming to. She was finally able to stop, for she had been kicked free. There was no end; she had spun in a circle and the circle had become her curse. Her dancing feet grew quiet and she slowly grew calm and came to. Shiva's body had brought her back; she could dance on him. And Kali grew calm and was once again herself. She came back to her essence, to the core of her being. The universe grew calmer, the dark forces grew calmer and everything fell back into balance.

"Kali and Shiva are alive in the city to which we are traveling It is the primordial story that the feminine powers, if they are no longer in balance, transform into a destructive quality that gets out of control and is only destructive. The feminine power is destructive, the feminine power destroys, but the feminine power is also the balance of the enlightened masculine that the power of Shiva lacks," Jesus told us.

"For that is the origin of this story. On this journey, you will pray the mantras of Kali so you immerse yourself in this darker power. For only when you have experienced the insanity of the feminine power can you return to the control and guidance over the feminine powers." He promised us that He and Simon would hold us, but He also promised us that we would have to dance on the edge of this insanity with our souls, in order to truly reconquer the powers of Shakti, for the powers of Shakti were wild and untamed. No one could control them. Only the complete soul of a Shakti soul, at peace with itself and with the insanity of the power of Shakti, could return, walk the path of initiation of Shakti themselves and pass it on to the people.

Mary Magdalene and I listened quietly. We sensed that something was coming. We had to break through our boundaries and only the insanity could help us break through these boundaries. We both began to sense that the boundaries we had experienced during our human existence could only fall in the transition to our origin if we break through these transitions while in the insanity. Jesus and Simon advised us not to allow ourselves any distractions. That night, after the fire went out, I lay in my bed and was ready to walk this path. If the dance into which I would enter was to carry me beyond the boundaries as it once did Kali, I knew that Simon would lay himself beneath my feet. So I could find the balance again, as Jesus would do for Mary Magdalene.

For nine days, we stepped in the dance of Kali's insanity, the Shakti. The Shakti which knows the insanity of the darkest, black light. The mantras grew more intense every night, as did our fire of black light. We danced within ourselves and our bodies danced, as we began to ignite, but as the days continued, the denser the boundaries grew. We wandered on the precipice as we walked during the day. Our escorts kept their distance. Simon insisted we wear the black dresses of Kali during those days. With jewelry that made us look wild. We wandered in this power. Sometimes I went out at night and danced beneath the sky to unleash the power of the rage released within me. The rage danced within me until the end of days.

It was also the rage that brought me back to the fire after nine days. When I saw myself sitting there, the rage burned within me, rage like I had never felt before. I didn't know what journey Mary Magdalene had been on, but I as I sat beside her at the fire, I sensed her power. There it was, as Jesus and Simon had promised, the feminine power. We had crossed through it. But it was not yet redeemed.

That night, we sat there at the thresholds of our insanity which burned within us as never before. Genius and insanity, the genius of our femininity and the insanity were in us at the same time. We were black and we were powerful. We were the black empress of Shakti who brought us back to our power. I spoke first. Simon had lit the fire. The more wild and powerful we became, the more I felt Jesus and Simon grow softer, without losing their power. They were the perfect balance to us. We were as unleashed as Kali herself and still ourselves because this gentle power, which Jesus and Simon bore within themselves held us together and reconnected us. Shiva and Shakti played with us during every phase we passed through. What had changed since the last moment of the last initiation of our journey was that we were no longer walking the path of Shakti, but instead this path, in an eternal dialog with the masculine, began a new conversation.

When we grew wild, Jesus and Simon grew gentle, flooded with the Light of Christ. I sat there in my rage which burned within me. The gentle fire that Simon had ignited within me brought me back in the moments in which I lost myself in this rage which burned like fire. But the rage did not control me.

I said, "The boundaries I crossed in the last nine days have brought me back to the boundaries of my own creative power. To create a feminine power that is more powerful than I am. It lives within me. It was born into me. Since the beginning of time, since I myself was created. Many experiences of embodiment and the material world transformed my creative power into rage, but I went deeper. I wove through the layers of my soul. I took them away. 'Go deeper,' I told myself, 'the rage is the source.' I went deeper and deeper. And I found it there. My sorrow. My sorrow lay on the primordial foundation of my soul like a sea, a lake full of tears. Tears I had cried long, long ago. My sorrow was so deep I was drowning in it. And I knew I had to wander on the boundaries of the insanity of my sorrow and I allowed myself to become the sorrow.

I became like these women who dress in black and wail and lose themselves in their sorrow. I allowed myself to lose myself in the sorrow. I lost myself in the insanity of the sorrow over my own tears. I did not have to remember why I had cried so much. I knew we had brought so much bitterness into the world with the loss of the light and now my own bitterness had grown larger than the bitterness. When a white flame suddenly appeared, I began to remember that on our journey, we had seen widows in India wearing white.

In Palestine, they wore black and here, they wore white. White transcendent light. It grew gentler within me. My tears became white tears and transformed into diamonds and one night, as I danced outside, I sat there and each of my tears found a place in the starry night sky. In my world, they became my stars which shone above me. I had reached my powerless limit, when you, Simon, murmured the last Kali mantra in my ear and I was free. Kali was my sister. We looked at each other and meditated. In my world, she sat across from me and we sank into our worlds.

We completed each other. I, who carried my stars above me which shone like diamonds around me. And Kali, who carried these diamonds within her, the Mother Kali. She was the universe. I was also the universe. But she was the mother who would always bring me back when I lost myself in the material of oblivion. And then I awoke: by meditating on our stars, I was allowed to awaken with Kali. But the rage returned. The rage returned the closer I came to my body and my human existence. So much rage. Until I understood that the rage is my creative power which had turned around. And now I need your help," I said to Simon and Jesus, "for I do not know how to solve this."

Mary Magdalene had listened to me in silence. After what I had released from myself, she took a long pause. She sat there and breathed deeply. I had never seen her power so black. Her black aspect suited her well. After a long time, she spoke in a warm voice. She said, "I already knew the insanity well. I no longer had to conquer my own insanity. I rode my insanity when you, my beloved, hung on the cross and I did not know if they would torture you right before my eyes and tear your flesh apart. I wandered on the boundaries of my own insanity then. I was alone and bore our daughter Sara. Even during her birth I wandered along the insanity of my existence. The pain was unbearable and it solidified within me because I did not know if you would return. I knew that I had to bring this child into the world because she would bring what none of us could. I know the boundaries of my insanity well.

What I did not know, however, was my sacred heart. My sacred heart which takes the form of flesh. On the first night, when you murmured the mantra in my ear, Jesus," she said, "a red, fleshy, ruby-colored heart blossomed in my heart. It placed a wreath of golden roses and blue light around this heart. I knew: That is me. I am this sacred heart. It was ruby-red and pulsated. Every night and every day, I took this sacred heart back into the space of the Black Mother. To Kali.

I sat in her spaces and began to illuminate my sacred heart. I illuminated the black with this ruby-red light; this was my meditation during these past few days. And the red wove through the black light. The gold wove through the black light. And it became sacred. My heart opened in carnal lust, beyond the boundaries and my desires and yearnings became flesh. They were so carnal they suddenly melded with me and became one with me.

There I am. As the embodiment of my desires, which are carnal and sacred. I yearn for life. In every moment. But the desires are different now. The desires I once had, when you hung on the cross and I bade life spare me this because I did not think I could bear it. Or the desire for you to have been there when our daughter was born, extinguished and ebbed in my soul. I do not know where they will lead me, but the beauty hidden in this carnal desire in my sacred heart is indescribable."

Her Light of Christ had become flesh. As I sat beside her, I could sense this and it began to transfer over to me. I felt waves emanating from her, passing over to my body. My sacred heart awakened and the rage became a flaming dance of my own fire. It wasn't just that Jesus' and Simon's powers came into balance with us and we found harmony again and again by encountering each other. It was also Mary Magdalene's and my origins in the powers of Shakti which began to complete each other and communicate with each other. Her light completed me. And put me under fire. Just as my light ignited her fire.

Cycle eight:
The Carnal Sacred Heart

The carnal sacred heart was our next cycle of initiation for the next nine days. Within us, the city of Kalikata, the city of Kali and Shiva came closer and closer although we were still a nine or ten-day journey from there. Now, we would conquer love. Since we had encountered Him, Jesus had always preached that there was only one religion, that of absolute love. That God is love, at His source. And that we must return to love. Nothing else was hidden in all of His teachings. His religion was love. Our mission for the next nine days was to conquer this love ourselves.

The mantras carried us day-by-day into the fiery love of our hearts. Yes, it was the sacred heart we were to conquer. The love into which were once born as God's children. Now it was about love become flesh, which is created when it finds itself in the human body. When it beats through the heart, as an organ, it becomes real. The heart was so filled with carnal, sensual desire, that it becomes the love we are ourselves. So we are only love embodied. Simon guided us through those days. He told us that we are born to find our freedom. That the freedom of the creatures of God can only be conquered in the human body. And that the secret that lies behind it is that we walk the path of love.

I didn't know if it was a coincidence, but I had the impression the Sadhus were beginning to accompany us. Or they simply appeared in greater numbers. Or they were on the path to Kali themselves. In any case, as I walked the path of love and absorbed my mantras, when I awoke every morning and went outside, there were more. They stayed within eyeshot and accompanied us during the day. I saw Sadhus everywhere, always at a safe distance. Either they were wandering themselves, or meditating. They spoke to me with their eyes. It was an eternal journey we spoke of with our gazes.

They had become my guardians on the journey to love. At the same time, I felt the gift I was giving them by being who I was and walking the path I was walking. Mary Magdalene and I sat together at least once a day and talked. We talked about ourselves. About our contemplation, about the life we had taken on. We told each other stories of the old days, of how we met to what we would do in the future or how it would be when we saw our children again. The past and the future found each other again during those days and in the present in which we were, in this foreign land, in sacred India, which gave us so many mystical gifts, we found our story again. Moreover, we had never had a future until that moment. Here, in love, we would find it.

Those days were full of yearning. They were silent and contemplative. The Sadhus wandered through my dreams. They were with us on our journeys. They were my guardians. Until we were two days from Kalikata on the ninth day and we gathered at the fire. Jesus and Simon disappeared for two days. They only came to give us the mantras and then went on their own journey. We walked our path with escorts from this world and other worlds, with camels and tents. We prayed our love continuously. That became our prayer.

Until that evening, the ninth evening, when Jesus and Simon came to us with the Sadhus. They had invited them, the silent men. They invited them to sit around the fire and they began to ignite it. The Sadhus kept their distance from us. Their consciousness was with the fire. Some prayed, others sat there in their bliss, others were on their inner path. So it hadn't been an illusion that the Sadhus were wandering with me in my dreams. They wandered and protected the Earth. I knew that the paths they walked were sacred paths. They were at different stations of consciousness. But this had no meaning here. They belonged to Shiva, the Lord Himself.

Jesus lit the fire. The Sadhus prayed, they prayed for us. Before we gave anything of ourselves, we listened to the eternal prayer of the Sadhus. They prayed and prayed and an energy field built up around us and spanned in a circle around our tents and spanned up into the night sky. Jesus and Simon waited. They approached the fire. We passed out rice and water. They did not ask for more.

That evening, no one spoke. Jesus and Simon were the fire. It turned ruby-red for us and shone like love itself. We were born from the fire. The fire of life would take us home. The fire became home in every moment.

The sacred heart of which Mary Magdalene had spoken had now awakened within me. It shone in my heart. I was the yearning of my life. We had found our future. Once, we lost it in Palestine, when Jesus was crucified. In Gaul, we found it again, but it was not the dream of our lives. India had healed us. We had found our future for the Earth again.

Cycle nine:
The Power of Devotion

We were a few days from Kalikata. The ninth cycle of the initiation we had begun, carried us toward the city of the Black Mother. We were to dedicate ourselves to the devotion as an aspect of Shakti and the path of Shakti. Devotion and reception. I myself thought in the beginning that this would be the easiest of my exercises. With each step I walked toward the city of the Black Mother, I noticed that it was, in fact, the most difficult initiation so far. I had thought I would become devoted and receptive, but I learned that the dimension that lay behind that overwhelmed me so much I lost all hold within myself. True devotion, true surrender, true reception was greater. It was the greatest power that moved this universe.

We walked toward the city and the events intermixed outside. It grew more lively around us. In the evening, Jesus started providing the people who lived on the streets near the city with food by simply multiplying and materializing what we had in the tent. We gave the pilgrims we encountered food every day. While we spent time in the morning meditating our sacred mantras in silence, we dedicated the remaining day toward feeding the people we met. Until we reached the city. The pulse of the dark mother who lived here came closer. We pitched our tents at the edge of the city again and Simon and Jesus brought us to a temple dedicated to the Mother Kali. The statue that looked down at us was black. The devotion and black power sought to reconnect here.

In those times, there were priestesses who guarded this black temple. Simon bade Amber, our escort who translated everything for us, our noble woman who was always with us, find out whether we women could participate in the priestesses rituals. She came back an hour later and nodded. The priestesses had allowed Mary Magdalene and I to participate in their rituals which only the black priestesses were allowed to witness. They brought us to them. The women wore black saris and were covered from head to toe. These women also had very dark skin. When we arrived, they ignored us. They lived near the temple and went about their business. Mary Magdalene and I stood there and waited. But hours passed without anyone taking notice of us.

When one of the women walked past us and nodded, that was our sign. We followed her across the fields to the temple. Our translator and protector came with us. The women knelt before Kali, their black goddess and began to sing. They lit fires and performed their Aratis, their fire ceremonies. They sang for several hours. They adorned them with flowers, they washed them. It was the first time I was able to experience how people worship their divine form so much it becomes real. The more the women presented their ceremonies and rituals to the form and statue of Kali, their goddess, whom they loved, the more alive she became before our eyes.

It took hours. Kali's presence became tangible among us. They drew symbols in ash on our foreheads. We went there every day while we were in Kalikata. We witnessed how the women washed the statue with devotion every day and awoke it to life with their rituals. Every day, Kali and the statue died before our eyes and was reawakened. In the silence of these rituals which we witnessed, something happened to us. It became a part of our cycle of initiation. The women never spoke a word to us. But after three days, they began to share their rice with us, for they ate when we came.

We began to bring flowers with us which we purchased at the market. Until, after three days, we were allowed to adorn Kali. Mary Magdalene and I enjoyed the game. But it was not a game. We adorned the goddess and it was passed on to us in the silence of devotion. With each flower we placed on the goddess, we adorned ourselves. The boundaries of devotion were wiped away in this devotion and were simultaneously rewoven. By worshiping the goddess, we became one with her. The goddess knew no boundaries. The goddess did not solicit their worship. The goddess exchanged it. It was a barter with her to become one with her.

In Kalikata, many fires burned every day. Many pilgrims came. The fires blackened the temples through which we wandered day after day. At the same time, death and poverty reigned here. The city lived from a severe polarity. The mother of death and the mother of life simultaneously drew all of the powers to us. The people accompanied this with the fires day and night. The people lived at the fire, sacrificed to the fire, and the priests fed the fire.

The fire was present in this city. It was a part of life. The people did not come to the rituals at certain times, rather they stopped when they went out onto the streets and came from their errands and made sacrifices to the fire that the priests and priestesses of Kali and Shiva kept lit around the clock. The priestesses were outside the city, for they did not perform their rituals publicly.

Kalikata guided our journey to devotion, to completely surrender ourselves and receive. We learned to face death on this journey, for the Black Mother was death because she was life. We only saw Jesus and Simon in the evenings. They were always out. But they did not want to reveal where they had been.

On the ninth evening at the end of this cycle, everything around us grew dark. Everything turned black. The night was so dark, like coal, and it grew so cold we froze. When I came to the fire, I was wrapped in several blankets because I was so cold.

Mary Magdalene wasn't there yet. She came out of her tent and sat down with us, calm and quiet. Jesus told us that we would not be alone that evening. We waited until a large, black priest came to us and bowed before us in greeting.

Simon and Jesus received him warmly and he sat down between them. He was dressed in black and had black skin. Since we did not speak his language, we could not understand what they were discussing. Until Jesus bade Amber, our translator, translate. This priest lived in secret, in the black city of Kali. He guarded a treasure that was brought to this city long ago.

While Amber translated for us, he unpacked something wrapped in black and a glowing, black stone appeared. Mary Magdalene and I shuddered, for as cold and black the night was, this black stone was so alive. Simon had Amber translate. The priest said, "This is a piece of anti-material, once given to this place by Shiva so the Black Mother can rule here. At the place on Earth where she receives her power. The priests in this place have protected this black anti-material since the beginning of time. It contains so much energy it could destroy the entire planet. But these priests are initiated masters. We know them, for they existed once and still do." Amber continued to translate, "The priest meditated on you for three days, then he sent word to us that he was ready to initiate you in the Black Mother because you have chosen to walk the path of devotion on your own. But believe me, this initiation will not be easy for you on your path of Shakti. But if you are ready, it will complete your path of devotion."

I was ready. "We have come so far now. Whatever happens to us, it is time to continue on. I am ready." Mary Magdalene looked at him. "I can sense what this will demand of us. Perhaps I will lose you, my beloved, for I sense this light will take everything from us first. We may no longer recognize that which we love." Jesus nodded.

We stood on a threshold at which we had to give up everything to accept our own greatness. Leave all bonds behind; that was what the Black Mother demanded. Forget everything that binds us. But there is no way to truly know what really awaits us. "No one knows what will happen with the beings when they are connected to this material," said Simon. "For each being, it is as his destiny requires."

We nodded. Jesus lit a fire and then went to get water bowls.

The only thing I remembered was that the priest came to me and touched my forehead with this material. Then I could not remember anything, for everything was gone. I fell into a trance and murmured mindlessly in fever dreams. Everything around me burned in black light. Everything. When I conjured up my sorrow, to mourn what I lost, it began to hurt until this pain became so merciless that I could no longer bear it. So I had to give it up. But the Black Mother was liberation. She liberated me from all material bonds until I was free.

When I awoke, I did not know how many days had passed or where I was. What awoke me was the heat, the sand and the gentleness in which I was carried onward and in which I slept. Where was I?

People surrounded me and were carrying me. Where was I? It was hot. I looked at my feet, walking in the sand and I was carried onward. I sat up and someone gave me water. In that first moment, I didn't recognize the people. Everything around me was so bright it nearly burned my eyes. I felt around me and felt fabrics, but they felt strange to me. When someone gave me something to drink, my body grew calmer. I began to feel my cells as living light. The drink I was given was something that revived my cells. I could sense that every fiber of my being was light. Who am I and where was I? Everything within me was light. I recognized the scent of the desert and knew there were people around me. I could feel her.

When I slept, someone murmured the mantras to me. The voices were familiar to me. But I was in another time. Until I awoke on another day. And stepped out of the litter. People tried to help me, but I waved them off. I went out and looked into the desert.

I recognized the man who came toward me. It was Simon and he was smiling. But I didn't know if there was a story that connected us. He said, "You will remember soon."

Cycle ten:
Embodiments of the Shakti

For days, we wandered in the desert. My being was unable to store memories. I was walking on the sand and the woman next to me was Mary Magdalene. I knew her. She was the most familiar being. She was my friend. But since we had no place to store memories, the only thing that was familiar to us was the sand we felt beneath our feet. That night, Simon murmured more mantras in my ear. I knew him. He was eternity for me. I also knew the mantras. I knew everything. But the only thing that was truly familiar was the sand, the wandering and the nights. Slowly, slowly, everything came back to me. And still, it was different.

Without a sense of time, we sat at the fire one evening and there He sat, the Son of God. In this dimension, I could see His full beauty. Simon was sitting there, lord of the fire, whose beauty and fire wove through the worlds. Mary Magdalene was sitting there, the red goddess and her light pulsated and nourished every being with the depth of life. I was there. And I was happy. A fire was lit and the more I looked into the fire, the more I came back to life. The fire brought me back. Until I heard Mary Magdalene say, "It is all right, I can remember everything. Yet I know that I am different. The Earth can touch me again, but I am free of bonds, I am happy."

I only now noticed how my light sunk back into the material world and I grew calmer. I said, "Thank you for this journey. I can remember you told me you didn't know what would happen. There were moments when I no longer knew who I was. I was everything. I am back. I know who you are, I know who we are. It is time for us to complete our journey."

I felt the need to stand up and I bowed before Jesus, touched His feet and kissed them. I did the same with Simon. I had never experienced such freedom in my body. The Great Mother, the Black Mother, had allowed us to take the tenth step in our journey. But I knew that I could never have taken it without the teachers who ensured I did not get lost in insanity. I had experienced the freedom in my human body. Complete freedom. I thanked them for this. For the journey began anew here. From a place of freedom. In freedom.

"There are people who have died on this path of initiation," Simon laughed, when we started our eleventh week.

"You will now embody yourselves," said Jesus. "When Shakti embodies herself, she finds her soul and she embodies herself in every cell of her body."

Cycle eleven:
Integration

In the days that followed, Mary Magdalene and I reacquainted ourselves with this world. Our memories slowly returned. In the mornings, we began performing the physical exercises with Amber, our escort, whom we had often watched doing them. She called them Asanas. Jesus had advised us to join her. Every morning, we immersed ourselves in physical exercises after our meditations and before we continued traveling. We turned to face the sun and followed her prayers. Her body expanded and she showed us how to breath into our bodies and take up positions of inner experience.

My language also returned to me. "Why didn't we start doing them earlier?" I asked Mary Magdalene. Our bodies needed a while to adjust to the flexibility of this energy flow, but after a few days, we noticed how good it was for us. "What are these exercises?" Mary Magdalene asked. Amber told us that these exercises were Asanas. That the sages in India had been searching for a long time for the form with which they could let the energy stream, the cosmic energy stream that always surrounds us flow through their bodies and make it fluid. So they could activate the flow of their chakras with the physical exercises. Their goal was to let the cosmic stream flow in their bodies in harmony. After we had fully elevated ourselves the week before, we found embodiment this week. My sense of smell returned, much more intensively than before. All of my senses awakened and came alive again. We even asked to be allowed to repeat the exercises at sunset and we found ourselves in the sand digging our hands and feet into it. Our bodies flowed in the exercises which they named and gave meaning to. We inhaled the sun in the morning and exhaled the sun in the evening. We become one with our bodies.

During the day, we rode on camels and came closer to a city.

Our escorts began to tell us it was one of the most sacred cities and the ancestors revered it and the gods are said to have lived there long ago.

Jesus and Simon listened to these stories as we walked. They simply let our escorts speak. After a while, I began to understand the words before they were translated, after all these weeks we had spent in India. After our escort had told us all about the city and its temples, in which the gods had once lived, Jesus said, "I think we will not visit this place." Mary Magdalene and I looked at Him, enquiringly. "Once, I studied at this temple and I discussed with the Brahmas for so long and, like the high priests in Palestine, I took them to their limits. We are looking for another place. I do not think the Brahmas want me to return to this place. They threw me out then."

He did not say more, but we all understood. Mary Magdalene and I knew that Jesus had broken the rules here too. He had denounced the caste system.

Sometimes people would walk with us for miles, because Jesus gave them food in the evenings. They followed us for a while with their children and then let us continue on alone. Until one evening after the eleventh week, after our physical exercises, we sat there and Jesus and Simon lit the fire, as always on the ninth evening.

We were not meant to speak. We sat there and were happy. Beneath the warm sun of India, in the midst of the beautiful colors that accompanied us. We were brought wonderful food and fresh fruits. During these nine days, life became a joyful celebration. After the state of unity, of being at one with everything, the cosmic expansion, we were hungry for life.

The body seeks it sensual fulfillments and that evening, there was nothing to tell until Jesus looked at us after dinner and His eyes took on an expression I had never seen on His face before. He grew soft and gentle. He asked, "What does happiness mean to you?"

"That is the most valuable question," said Mary Magdalene, "you have ever asked me, Jesus. I don't think I have ever asked myself this question. I have always had the impression I am here to serve. But what is happiness?"

"If you do not choose life and service as your own happiness and you do not first ask yourself what your happiness is, you will never understand what it means to serve," said Jesus.

"But Jesus," I said, "you knew from the start that you had chosen this violent crucifixion on your path. But you came only to serve the people." I looked at Him and the fire between us turned golden. It turned liquid and golden.

"Of course," said Jesus. "Before I even asked myself and stepped into this world, I asked myself this question. What does happiness mean to me? Happiness for me is to come and serve. I am happy all the time," He said. He took His hand and tapped His index finger on His heart and said, "I am always happy."

Simon began to laugh so loud that Mary Magdalene and I looked at each other enquiringly. We waited until the moment passed and our beloved husbands told us what they wanted to share that evening. Simon took a handful of sand and threw it in the fire. The fire grew even more golden and liquid before us and he said, "Happiness and joy are the source of all life. The reason why God created everything was for happiness and joy. The source of all Creation is joy. Creation was happy and joyous when it was created. The Indians called it Ananda, bliss. It lives in every source and every flame. And those who return to joy, return to Creation."

"So what do joy and happiness mean to you?" Jesus asked again.

"For me," I said to Jesus, "happiness is when I am connected to myself. When I am connected to myself and connect to life from that essence. When I know I am so connected to myself that I experience everything around me. The space, God and everything all at once, that is happiness for me. For me, happiness is to be permitted to live." I suddenly sank into myself and touched what I had just said aloud. For me, happiness was to be permitted to live. Mary Magdalene was weeping. She said, "For me, happiness is everything that exists. Happiness is what I have been permitted to experience with you all. Happiness is that I have found you again. Happiness is that we are here tonight. Happiness is that we will always find each other again."

Our path of Shakti, our initiations had led us to this point, on this evening, as we honored life. We told each other stories. Jesus told us of India and for the first time, we learned from Jesus why He broke with all religions. He said, "There are no religions that can exist if they do not acknowledge that heaven is here and now. That the fulfillment of heaven is always present for everyone."

"Why do we come to Earth?" I asked Jesus and Simon.

"Why? Because we want to learn," said Simon. "Every time we come to Earth, we dream this life and we try to make it real in this material world. We learn with each life we live."

"Do you learn too?" Mary Magdalene asked.

"The principle of life is eternal learning," said Jesus. "Eternal learning." That wasn't enough for me. I wanted to know, "Where does this journey lead, Jesus? You brought us here, we have completed eleven cycles, what is the goal of this journey? What is the goal of all our journeys?"

"What do you think?" Jesus asked. "What is the goal of all our journeys?"

"The goal of all our journeys is God," I said.

"And there are thousands of paths to Him," Jesus said, "but there is only one for you in particular, and you must find it."

"Why are you bringing us to India alone?" asked Mary Magdalene. "You have dedicated yourselves only to us for weeks. So we can walk our path of initiation. You hold yourselves back. Why do you do this for us?"

"Because you are capable of raising up the banished Shakti on Earth again and breaking her banishment. Because you are capable of conquering the feminine power and rediscovering your feminine path of initiation. Because you can break through the barriers and release the waves for the Earth." Jesus was divine.

"I feel as though I am in heaven on Earth," I said. "I don't think I have ever been this happy in my life, except for missing our children. I miss Sara and John and our family, but I have the feeling that heaven is tangible around me." Simon said, "Shakti is heaven. Shakti is the soul. If you return home, heaven will return to Earth and you will open heaven to others who will in turn be able to open heaven to others."

Cycle twelve:
The Resurrection of the Prophetess

The eleventh cycle had been sealed and we began our twelfth cycle. On the way to the sacred site of Jagannath. Every morning, Simon and Jesus came and drew symbols on our foreheads in sandalwood. The mantras were so old and sacred they nearly enchanted us. They said, "There is nothing left to do except initiate you, so you become female prophetesses again who go out before the women to prepare their path on Earth. To raise the feminine power up again and help other women elevate this feminine power. To allow the mothers to arise again and her daughters. To heal the ancestors, the mothers who were broken by the wars."

Every morning, when the oil touched my forehead, a part of the ancestors was healed. The fragments of the shattered worlds around me reconnected. That which was disconnected began to interweave without my knowing what was really happening. I sensed only that I was connected to many powers of Shakti and feminine powers of all women ever born. All the feminine powers that reside in this universe pulsated in the Earth. What happened during those days was sacred. It simply guided us through the song of the mantras and into ourselves. We walked during the day and step-by-step, we interwove with the Earth. I did not ride on the camel, for I wanted to feel the Earth beneath my feet. I wanted to walk this sacred path, embodied in my body, the sacred Mother beneath me. My sacred self within myself.

Until, on the evening of the seventh day, we arrived in Jagannath, where Jesus tasked our guide with pitching our tents nearby instead of taking us to the Jagannath temple. We were looking for the Shakti temple, which was old and sacred. Our guide refused and said, "There is no such temple." But after asking around, he discovered that this temple lay outside the city by a river. But that it was full of witches' powers and full of evil Siddhi powers and the people avoid the place for that reason. Jesus laughed and said, "That is exactly why we want to go there."

The Beginning of All Journeys

It was already dark when, after this labyrinthine journey, we finally found a place on the river where we could pitch our tents. Raj Sing, our guide, had given up on us. He repeatedly tried to convince Jesus that He was mistaken, for the temple He sought was the sacred place of Shiva and the temple where the King of the Lingams ruled. Jesus, however, insisted that He was looking for a small, powerful Shakti temple. It took a long time for our guide to ask around, still trying to prove to us that Jesus was mistaken. Until he was finally told that the temple was on the other side of the river, but one could not get there uninvited. It was a secret place. At first, he didn't want to tell us. "They say it is an eerie place protected by magic and the women from the primordial tribes. They say there are Siddhi powers there." "Yes, exactly," Jesus said, unimpressed.

I listened to Mary Magdalene, off to the side singing mantras, unheard by those who did not know the syllables. But I vibrated with them; they had become flesh and blood within me. She had to be somewhere out there by the river. Her vibration was powerful. I could feel her singing herself into a trance. Her red power of Shakti came to me in waves.

The place did not allow our Kundalini to sleep, nature meandered like snakes in our vaginas.

"The powers of Shakti must first find God within them, then they can awaken." This is what Jesus had been teaching us the entire time. And we would soon discover what He meant.

Tribhubaneswar

Mary and I did not sleep that night. I spent the hours in meditation in my own tent. I sense when Jesus and Simon were meditating and when they were sleeping. Each of their movements came to me as vibrations. I felt when they dissolved into the vigilance of the eternal light of being at one with everything and when they delved into the dream state. The energy of the place kept me awake; I was surrounded by magic. I couldn't say that I liked this energy. It felt uncanny to me. But my dark side was calm, relaxed. If I hadn't trusted Jesus and Simon as much as I did, I would have fled.

"Om Gam Maha Devi Gam Devi…" Mary Magdalene conjured up her powers of Shakti.

"I will show you something." It was four in the morning and Simon was standing before my tent. "No, the red sari and regal jewelry," he requested as I came out of the tent. I went back in, quickly changed and reemerged, regal, red, in the world of India, in the world of Bharat. I saw Mary Magdalene and Jesus out on the field and we followed them.

A round, red temple spanned the landscape, seemingly appearing from another world behind the green thicket. The aura was red like blood, as was my world. This was the goal of our journey which Jesus had promised us. Our preparatory initiations had lasted 108 days. 108 prayers had been fulfilled since we set out to fulfill Shakti. The most powerful, ruling place of Shakti on Earth was 108 steps away from me. We had arrived. Hidden at the end of the world, the little, round temple held the primordial powers of Shakti in the material world with all its might; the powers that had been shattered on Earth. I counted each of my steps, for I wanted to remember for the rest of my days, what it was like to encounter the feminine power awakened within me. Each step should count. The magnetic powers of the Earth pulsated and flowed from here like a black hole in the universe.

We were so close we could see the priestesses were already performing their early-morning temple services and singing their mantras.

The four of us exchanged thoughts via eye contact. "Until we arrive, you must remember your powerful Shakti," Jesus had told me. It sounded like massive claps of thunder in my ears. I looked into Mary Magdalene's eyes and fell into the wildest land of the goddess. That power, which could never be possessed, could not be tamed. It knows it was created to be free.

My beloved soul mate and I were enveloped in ethereal, blood-red and our red chakras roared in our womb like an anarchic, greedy animal as we entered the round temple. We moved in roaring synchronicity. The shock of the indescribable beauty made us freeze when we saw what had been invisible from outside. A powerful circle of female Yoginis was the living radiation of the eternal here in the stone. The priestesses were much smaller than we were and looked as though they would attack us any moment like angry cats because we were in the temple which was small, yet contained the entire universe. We showed respect by sitting down and silently immersing ourselves in the prayer of the mantras. With our eyes closed, they had no way of convincing us to leave the temple with their gestures.

The feminine power was uninterrupted here. We wondered which sacred commandment we had just broken. The priestesses completed their temple services and then left us alone. When everything was quiet, we both took a deep breath and danced, breathing with the pulsating rhythm of the temple. Until an impulse told us it was time to go. We stepped out of the temple. We could not see our husbands anywhere and suddenly, out of nowhere, small women surrounded us, all dressed in red and they regarded us with suspicion. Their vibration was very earthy and wild. An old woman stepped out of the circle, smoking a roll made of leaves. The smoke made me dizzy as she sniffed at me.

They began to sing. Their voices united into drumming, guttural rhythms and they stomped their feet on the ground which molded around them.

Mary Magdalene and I stood beside each other and avoided eye contact; we were overflowing with the feminine powers we had mastered over the last few weeks. We were elevated and regal and looked at the women with kind, loving eyes. Mary Magdalene and I were one, without fear of the foreignness of these shamanic women. I could also sense that Simon and Jesus were nearby and would protect us if we needed it. Without discussing it, we both knelt and held out our hands. The leader of the tribe was a high priestess and initiate. She grabbed my left hand and pulled it to her and ran her dark, rough fingers along the lines on my palm. She murmured and won me over with her earthy, uncultivated devotion. She looked at me with her knowing black eyes, the landscape of the goddess resided in this wild body and she kissed my hand. She gave instructions and a few priestesses left the circle and ran away to get something.

"You are rich. You are the goddess of this place." Mary Magdalene's voice was so loving I instantly dissolved in a thousand explosions. "They recognized you." I fell into her arms and out of the eternity I had forgotten, my soul voice said, "You help me recover my empire. When we return, I will support you with all my power in building your empire and your church which they will follow." I felt something at my feet, the priests placed flowers at my feet and murmured, "Ma, Ma, Ma, Ma, Ma, Ma, Ma."

MA

I made internal contact with Simon and Jesus. "Where are you hiding? Are you watching what is happening here?" The telepathic response came immediately. "You have done it. They trust you. That is the beginning." My palms were still open, offering my innermost heart. It began to tingle and when I looked, a red paste that smelled like flowers materialized in the middle of my hand. I was old and new. I knew everything and everything was familiar to me. I took my finger and drew on the initiated tribe leader's and head priestess' forehead. She grew soft and tears came from here wrinkled eyes which had been tanned by the sun and life. It happened on its own. The priestesses each came to me and I drew on their foreheads. I sang old mantras and remembered. Then they lay their faces in Mary Magdalene's hands and hummed.

It was over when every woman had come to us and been filled with love, when we arose and I sent out the inner call, "Thank you for the miracle." My hands were sated. Jesus and Simon were the cause of this mystery. I was Shakti, who received the miracle. Many hands pulled us into the temple. We were to sit in the middle, in the heart of the temple. They danced in a circle around us and sang to honor us. I had never experienced women melting into the unity of Shakti before in my life. At the end of the world, there were women who could conjure the primitive cults. They had recognized us and taught us what femininity truly feels like.

As we came back to our tents in the darkness, we did not have guards with us, but we were not alone. The potent power of Shakti was in us and spiritual beings were with us and they were our legions. Jesus and Simon were sitting at the fire. "What an adventure!" I was in a trance when Simon threw his arms around me. Mary Magdalene was intoxicated and had I not known better, my first thought would have been that someone had drugged us with plants, putting us in this ecstatic state. But we hadn't taken anything. The magic of the place alone had put us in this state. Mary Magdalene danced, sacred and wanton, before the fire and unhinged all of the laws. The feminine had been kindled in its tantric power. "Is this what you wanted?" I looked at Jesus. Everything spun within me; I had never been this drunk. "This is the feminine power that creates the universe," said Jesus and I don't remember anymore how Simon picked me up and carried me to my regal, nomadic sleeping chamber.

At four in the morning, Simon and I awoke. We sat up silently and meditated together after the 108 days of initiation. I had never experienced anything like the gift that was given me now. My awakened, feminine power moved in a cosmic dance with his awakened, masculine power. The golden snakes spiraled into each other and spun in a dance in the source of the universe. We were united and separated from each other in the rhythm of the tides of Creation. There was no separation anymore and the ecstasy of the union was the ecstasy of the merging. My ego was reborn therein.

The primordial power dances through the universe sexually and without inhibition. Shakti is the powerful creative power of the cosmos. It becomes the conscious creator's own, who has freed himself from ego. It awakened us in this place. When I came up from the river that morning and the morning mist still surrounded everything in gold, Mary Magdalene came out of the tent and was marked by the traces of a night of love-making. "Believe me, we did not touch each other. But I finally know what He means when He says, 'Merging is the orgasm of the universe.'"

Mandalas made of red flowers had been placed before our tents, a path of white jasmine petals lead from that to the Shakti temple. This invitation was for us. It didn't take long before Jesus and Simon came out of the tent and we showed them this invitation with our glances. We waited until evening. Silent, because our Shivas were meditating on the river in silence. We did not eat or drink; we spent the day in asceticism. "Now," Simon smiled and gestured, inviting us to take the path.

It was clear that we walked the path together and were guided to the entrance of the temple by a thousand kisses that prepared our path as buds. We stood there and weren't certain if we were somehow violating the sacredness. We stepped into the inner circle with Simon and Jesus. Priestesses were there, praying silently. They were not disturbed by our arrival. The four of us walked around in a counterclockwise circle three times. They began to sing and we sat down with them. We did not encounter any resistance.

Other priestesses joined and brought flowers and red and yellow pastes. They washed the stone Yoginis with water from the river and adorned them. They bowed before each statue, brought them to life and prayed. Jesus arose, my heart stopped and He stood before one of the statues. "Give me your left hands!" What was He doing? He took my hand and laid it on the heart of a Yogini statue. The stone breathed so alive I jerked back for a moment. Then I held on. We had the priestesses' attention. They stood there, motionless, staring at us with inquiring eyes, wondering what we were going to do. Jesus took Simon's hand and placed it over mine. He took Mary Magdalene's hand and placed it over Simon's. When His hand joined ours, the stone began to glow and shine. The face of the Yogini turned into living light and radiated. Their animal heads or unusually beautiful faces awakened from a spell. The priestesses ran away, with sounds of admiration and we were alone. "We are awakening them all," said Jesus.

It had grown dark. And then the temple filled with priestesses who stood in awe before the miracle. We awakened Yogini after Yogini and walked to the next by drawing a counterclockwise circle with our movements. We later learned that men weren't actually allowed in the temple, but what was happening here was healing, a miracle and Creation. The feminine was wild in its primal power; it requires the protection and illuminated power of the masculine to be illuminated itself. Only when the masculine and feminine united would the light come to life. And the Yoginis shone in the darkness of the night under the starry sky.

A roar like a terrible thunderstorm startled us all. The sky suddenly grew dark with clouds before our eyes, forming a black hole. I thought we would be pulled into the powerful vortex, but we stood fast and grounded and became witnesses as the sky inhaled itself and spit itself back out. The Great Goddess appeared in the sky. She was black and full of glowing stars and filled the entire horizon with her all-penetrating love. We were her children and were astonished in humility by her blinding beauty. She was the mother of all existence, the mother of all gods and goddesses. She who existed before everything.

The middle of the Shakti temple began to shake, the Earth was quaking. But everything was quiet where we stood. "Draw the powers in," Jesus said. In the roaring storms, where the black sand whipped in the spheres, we offered all of our power and Mary Magdalene and I knew what He meant. We drew from invisible currents that flowed from the womb of the Great Mother. We needed all of our powers, we drew them to Earth, we hung ourselves in the spirals, we drew and drew until we had them under control and they were anchored.

In the middle of the temple, a black statue suddenly appeared and when it had materialized, the roaring stormed grew calm. She was with us in the material world; she was black and embodied all of the pain that had been liberated. We had no inhibitions. The priestesses took the miracle and made it their own. They retrieved flowers and adorned her, knelt before her, prayed to her, kissed her feet and hands. They also did so with Simon and Jesus. They did so with Mary Magdalene and me. The red intoxication of sacred, insane joy roared beneath us.

"Lift her up," Jesus said to me as the first commotion abated. That was impossible, for the Black Mother was made of heavy material. I could not move her an inch. He laughed. "Try again," He insisted. She was now so light she slipped from my hands because I tried with the same force as before to lift her. She weighed nothing. She had absolutely no mass. I was connected to her and understood her needs. I carried her to the river and everyone followed me. Until I stood knee-deep in the water and held the materialized mother in the water like a child. I invited Mary Magdalene to join me and we washed her with our hands in the flowing river. We sang. When the cosmic stone touched the water, it turned it blood-red and carried it away in the flow. We nodded to the priestesses to join us and they watched the miracle and laid yellow petals around her.

The spell that wove between us, the Black Mother, the river and the women shimmered with the spheres from all the heavens. Cosmic love burned in our hearts and we all interwove with each other. Jesus and Simon had been watching everything from the water's edge and now they left us alone. We remained a while and digested the experience. We had penetrated the heart of the Cosmic Mother. We brought her back to the temple in a silent, sacred procession and remained with the priestesses for a while. They lit a fire and began their watch of the sacred.

When we returned to the tents late at night, Mary Magdalene and I held each other's hands. We were ready to learn from this place. We were initiates and were ready to pass on our knowledge, just as we were open to learning from the priestesses.

The Temple of Shakti

Jesus and Simon left us and made their way to meet Thomas. They had sent him a message from Shrinagar and agreed upon a meeting place. They wanted to return in twenty-eight days. It was new moon and we saw Jesus and Simon disappear on the horizon. Amber and our escorts remained with us. Amber would be our translator, but the strong dialect of the women made it difficult for her to understand them.

Mary Magdalene and I were accepted into the women's tribe, but we made it clear that we would sleep in our tents and would eat with our people, for Simon had advised us to do so. We were in an archaic landscape learning about the initiation rituals of the women who knew and worshiped this place as the legacy of their mothers and grandmothers.

We observed them as they paid homage to the goddess of the moon and truly worshiped her. We often saw the women squatting, breathing in the moon goddess. They followed her rhythm and listened to her. They drew spirals in the sand in the temple and transformed her on the full and empty moon. On the new moon, they drew a spiral that turned counterclockwise and in the evenings, the priestesses came and placed stones in the spiral. We found out that there were no essential rules, they simply did it based on their intuition and the stones wandered on the spiral based on their impulses which sprang from the river with the moon goddess. On the full moon, they erased the counterclockwise spirals in the sand with rituals and then drew a clockwise spiral, from the inside out, which they also cultivated.

We learned that the women didn't always live in the tribal community of the priestesses. They had families, but when their time came, they communed with their Yoginis. They spent as many moons there as needed to perform their feminine rituals and initiations in order to then return to their families. Some only came once, some came many times during their lives.

They taught us their rituals in which they praised the feminine power of Creation. Their symbols for this were Yonis, the female gender turned to earth, which they animated everywhere with mantras and oil rituals. They believed that everything followed the rhythm of the great womb in which everything alive was born and to which everything returns in death. The Yoginis then became powerful women with magical powers who returned to their families. When a Yogini awoke, her statue was carved by stonemasons from the region and placed in the sacred circle in the temple. The statues changed. When a Yogini had concluded her sphere of influence of power on Earth, a new Yogini took her place, voluntarily, and received her own, new statue. The Yoginis were sent off and greeted in a ritual. They were a perfect fabric of feminine creative powers which rewove themselves over and over again.

Mary Magdalene and I learned about the magical powers of the Yoginis through their initiation of us. On the full moon, the time had come. We were brought into the temple and Amber translated for us so quietly and respectfully in the silence of the magic that wove around us. The highest priestess, Mokhsa, wiped oil on our foreheads and the Yoginis surrounded us in a circle, humming sacred mantras. The tones began to vibrate in our bodies. Mokhsa passed us a bitter drink.

It didn't take long before animals grew within me in my trance, sometimes my head mutated into a tiger's head, a lion's, sometimes completely into a black leopard. In the end, I was a she-wolf and felt her hair which sensed everything and her fully awakened instincts. It was not monstrous to me, rather it was familiar for me to slip from the fine skin of my existence as a woman and ex-perience myself as an animal power which awakened within me.

Then there was silence. I sought within me for Mary Magdalene and ensured myself everything was all right. I felt her, as soft as a doe beside me; she was calm. Then we were given the next drink. My body became real and I became golden. I grew ten arms, each carrying a tool of power. I became aware of them. I was powerful.

The initiation of the Yoginis was not relieved and there was only light; it brought me back to my body. I grew more and more awake, my cells pulsated until I awakened and my eyes opened. I was looking directly into Mokhsa's eyes She nodded and left.

I looked at Mary Magdalene. She had awakened as I had.

The Yoginis did not make a fuss over us, they simply left us alone and treated it as natural. After a while, a young Yogini came to get us and gestured clearly, indicating we should follow her. She brought us to a circle of the others performing their Sadhanas. They moved in synch in the yoga of the Yoginis. They taught us to transfer everything into physical movement, to bind every emotion, every desire, every pain into dance and a physical form of expression. They taught us how to use our pain as movement.

"What did you experience," I asked Mary Magdalene at the fire our escorts had lovingly lit for us outside our tents. "It was without compromise," she responded. "I was a snake, drawing knowledge from the earth with every fiber, lying on the loamy ground. I was the doe woman who returns to Gaul and amazes everyone. I was prepared and trained for my mission in the future. And you?" she asked.

I told Mary Magdalene that India was familiar to me, yet foreign. I held the memory of the prehistory of power and the present which was dwindling. "I think these temples will also disappear and be reborn. I want to carry the path of Shakti throughout all time. I want to return and renew this path again and again."

"You will," she said. We lay in each other's arms and from then on, it seemed to take forever for Jesus and Simon to appear on the horizon. We participated in all of the rituals. We moved the stones, we performed our Asanas. It became clear that we were both cosmic nomads, for no place fascinated us long enough to remain there. We came, absorbed, recognized and traveled on. Because we ourselves could not be changed.

The Yoginis had trustingly initiated us in all of their knowledge. And now nothing held Mary Magdalene and me; we had experienced deeper levels of ourselves.

We were hungry for new life. Mary Magdalene and I had the same dream for several nights.

The Black Madonna

Our joy was immense when Jesus and Simon returned. They had met with Thomas who had continued traveling north toward Kashmir. Jesus had given him the responsibility for the council of religious leaders. Until then, he had found fertile ground in southern India. His teachings of Christ had been taken up and integrated into the existing temples. He was the ideal apostle for connecting the religions in love and teaching tolerance. He was respected as a religious leader and was recognized in the palaces of the rulers.

It was time to leave. We passed the fire on to Amber, which she brought to the masters of the Himalayas as they had requested. Every evening, she lovingly lit the fire on the way there and by day, she carried it to the next place so it would arrive in the Himalayas alive. We also gave her a fire as a gift for Ananda Gopa, the ruler of Kashmir. This path was her destiny.

We said farewell to the tribeswomen, the sacred Yoginis who had shown us the end of the world and that the power of the Great Mother lived, no longer enslaved.

We now took a different path, straight across India. Amber gave us Ananda Gopa's escort as he had ordered her to do.

We were being drawn home to Gaul. Jesus and Simon had planned our return journey to Egypt via Abyssinia. The red soil awaited us. The news of our arrival in a few weeks preceded us. We were expected by the ruler of the red soil in Africa and by Marc and Seraphim.

We carried with us the secret of the black statue. Every night, Mary Magdalene and I dreamt of her and our messages were the same. She was primordial material, destined for the land of the Celts and the new seeds of Christianity. She was destined to unite the land of the Earth with the creative forces of the Great Mother. She had come to divide herself hundreds of times and to let her miracles take their effect in the hearts of hundreds of statues distributed across the land. We were her guardians until she reached her destination. She was destined for Ia-hr-ra, the Queen of the Celts.

And we had been tasked with bringing back this secret of how to anchor the primordial powers of the Great Mother in the Earth and creating the sacred sites.

The Horizon

After forty days, we reached the harbor where we first sailed to Arabia Felix and then on to Abyssinia.

At sunrise, we stood barefoot on the white sands and looked out at the sea.

Jesus, Mary Magdalene, Simon and I.

We carried two secrets with us. The Black Mother was wrapped in my clothing and pulsated as she neared her destination.

Mary Magdalene bore the second secret in her womb.

Glossary

of important terms and geographic names

Abyssinia	East African country, modern-day Ethiopia
Africa	Latin name for a Roman province, modern-day Tunisia and parts of Libya
Amrith	Immortality of the Indian gods
Anatolia	Asia Minor, Near Eastern part of Asia, modern-day Turkey
Arabia Felix	Southern part of the Arabian peninsula, modern-day Yemen
Arati	Light ceremony with incense sticks and a camphor lamp
Arhedaes	Modern-day Rennes-le-Château in southern France, also called Areda
Arles	Latin for Arelate
Asana	Resting posture in yoga, e.g., the lotus position
Asia Minor	Anatolia
Asura	Evil demon
Bharat	Name for India in Sanskrit
Brahma	One of the primary Hindu gods
Brahmans	Members of the top caste in India, the priest and scholars caste
Britannia	Latin name for modern-day Great Britain
Damascus	Capital of Syria

Devi	Hindu goddess, the creator of the universe
Ephesus	Latin name for the Greek Ephesos in Asia Minor
Eran	Persian name for modern-day Iran
Essenes	Religious community that once left behind their sacred scrolls in Qumran and later built a new community in Southern France
Gaul	Latin Gallia, modern-day France, Belgium, part of the Netherlands, Switzerland and the part of Germany west of the Rhine
Gopi	In a narrower sense, a shepherdess; in a more general sense, a servant; in this case, Krishna's consort
Himalaya	Asian mountain chain, seat of the Hindu gods
Hiranyagarbha	Hindu god of creation
Homa	Ritual fire ceremony
India	Latin name for India
Jagannath	Site and temple in the city of Odisha, important Hindu pilgrimage center and gracious pilgrimage site
Japa	Repetition of a mantra
Kali	Hindu goddess of death and also goddess of destruction and renewal
Kalikata	One of the three places unified to create the city of Calcutta (Kolkata)

Kashmir	Indian state, located in the Himalayas
Kashi	City on the Ganges, called Varanasi in Hindi
Asia Minor	See Anatolia
Kundalini	Ethereal, spiritual power in humans
Kushan Empire	Old, Central Asian empire, spanning from Tajikistan across to modern-day Afghanistan up to Northern India
Lingam	Symbol of the god Shiva for the masculine power of creation
Mahababa	"Great Father"
Maharani	"Great Princess", "Great Queen", the female form of the Indian ruler title Maharajah
Mantra	Sacred syllable, sacred word or sacred verse, effective when recited repeatedly either spoken, sung or in one's thoughts
Massalia	Or Massilia, modern-day Marseilles
Mudra	Symbolic hand gesture in the religions of India
Narbo Martius	Latin name for the French city of Narbonne
Nemausus	Latin name for the French city of Nîmes
Northern Sea	Black Sea, Pontus Euxinus in Latin
Palmyra	"City of the Palms", ancient oasis city north of Damascus on an important caravan route in Syria

Persia	Near Eastern state, modern-day official name is Iran
Qumran	The sacred city of the Essenes in modern-day Israel
Rajagriha	Ancient Indian name for modern-day Rajgir
Redonen	Also Rhedonen, Celtic tribe
Rishi	Hindu seer, sage
Rishikesh	City in Northern India, pilgrimage site
Sadhana	Spiritual path to achieve a spiritual goal, for instance to achieve enlightenment
Sadhu	A person who has dedicated themselves to a religious, usually ascetic life
Samadhi	Highest level of spiritual gathering, spiritual state of consciousness of unity
Shakti	Feminine primal power
Shiva	Primary Hindu god, embodying both creation and destruction
Siddhi, Siddhis	Supernatural powers obtained through spiritual practice
Shrinagar	City in Northern India
Southern Gaul	Latin, Gallia Narbonensis, modern-day Southern France
Swaha	"Well said", the end of a mantra; the feminine aspect of Agni
Syria	Near Eastern country, Latin Syria

Taxila	Capital of the ancient Gandhara Empire located in modern-day Eastern Afghanistan and Northwestern Pakistan
Tribhubaneswar	Modern-day Bhubaneswar, known as the "City of Temples" because it houses several hundred Hindu temples
Upanishads	Collection of philosophical Hindu scrolls
Veda, Vedas	Collection of religious Hindu scrolls
Via, Viae	Latin word for road, roads
Via Domitia	The first Roman road in Gaul, named after its commissioner Gnaeus Domitius Ahenobarbus
Vibhuti	Sacred ash in Hinduism
Yagna	Sacrificial ritual accompanied by mantras
Yogin	Indian ascetic who practices yoga
Yogini	Companion of a Yogin
Yoni	Symbol of the feminine womb representing the feminine power of creation

Contents

8   Ephesus - The Beginning of a New World

14   The Sacred Red

15   The Essene Village

54   The Sacred Oils

58   Healing Our Inner Country

63   The Ruby-Red Night

68   The Grail and its Destiny

71   The Powers of Shakti Return

74   Unleashing the Feminine Powers

79   The Awakening of the Feminine Powers

83   Lazarus and the Gladiators

88   The Secret Realm of the Celts

89   The Queen of the Celts Appears

98   The Journey to Arhedaes

114   The Grail of Renewal

120   The Council of Tribes

130   The Star of Destiny Wanders Onward

132   Time is a Circle

134   The Departure

141   Damascus

148   The Golden Leaves

156   The Roads of Silk - The Journey to the Self

165   The Enchantment

170   Kashmir

180   Rishikesh

182   The Masters of the Himalayas

186   The Path of Shakti - The Path of Feminine Power

190   The Sacred Mantras

192   The Sacred Cycles

193   Cycle one: The Power of Prayer

196   Cycle two: The Power of the Shadow

201   Cycle three: The Power of the Threshold

205   Cycle four: The Power of Silence

208   Cycle five: Reading the Seeds of Light

210   Kashi

218   Giving requires taking

222 The Dissolution of the Castes

227 Reconquering Our Sexual Power

230 Cycle six: The Power of Shiva and Shakti

234 Two days later

236 Cycle seven: Kali, the Black Mother

241 Cycle eight: The Carnal Sacred Heart

244 Cycle nine: The Power of Devotion

249 Cycle ten: Embodiments of the Shakti

251 Cycle eleven: Integration

255 Cycle twelve: The Resurrection of the Prophetess

256 The Beginning of All Journeys

258 Tribhubaneswar

261 MA

265 The Temple of Shakti

268 The Black Madonna

270 The Horizon

THANK YOU,
for traveling with us this far.

This is the time we have been waiting for.

The story of Jesus is arising now. It does not come as a messenger, as a priest or a savior from outside. It is arising within us. The promise that Jesus made for our time lives in the books we have written for you.

The Light of Christ is special. It has influenced this world for a long time and calls forth to different kind of revolution. The Light of Christ does not bring change through destruction. It awakens everything we experience today and inspires women who are awakening, children who turn everything upside down, and social media to lead the revolutions. It connects with new technology and the collective consciousness that is currently awakening. We live in an incredible age.

We move at a "hellish" speed in the age of love. You have the ability to melt hearts. Use it.

Our promises are important now.

We are entering into the collective consciousness of Christ together.

"Jesus the Book" and the "Series of Sacred Stories" does not end here. It continues. But we realized that these books inspire hearts and create new communities. We look forward to any creative ideas you may have as the movement grows larger. Let us know.

thefemalegrail@gmail.com

Where does love lead you?

The "Series of Sacred Stories" has become a journey that awakens the prophecies of Jesus to life with each book. The series accompanies us into the new era. Jesus always prophesied that his teachings would be understood in 2,000 years.

The seeds are beginning to bloom. Jesus' prophecies are online. The message Jesus sowed for this age is in the book. It will be revealed to you as you read. Whatever you are seeking can be found therein. But you have to find it yourself.

The paths we walk through the universe are crossing each other right now. This book sought you out because your yearning wrote it. You don't really believe this is a coincidence, do you?

We have found each other again.

We wish you an exciting journey.

Durga & Agni

Durga is the storyteller of the "Series of Sacred Stories", back then, she was Miriam. But only together can we completely remember ourselves by recognizing ourselves in others. Together with Agni Eickermann she remembered her story.

HOW we can meet:

We work internationally, holding lectures, workshops, seminars, retreats and meditations. Durga regularly writes about spirituality on her website www.durgaholzhauser.com.

If you wish to contact the authors, you are invited to do so. You can find us online at:

Durga:
www.durgaholzhauser.com
https://www.facebook.com/groups/TheChurchoftheSacredFeminine/

Agni:
www.agnieickermann.com
https://www.facebook.com/groups/1957653731228579/

Jesus The Book

Book One of the untold chronicles of Jesus of Nazareth and those who love Him. Travel through time and wander, seeing through Miriam's eyes, through Jesus' story in Palestine 2,000 years ago.

In her stories, the nights in Canaan come alive and we delve deep into the mysteries of the Light of Christ and the Sermon on the Mount, where Jesus redeemed the people and whispered the word "forgiveness". Recognize yourself in the stories of the people: in weeping Roman soldiers, praying mothers, devout followers, families falling into each other's arms, trembling doubters, grateful beggars, touched seekers, lost souls refound, thousands of lovers... Witness the stories of the lost traditions of the sacred feminine and learn who Jesus really was: a revolutionary, a reformer and a healer. Find yourself in these archetypes, which have come to heal.

Jesus The forgotten Years

Book two of the untold chronicles of Jesus of Nazareth and those who love Him. A new world is born out of desperation.

Miriam was incarnated 800 years ago during the age of the last Cathars. They are facing the last days of the early Christians on Montségur. Jesus appears to Miriam and bids her, in the face of the death that awaits her on the pyre, to tell about the forgotten years.

Return with her, the storyteller, to a time when she lived in Southern France when Jesus was alive. Jesus survived the crucifixion and traveled to India. Mary Magdalene is pregnant. Together, they have to face the challenges of life alone, for the others come and go. Celebrate with them as their yearning prayers bring Jesus back. "Jesus: the Forgotten Years" intertwines two stories from different ages and tells the story of the early Christians.

Made in the USA
Middletown, DE
26 March 2021